Pat

(CALTER CREEK 2)

LizAnn Carson

Thank You

To Min and Kate, diligent readers, honest critiquers. You pointed the way for me to improve *Pat* and make the book stronger.

1

"Pat! Pat Fraser!"

Pat stopped in her tracks, hoping against hope she hadn't heard what she'd heard. Of all the possible outcomes to the presentation she'd just sat through, it looked like she was about to experience the all-time, absolute worst.

Alan Carmichael, hailing her across the parking lot. Alan Carmichael, who had stood on the stage half an hour ago to tell her and two hundred others how much they were going to *love* a new mall and office complex in their neighborhood. How thrilled they'd all be to live side-by-side with the monstrosity, morning, noon, and night, for the rest of their lives.

His velvety baritone voice from her past, the voice of her own personal devil, triggered memories she thought she'd left behind forever. As her supervisor on her first and only engineering job, Alan Carmichael had made her life a living hell nineteen years ago.

No way. Not again.

He'd steamrollered back into her consciousness with this proposal to destroy her quiet, 1940s neighborhood, and she'd been on edge for weeks, trying to figure out how to fight him and avoid him at the same time.

Agitation gripped her vital organs and twisted.

Damn.

The mild September evening should have delighted her, but didn't. She heard his feet on the gravel, coming at her like some kind of heat-seeking, shrapnel-loaded missile. ETA about five seconds.

Egotistical, demeaning, bullying…

1

The evening hadn't gone well for those who opposed a new mall in Calter Creek, an Ohio town southwest of Columbus. Facts and figures galore had battered them, demonstrating irrefutably how much they needed it. As orchestrated by the county, and by Carmichael and Caine Developments, the presentation had been slick and oh so predictable, as if their mall was a slam-dunk.

He was instantly recognizable, even after nineteen years. She'd studied him on stage. Lines framed the sides of his mouth now, and fainter ones radiated from the corners of his eyes. Not laugh lines though, not this man. The gray in his near-black hair gave him the distinguished air of a senior politician—damned alluring, but she was better off not going there. He'd stayed in shape, based on the panther-like way he moved. Back then he'd been muscles on a whip-thin frame, and she'd bet he hadn't gained more than a couple of ounces over the years.

Unlike her, but that was *really* another story.

Yes, with his sleek air of entitlement, Alan Carmichael was the same as she remembered him—and the one person she'd happily have gone through life never seeing again. But the only route to stopping the mall led straight to Alan Carmichael.

Double damn.

She'd hoped he wouldn't remember her at all, wouldn't notice her in the audience. Why should he? She'd been just another recent graduate engineer he'd chosen to give a hard time to.

Because I'm a woman, and engineering is a man's domain, right?

All the hoping hadn't done the least bit of good. Obviously, he remembered.

Pat stood statue still, not turning. She consciously relaxed her fists.

Her five seconds of grace were up. With those long legs, he didn't waste any time. He stepped around her and—the man positively *beamed* at her.

"Pat. Hello." He reached for her hand and held it with both of his own.

2

"Alan." She kept her voice neutral while she inched her hand free.

He didn't pick up on her reluctance to engage with him. Instead, he turned on the stage charm, a mix of debonair and enthusiastic. "I'm glad I caught you. I've been looking forward to seeing you again since I saw your name on the objection letter you filed."

Good deeds never go unpunished, right?

"Until then I didn't have a clue you lived around here. I gather you're part of the opposition?" He said it lightly, as if opposition was a trivial annoyance. Which, in his world, it probably was.

"Adamantly." She dodged to the right and made her way toward her car. Naturally, he came along.

Oh, joy.

Cool, Pat. Play it cool.

She tried, but cool had never worked where Alan was concerned. The man was a master at manipulation. She'd seen him in action, and had been on the receiving end. She sped up her pace; the sooner she was free of him, the better.

"Please don't expect me to be thrilled. Your mall's going to be the view out my living room window. How would you feel?"

He ignored her question. "It took me a while to spot you in the audience. You've changed, you're more sophisticated. You were sort of a scruffy kid back when we worked together."

She had forgotten his height. At five feet seven inches, Pat wasn't short, but his voice came from just above her left ear.

She'd forgotten the effect of that voice, too.

Seductive as trade winds and a Mai Tai on a hot summer day.

Wait a minute. Scruffy?

Time to shut him down. "Good night, Alan. It's late, and I'd rather not have this discussion right now."

They'd reached her car. She clicked the unlock button on her fob and pulled the door open.

"Hold on." He managed to surround her—not touching, thank God—by gripping the top of her car door and stepping into the gap. Far too close for comfort. "That was a compliment. You look good, Pat."

She stopped lowering herself into the car and pulled upright again. His eyes glittered in the semi-gloom of the parking lot lights. "So do you," she said sweetly. "Did sell your soul to the devil, by any chance?"

He stepped back as Pat dropped into her seat and yanked the car door closed. She carefully backed out of her parking place — wouldn't do to flatten the man, however tempting. She could feel those eyes following her car as she tore from the lot.

Alan eased his car — a silver BMW Roadster that wasn't in the least practical, he owned an SUV for that — onto the Interstate for the half hour drive to his home on the outskirts of Columbus, and thought over the parking lot confrontation. What on earth was wrong with Pat Fraser?

Pat had grown up. The sandy hair now swung in a reddish-blonde fall around her shoulders, instead of looking like she hacked at it with fingernail scissors. Her clothes — well, they worked, a balance between casual and businesslike, subtly suggesting enough while revealing next to nothing. She'd never been overly slender and still wasn't, but it suited her — and suited him. When he'd spotted her in the audience, he'd taken notice. Which was ridiculous, because she hadn't crossed his mind in years.

Quite a contrast to Danielle, who was skin and bones underneath her fashionable wardrobe. She looked like dynamite when they went out, or for that matter, when they stayed in, but sometimes he suspected an elbow or hipbone might do serious damage if things got uninhibited. Not that they often did.

He wondered if he'd see Danielle tonight. She might have gone to bed, or she might be out somewhere. They didn't live in each other's pockets. Lacking any emotional involvement, theirs was more a partnership than a relationship, which suited them both.

Hearing about his encounter with Pat would amuse Danielle, but he had no intention of sharing. Seeing Pat in the audience had rattled him. Mildly, true, but definitely given him

4

pause. Even before, it must be eighteen or twenty years ago now, when she'd been a ragamuffin in her hardhat and shapeless overalls, she'd affected him. He'd chosen not to explore his reaction then, not with his career and his foundering marriage at stake. Now, he couldn't imagine this polished woman, who obviously wanted nothing to do with him, in a hardhat.

The marriage was ancient history, replaced eventually by his and Danielle's carefully crafted arrangement. The career flourished, and Alan didn't doubt his ability, personal and professional, to continue carving a successful path.

Maybe, on reflection, he could imagine Pat in a hardhat. The thought nudged something in him that hadn't been nudged in a long time. His mind paired the hardhat with bib overalls, with nothing underneath. A cocky attitude, a jutting hip, maybe a power tool in her hand...

He'd pulled off the Interstate and was working his way to his own suburb when a shadow darted across the road in front of his Roadster.

Alan slammed on the brakes. He heard and felt the thump before his mind caught up with what was happening. He hadn't been speeding, so he had the vehicle stopped and himself out of it in a matter of moments.

In the light from a streetlight down the block, he saw a dog lying on the road, half under his car between the front and rear driver's side wheels.

Thank God he'd been able to brake.

For a moment he stood there, stunned. Was the animal dead? What did you do with a dead animal? He'd seen animals left on the side of the road, but that didn't sit right with him. Was there a number to call? No other cars moved on the street, and most houses were dark. No one appreciated a knock on the door at this hour. He was on his own.

He squatted. In the dim light he saw enough to suspect this dog had been homeless for a while. Matted coat and very thin. It wasn't a big dog, perhaps two feet long, plus tail. Impossible to tell what color it was under the grime.

The dog's tail thumped. It opened an eye and raised its head.

5

The animal whimpered at him.

A dead dog was one thing. A live one? Alan got back in his car and paged through his phone until he found a twenty-four-hour veterinary service. Phone call made, he settled in to wait.

Someone would claim the dog, but he didn't imagine a vet would work for free until that happened. He'd bet he was going to be stuck with the bill for the animal.

Another whimper came from under the car. Alan got out and checked on the dog. It looked more alert, and he had a peculiar feeling that the animal was glad to see him.

What if no one claimed the dog?

He squatted, looking down while the dog looked up. "Don't get your hopes up," he said, and then wondered what he was doing, talking to a mongrel.

Twenty minutes later a van pulled up behind him. A young man in a fleece and jeans, not much more than a kid, got out, pulling a clipboard and a medical bag with him. "Sean," he said, and stuck out his hand. After perfunctory introductions, Sean shoved a flashlight in Alan's hand and knelt next to the dog. The mutt turned its muzzle into Sean's hand and whimpered some more. Sean muttered endearments back.

After a minute he stood and brushed off his knees. "Nice dog. His right hind leg's injured, I can't tell how severely until we get him to the hospital. But he's also starving and dehydrated, and probably has worms and who knows what else. No way to tell if he's been vaccinated. My guess is he'll pull through, but it's not going to be cheap. We'll check him for a microchip, but there's no collar or tattoo, so I'm not holding my breath. The question, Mister Carmichael, is how much you're willing to pay for."

Alan stood beside Sean and looked at the dog. He'd swear the dog looked back at him with hopeful eyes. The animal recognized a meal ticket, and certainly needed one.

He'd had half an hour to think. He had the money, so why not give the beast a chance?

"Fix him up. I'll pay. But find the owners. I don't have room in my life for a dog."

"They can surprise you," Sean said. "I have forms to fill out, and a credit card slip. One of the forms lets you specify the maximum we can bill to you without further authorization."

"Give me a clue. How much does it cost to fix a broken leg?"

"It looks bad. Surgery, possibly amputation. With boarding until he's well enough to go to a shelter and all the medicine he's going to need, it could be thousands."

Alan took the clipboard, glanced at and signed the forms, and filled in the amount while Sean went to his van, returning with a credit card machine and a large board.

"Ten thousand. That's generous of you, Mr. Carmichael." The young man processed the card and passed the paperwork over to Alan. "Want to give him a name? They like it better at the vet if they have something to call him."

"Pete," Alan said without thinking. The name he would have given a dog, if he'd ever had one.

"Pete it is. Could you help me here? He won't weigh much, but the less disturbance, the better. I'll lift while you shift the board under him."

Alan grimaced and once again squatted next to the dog. The animal whimpered nonstop, and once growled, but they got him onto the board.

Sean installed the dog in the back of the van, then turned to Alan. "Call the number on the form tomorrow, and they'll be able to tell you how he is. Seems to be a sweet little guy. I hope they can save him."

Alan drove off hoping the same thing. He wondered how much it would cost him. Even if the dog lived, his return on investment was nil.

He considered dumping the whole mess on Astrid, his office manager, who ran his operation with an iron fist. Even he couldn't bamboozle Astrid. But no, this wasn't company business. Besides, he preferred to keep his professional and personal lives strictly separate.

He wanted the little guy to make it. Those needy eyes... yeah, he hoped the dog had a chance.

7

At long last, he pulled into the circular driveway in front of his house, an event that never failed to give his spirits a boost. The portico over the driveway reinforced his sense of his own value, as if, in another era, a butler waited to open the door. Ahead lay elegance and regimented peace. Dark oak in the library, rich burgundy Aubusson rug on patterned parquet flooring. His home stood as a tangible reminder of his success. What was the point of being the best without the trappings?

He found Danielle curled up in one of the buttery brown leather chairs in the living room, reading. Sleek as they come, Danielle, even in a terrycloth robe, probably fresh from the hot tub or sauna. Her damp, dark hair balanced on her head by some miracle of structural integrity, since it seemed to be tousled but stayed put.

Her chair faced the fireplace rather than the door. Alan leaned over her, putting his hands on her shoulders. "Hello there."

She twisted up and around to smile at him. She held the patent on that cool, frosted smile. "Hello, darling. Did it go well?"

"According to plan. I expect we'll be breaking ground next spring."

In all probability Danielle wouldn't be any more interested in sex tonight than he was. Or to be strictly honest, his interest in sex had received a jump-start, but from somewhat more padded curves than Danielle's flat abdomen and fashionably thin thighs. But there were expectations between them, a kind of dance weaving through their odd relationship.

He slipped his hands over her shoulders, inside the robe, moving slowly down—as she no doubt expected. As he expected, she caught his hands before they grazed the tops of her diminutive breasts. "Not tonight, darling. It's late, and I have an early appointment tomorrow."

It wasn't all that late, but he readily accepted her words. He dropped a kiss on one shoulder, then smoothed the robe back in place. "You didn't need to wait up."

"I wanted to finish a chapter." She closed the book. "Let's get our beauty sleep, shall we?"

8

Alan circled the chair and offered her a hand. She rose gracefully and led the way to the stairs. Another step in the dance, each move expected. The only surprise would be if she accepted his advances. Sex was an occasional perk, not a given.

They were part of an elegant core of successful mid-career professionals, well off and well connected, and they both played the role with practiced ease. They'd declare, if asked, that they adored each other, but he was well aware that Danielle considered him a useful prop, much like the vases and swags and what-have-you she dealt with in her interior design work. They had a deal. He set the stage for her, as she did for him. With striking similarities to a business partnership, their relationship, not quite personal, not quite business, suited them both.

He settled next to her in their bed, toying with the idea that there might be something missing in their arrangement...

No. He'd explored that path already and wasn't going down it again. His life, including his arms-length relationship with Danielle, ran according to plan.

Tuesday, the day after the presentation, Pat got home from her work at the county's Social Services Department, where she had a three-quarter time contract, a little after three. Today, like most days, she'd visited a couple of the foster families on her roster. Tomorrow she'd lead a circle where the kids could let off steam in a safe setting. For some of these lost kids, it wasn't enough. When you worked at Social Services, being emotionally wrung out was a way of life.

At least she didn't have any private clients today. Maintaining her private child psychology practice could be a struggle, but it had its rewards.

She hauled down her garage door, the old, manual kind, then stood on the driveway for a minute, gazing up and down her quiet, tree-lined street. These were the homes of the people who called good morning, invited her to their barbecues, and watered her garden when she went out of town. She shared their worries and joys, sympathized with their increasing aches and pains as age crept up on them. The mall threatened the

9

slow pace of their neighborhood. At forty-one, she had long been one of the youngest on the street, although younger families were moving in now, and tricycles littered front lawns.

She went indoors. Pat's two-bedroom house reflected the way she lived, comfortable, a little worn at the edges, but neat and cheerful. A place to come back to, to relax, to put her feet on the coffee table if she wanted to.

She set her laptop on the small desk tucked into a corner of her living/dining room, opened it up, and found a note from Alan Carmichael in her inbox.

How on earth did he get her email address?

How else? The letter she'd written, months ago, protesting the mall. Her letter, which had taken her a week to craft, had triggered a form reply full of platitudes. Through it the county knew where to find her, and Alan was in bed with the county.

She deliberately bypassed this particular time bomb for the moment, in favor of her updated kitchen. With a pot of tea steeping on the black granite countertop and a chocolate chip cookie waiting on a plate, she returned to the computer, glaring at it as if the email were its fault, then opened the note.

"Hi, Pat," it said. "*It was good to see you yesterday.*"

The thrill of a lifetime.

"*I wonder if you'd be free to drop by the office one afternoon this week. I'd like a chance to talk to you.*" The note concluded by directing her to Brandon Caine's realty office on the outskirts of town.

Do I really have to do this?

Remember the mall. Think of yourself as a sacrificial lamb.

She hit Reply. "*I'm free late tomorrow afternoon. I'd like a chance to present my arguments against your development in person.*" She pressed Send before she could give herself time to reconsider, then retrieved the cookie from the kitchen.

The reply came in as she chewed. "*I'll be here. See you tomorrow.*"

And isn't that a great way to stab your own back? Clever, Pat.

If it were only the blasted mall, it would still be pretty bad, but it wouldn't be *so* bad. All day her mind had flirted with the memory of his hands on hers the night before. This was new. And was absolutely not supposed to happen. Why should she care anything about his hands?

Because they've never touched you before? Because you liked *it?*

Thanks to those hands, any face-to-face meeting with Alan Carmichael held more potential for catastrophe than she'd expected.

The email time bomb detonated, she bit viciously into the cookie and stomped to the kitchen to pour her tea.

2

"You don't mean that." Pat kept her voice mild. As usual on a Wednesday afternoon, she was sitting on the floor with a group of kids, all of them in foster care, their ages ranging from seven to thirteen. Every one of them came with a gripe.

"Yes, I do. She hates me."

"Because she thinks you ought to turn up for supper?"

"Who cares about her stupid supper?"

"She does, I expect. It can take an hour or more to make supper. If you figure in shopping, menu planning—"

"So? She gets paid."

"Jason. Take a breath." One of the older ones at just-turned-twelve, Jason usually gave her attitude, and today was no exception.

The whole circle, all seven kids, breathed.

"Now, back to basics. Do you like her cooking?"

Jason shrugged.

"Okay, we'll take that as a yes. What about the rest of you? Do you like the food?"

"Stinks," a nine-year-old girl said. "It's always frozen or takeaway."

"We get lots of frozen too. It gets old after a while," one of the older kids contributed.

"So a pot roast with potatoes and broccoli doesn't sound terrible by comparison, does it?"

Jason shrugged again. Pat took that as a no.

"Given that the grub's good, it sort of makes sense to show up to eat it, doesn't it? Where else do you need to be at suppertime?"

More shrugging. Jason studied the carpet, excavating lines with a finger.

"Make me a deal?"

"What?" His long-suffering tone belied the curiosity, a slight lessening of tension, on his face.

"You commit to being home for supper every night this week, and next week I'll bring brownies. With chocolate icing." Faces brightened around the circle, but she kept her focus on Jason.

"What kind of a dumb deal is that? I can buy my own damn cookies."

Pat let the 'damn' go. She never called them on their language. "Call it peer pressure. Plus, you'd have to use your own money. You're the one who told us last week you never have enough spending money."

She remembered things like his comment about money, helped a lot by the mad brain dump she documented right after each circle. She never wrote anything down during their time together.

The drama wasn't quite over. Jason treated them all to a dramatic sigh—she sensed the rest of the circle holding its collective breath—and said, "Since I'm stuck in this crappy group thing, we may as well get brownies."

He wasn't stuck. Attendance was voluntary. Something else she wouldn't mention.

"Good. That's settled. What's next?"

She kept her attention rigidly on the group, but it was a struggle. Because after the kids came that rarest of privileges. She'd get to spend time with Alan Carmichael.

Sarcasm kept her grounded.

The prospect had her stomach dancing salsa with her nerve endings.

She shouldn't be reacting so strongly to the thought of time alone with Alan.

Shouldn't be. Was anyway, worse luck.

13

What are we talking about here? His hands? His voice? The mall? Remember the mall?

Pat shifted her gaze around the circle. The kids came with complaints, the irritants that could make or break a typical fostering experience, and after they'd attended a few sessions they weren't shy about airing them. It didn't always work, but often enough it did. Who'd want to be dumped into a strange family? Who'd want to live with rules and behavior patterns they didn't understand? Or with the subtle distinctions between themselves and the foster parents' own children?

Every one of these kids had once had a home of some sort. A couple of them were the victims of a disintegrated family. That was the case with Jason, a decent boy underneath the attitude. She'd seen him stand up for the more timid ones in the circle. She liked Jason, beyond her usual liking for these bruised kids. Hopefully he'd make it through the system unscathed.

Others in the circle had experienced abuse, neglect, filthy homes, beatings, or worse. She had studied all their stories, and never referred to them.

She turned her attention to a ten-year-old girl who complained about restricted television privileges. Until fostering, this child had never voluntarily held a book or participated in any extracurricular activities. Breaking the television habit would be tough. Pat fastened her gaze on the child, listening to the undercurrents of pain and betrayal and too much changing too quickly.

An hour later, her circle concluded, report filed, and brain dump documented, Pat headed for her next meeting, the one involving her nervous system as much as her logical mind. The one with Alan Carmichael, his voice and his hands and his bloody mall.

Brandon Caine's realty office occupied the end unit of a strip mall south of Calter Creek. The unoccupied receptionist's desk lifted Pat's mood from defensive to merely cynical. Anyone who appeared at the door fended for herself. She loved the idea that Brandon Caine, whom she disliked and distrusted almost as much as she disliked and distrusted Alan Carmichael, albeit for different reasons, couldn't or wouldn't splurge for a receptionist.

Alan looked up when she came in. He rose from behind the desk in a small office off to the side of the reception area, like some kind of evil angel. He wore a white dress shirt open at the collar, no tie, and dark slacks. He had the air of a man who might spend today in the office making technical calculations, then tomorrow in work boots supervising a building site. In short, a man in control and fully capable of taking on any challenge his chosen career presented.

He strode around the desk — *Did the man ever just walk?* — and held out a hand. "Pat, I'm glad to see you. Not that I wouldn't have been anyway, but you've acquired mystery status."

"Hello, Alan."

His firm, dry handshake left some kind of energetic imprint on her palm after he released her. The same way his two hands on hers had done in the parking lot.

Think about it later.

Or never.

He led her to one of the hard, molded chairs facing the utilitarian desk. "Not the most elegant meeting place, but it serves the purpose. Brandon uses this office when he needs extra personnel to push one of his housing developments." The room, with beige walls and a window behind the desk looking out onto a vacant lot, was devoid of decorative touches.

Pat sat, leaning forward, tense and alert. Rather than returning behind the desk, Alan commandeered the other guest chair and folded into it, leaving them almost knee to knee.

More distance between them would be good. Very good.

The silence became awkward. "Are you waiting for me to say something?" she said.

"Yes, I am. I told you that you have an air of mystery about you. Your obvious next move is to ask about it. Since you didn't, I'll tell you I made a stab at tracking down who you're working for these days. I came up empty. I couldn't even find you in the roll of professional engineers. Want to tell me why?"

15

Pat settled into the chair, crossed her legs, and put her oversized purse down beside her. "It's no secret. I left engineering years ago. Not long after you made my life hell, actually. I have a Ph.D. in child psychology now."

"You're kidding." His mouth went slack for a moment, while his eyes focused on her with an intensity that would have made her squirm, once.

"No, I'm not," she said without elaboration.

"But why? You were one of the best entry-level engineers at Gaiman Engineering. To tell the truth, I asked you to come by to see if you'd be interested in working on the mall project with me."

"I beg your pardon?" Whatever Pat expected from their meeting, it wasn't this. She was too stunned to say anything more.

"I understand you plan to fight the mall, but it's certain to be approved. Basically, we hold all the cards. But you know as well as I do there'll be changes to the plans before we break ground. I thought I'd stumbled on a match made in heaven. Someone who's in touch with local expectations and has the professional competence. Being opposed, you'd be invaluable for identifying desirable modifications."

Well, hell. He'd thrown her off balance, and the meeting had barely begun.

Pat pulled herself together. "Sorry, Alan. I can't imagine any set of circumstances in which I'd voluntarily work with you again." She kept her voice level, but behind the façade she was flustered. She wanted her anti-mall presentation on the table. Her game plan involved rationality, facts, and staying one step ahead of him. He'd shot her strategy to bits, and she didn't have a Plan B.

"Pat, what's going on?" Alan leaned forward, resting his forearms on his thighs. His shockingly blue eyes looked up into hers. She'd forgotten his eyes.

His hands. His voice.

Pat experienced the lessening distance between them, not to mention his eyes, like a kick in the gut. He manipulated space to his advantage, and not only in structural design. Strategically,

16

it would be a mistake to shove her chair back a foot or two, but oh, how she wanted to.

"You weren't this outspoken all those years ago," he continued, clearly not receiving her unspoken plea to the universe to take his eyes off her face. "You'd get this belligerent look but never say a word. I get the message, though. I insulted you back then, and you'd rather not deal with me now. Is that about the sum of it?"

She nodded briefly. The shock of his closeness was finally receding.

He leaned back at last. "I can see I might have gotten your back up a time or two, but that came with the territory. As your supervisor, it was my job to point out any slip-ups you might make, so you'd learn from them."

A dozen emotions swirled around inside her, invisible energy threads tangled together. In deference to her nerves, she got up and began a slow prowl of the room while she chose her words.

"Are you even aware that you never once, during my time with Gaiman Engineering, said anything encouraging or even polite to me? You criticized everything I did, every step I took. You never quite said so, but you always left me with this feeling that it was because I was the only woman on the team."

She'd believed she wasn't angry anymore, merely regretful, and with a justifiable uneasiness when she thought about dealing with him again. But the anger hadn't dissipated after all. She felt it percolating up through her words, not to mention her stomach lining.

She stopped behind the desk. "Ring a bell?"

"No." He shook his head. "No, it doesn't. I'm sure I gave you a hard time occasionally, but did I ever treat you more harshly than the other rookies? I doubt it."

She hadn't meant to get angry. She hadn't known she still *was* angry. "You don't remember the girlie calendar in the construction trailer? The skanky, sexist jokes you never put a stop to?"

"A work site's rough, Pat. You must have known that going in."

17

"First you deny it, then you justify it." From behind his desk, Pat turned away and stared out the window at the desolate vacant lot next door until her rampaging emotions were back under control. "Some people respond to harsh criticism by trying harder," she said quietly. "I'm afraid I was more likely to shrivel. On the plus side, leaving's turned out to be the best thing I ever did. I'm poorer, but I'm much, much happier."

"Please sit back down. Can I get you water or coffee?"

"No, thanks." She circled the desk to her chair and sat, straight-backed. Striking a note of defiance, she pulled her water bottle out of her purse and drank.

Alan sighed. "You're fighting the mall, right?"

She nodded once.

"Because of the mall, or because of me?"

Despite their shared history, that one was a no-brainer.

"Because of the mall. Maple's one of the bordering streets. I live on Maple, as do a number of extremely upset elderly people. They don't want to see an upswing in traffic. They don't want some monolithic three-story building cutting out the light and the view. They don't want to lose their walks for the sake of your megalomaniac dreams."

"There's a fair number of younger families in your neighborhood as well. Demographics suggest they'll be delighted with a facility like this so close."

Pat was silent. With large lots and lower property values, of course young couples sought out her neighborhood. Should she admit it? Hell, no.

"Is there any way you'd consider working with me on this instead of fighting me? You're not going to be able to stop it, so if you want to have any influence over the final product, you'd be better off having a platform to make your voice heard."

This time the silence stretched until it was ready to snap. Or she was. Pat took another drag on her water bottle and set it down on the desk more forcefully than necessary. Because he was right, she wasn't going to be able to stop it.

But she could try.

18

"Understand that I intend to fight this mall with every approach I can come up with. Don't think you can bully me or my neighbors into rolling over and playing dead for you."

"All you'll do is delay it. It's going to happen, Pat. The county wants it, we've got the investors. There's really no way to block it."

"How can you even think it's worthwhile? You're taking a peaceful neighborhood of older homes and adding a monolith. You're affecting traffic patterns—"

"I've already told you we've considered that point from your letter. I can show you the modifications to the plans if you want."

"I do, but not this minute. Nothing you've changed will reduce the impact visually, with this thing towering over the neighborhood. For the families on the north side of the street, it'll be in their backyards. It has the potential to increase the traffic on Seventh Avenue—"

"Which downtown Calter Creek will love, if more people are drawn into the downtown core."

"And it doesn't provide any identifiable amenities to justify the disruption."

"A place to go for afternoon tea, perhaps?"

Pat stopped talking and took a breath. He had an answer for everything. She swallowed and got a grip on herself. "I came here to make a presentation. I suppose that would be pointless."

"No, but it's unlikely to succeed. However, I'm well aware that you have the ability to make a difference. You will, if you come on board."

She stared out the window behind the desk while she contemplated her next move. "Okay," she said finally. "At the presentation you talked about a community round table. One of your better ideas, actually. I want to be on your committee. Maybe I can at least stop it from being a rubber stamp."

"I'll make sure it happens."

"It doesn't mean I'll stop fighting to block you."

"Understood. Why don't I meet you one day next week? I'd like to walk the site with you, show you what's planned and why. It'll give you a better perspective than the presentation

19

did. Even if you aren't practicing engineering, you've got the training. The point of all this isn't to railroad the development into the community, no matter what you believe. I'm not hiding any secrets here, and I'd genuinely like to get your opinions."

She fished a sheaf of papers from her purse and handed them to him. "What I intended to say. Would you read it?"

"I'd be happy to. If you like, we could go through the plans now."

"Not today. I'd rather have time to think first. About walking the site, I'll get back to you." She shoved her water bottle into her purse and rose.

He circled the desk, took a card from a drawer, scribbled on the back of it, and held it out to her. "This is my private line. Call or email, whatever you prefer. I'll try to find some time next week. What hours do you work?"

"Mostly my own." She took the card, careful not to touch his hand, then gave a short nod and left.

By the time she'd made it to her car, Pat needed scream therapy.

You honestly thought you were going to sit opposite him and make a composed presentation?

Steady, Pat. Breathe, Pat.

A calm demeanor required massive amounts of interior command, which was starting to crumble. She settled down by sheer force of will, taking several lungsful of calming breaths before risking driving. How was it possible that this man could still tie her in knots? Her job required her to be in control, but control wasn't in the picture this afternoon.

How did he do it? He'd even had the nerve to compliment her, offering her a job on the mall project.

Pat took her time pulling out of the parking lot and into traffic. She hadn't calmed down, but at least rush hour prevented her from speeding on the way home. During a stop at an intersection she fished some mints out of her car's glove compartment. By the time she pulled onto Maple Street she had eaten them all—crunched, not sucked.

The feel of his hand plagued her—lightly callused, not the hand of a man who spent his life in an office. Where had *that* come from?

Parked in her detached garage, she rested her forehead on the steering wheel for longer than it should have taken to pull herself together.

A few minutes later, inside the house, she discovered she'd neglected to close the spout on her water bottle. The inside of her bag was soaked through.

She needed a drink. She needed to get a grip. She needed to put her head down for a cry.

Chalk up another negative to Alan bloody Carmichael.

Alan stood at the door and watched her go. Something suspiciously like excitement filtered into his awareness.

So this was Pat Fraser today. Brown eyes didn't usually flash, it took blue or green to catch fire. Brown meant quiet nights, fireplaces, deeply intimate moments. But Pat's eyes had blazed when she lost her temper, and wasn't that exciting?

Her career change astonished him, as did her obvious dislike of him. He'd been a tough taskmaster. Hell, he still was. But he was confident he hadn't singled out Pat in any way, despite resenting his low-grade attraction to her.

Now, an adversarial relationship presented intriguing possibilities. In the case of the mall, finances and politics both weighed in his favor, but she'd add an element of challenge and excitement to the upcoming negotiations. She'd lit a spark of interest, and that hadn't happened in years.

Yes, he looked forward to going toe to toe with Pat Fraser. He didn't question the nature of the contest, or need any justification to engage in it. In a battle between them, he'd come out on top.

There was a disturbing image.

If she didn't get in touch with him, he'd find her. From her earlier letter opposing the mall, he already knew where she lived, her phone number. Pat Fraser and he were at the beginning of a most entertaining relationship. She just didn't know it yet.

21

3

Pat yawned. Social Services held staff meetings at nine o'clock Thursday mornings, and despite the—to her—ungodly hour, Pat usually enjoyed getting together with her colleagues. This morning though, the welfare of the underprivileged failed to hold her attention.

Note to self: meeting with Alan Carmichael is not conducive to a good night's sleep.

Social Services maintained a cheerful, if shabby, suite of offices and meeting rooms in the County Building, a block from the main strip in downtown Calter Creek. Riding another yawn, Pat slumped into her uncomfortable bucket chair in their conference room and stacked her file folders on the table, grateful she didn't have much to say.

Well, they all had off days. The pressure of the work meant no one got through unscathed. Without intending to, she zoned out...

Pat snapped back to attention as her colleague and work partner, Linda Gonzales, a motherly woman in her fifties, concluded her summary. "Wait," she interrupted. "Sorry, mind wandered. What about Jason Jarvis?"

"No more late nights and hot dates for you," Linda quipped, and scored a comfortable laugh from the others around the table. This was no high-pressure meeting. The small Social Services team relied on their camaraderie to relieve some of the stress, because the work itself could be uncomfortably intense. "Jason's foster family reported two curfew violations—I'll talk to you about it after the meeting."

"Surprises me. Some of the kids sit in a circle and say what they think we want to hear, but Jason doesn't go out of his way to ingratiate himself."

"Surprised me, too." Linda returned to her summary.

When they'd all checked in and worked through a couple of administrative glitches, she and Linda walked in the September sunshine to the downtown Coffee Shack.

"Trouble, Pat?"

"My middle name."

"And aren't you grumpy this morning." Linda grinned. Pat had worked with Linda since joining the team six years before, and they knew each other well, a necessity in their business. They had each other's backs, provided shoulders to cry on, and, more rarely, celebrated triumphs together. "I've sniffed out trouble. Spill."

At the Coffee Shack they dropped their jackets on a free table before joining the line at the counter.

"It's nothing new. They held the public meeting about that damned mall Monday night. It left me riled up, so I haven't been sleeping enough."

"Hmm." Linda placed her order and stepped aside to wait while Pat did the same. Lattes in hand, they worked their way through the crowd to their table. "Is it going to go through?"

"Based on Monday, yes. They've got the county's backing and no organized opposition. Their team came armed with numbers and cool heads." Pat didn't sip so much as gulp the hot drink. She briefly raised her mug heavenward. "All praise to the goddess of caffeine."

"All that keeps us going, some days." Linda echoed her toast, then drank.

"Anyway, I actually met with one of the developers yesterday, for all the good it did. I'm not sure what avenue to take next. A *little* mall wouldn't be wonderful. The size they're talking about, it'll destroy the neighborhood, mess up the traffic patterns—"

"Easy." Linda put her hand on Pat's arm. "This is old news."

23

If possible, Pat got grumpier. "The county's firmly behind it, so I don't have any clear avenues to fight it. And then there's the developers. Brandon Caine—"

"The guy who stuck up those billboards as soon as you're outside the town limits. We looked at a house in one of his developments a few years ago. He's scary smooth."

"He's an operator. A friend of mine was involved with him a few years ago. Let's say we didn't hit it off. I doubt he'd remember me, but if he does, I can rely on his not being thrilled about it."

"I assume there's another name?"

Pat chuckled. Linda definitely knew her too well. "Alan Carmichael. Ancient history, but he remembers me for sure, he cornered me in the parking lot after the public meeting. It was a work relationship, but it consisted mostly of him telling me how useless I was. It's fair to say Alan Carmichael is one of the main reasons I switched to psychology."

"Psychology's grateful. He's the one you met with yesterday?"

"Yeah."

"And the reason your focus was shot this morning."

Pat released her breath in a whoosh. "Butter wouldn't melt, the man is so smooth. *Dammit,* I wish I'd drawn a break on this one."

"Want to change the subject before you crush your mug?"

"Oh." Pat released her grip and flexed her fingers. "I need an infusion of sunshine and daisies."

"It won't be daisies, but here's what's going on with Jason."

Pat pulled a pad of paper and a pen out of her purse, which was easily large enough to carry them. "Tell."

Linda swallowed down some coffee. "Started last Friday. Two hours late getting home from a movie. It sounds like his foster parents were reasonable about it, even though he didn't have a credible excuse. They sent him to bed with a warning.

"Then on Monday he swore he was meeting up at the library with a friend whose mother could bring him home.

Library closes at nine o'clock. This time they caught him trying to get in a bedroom window around eleven. They laid down the law and grounded him for a week. Got lots of fury and acting out. Then they notified us."

Pat had been silent. Now she looked up from her notes. "What else is new?"

"Old story."

"Wish we could provide phones for these kids."

"Dream in Technicolor, woman. You know what the budget looks like. How was he in the circle?"

"Sullen, as usual. I'll keep you posted." Pat swirled her coffee around in her cup and thought about a skinny boy, mad at the world but still turning up every Wednesday, willing to speak up for the younger ones.

"I'm meeting the foster mother this afternoon. She's reaching the end of her tether with Jason, I'm afraid."

"And they're one of our better foster families. Jason's so busy fighting the system that he doesn't know when he's got it good."

"Speaking for myself, I hope never again to have to deal with a pre-teen of either sex on a personal level." Linda had been married forever, and had a son and a daughter in college.

"He's a good kid. There's something about him," Pat mused. "Sometimes I want to yank him out of the system and take him home with me. Does that make any sense?"

Linda eyed her. "He's handling a rotten situation better than most twelve-year-olds. He can be likable. Watch out—I've got enough worries."

"No fear. He's not getting special treatment from me." It was hard to avoid favoring one child over another, but it was necessary, both to maintain objectivity and because the departmental rules dictated it.

Telegraphing intent, they both shrugged into their light jackets, took their mugs to the bussing station, and headed back to the Social Services office.

"And now," Linda said, "to hopefully happier events. Tell me about the wedding."

Pat relaxed. It had taken them long enough, Amanda and Jacob, to sort things through and get to the altar. Amanda Sinclair, now McKinnon, her best friend since college, was president of Sinclair Imports, and SI had dominated her life for too long. Pat regularly offered a thank-you to the heavens for sending Jacob to lure Amanda out of her closed-in, workaholic ways.

"Don't expect dewy-eyed from me. A wedding's a wedding, but this one was nicer than most. Family and close friends in the Sinclairs' back yard, a larger reception at the hotel ballroom, hors d'oeuvres, dancing. Amanda can pull off white, and she kept it simple, no veil or train. No one I know wants to be a bridesmaid—do you?"

"Nope. Stupid dress, too much expense."

"Exactly. The dress wasn't too bad. She caved in to her new daughter on the matter of pink and let Norah be a bridesmaid instead of a flower girl, but at least she chose a dark rose shade and a simple style. Jacob fills out a tux very nicely—I tell you, if he'd ever sent out the slightest signal before he laid eyes on Amanda..."

Linda laughed. "Lusting after the bridegroom?"

Pat gave her an answering grin. "Not seriously. I like it when things work out. The two of them did the expected floating-on-air things. I think the staff at Sinclair Imports got a kick out of seeing the romance side of it. Simple ceremony involving an exchange of roses and a curl-your-toes kiss. What's to say? It was a wedding."

"But you had a good time and came home happy. That's what matters."

"Nah. What matters is they left happy. And they assuredly did."

"You're next?"

Pat rolled her eyes. "Like that's going to happen. With no one even on the horizon? Shawn the Creep was enough to scare me off the whole institution."

"One lousy marriage does not a life make. Take Mister Carmichael, for instance. He seems to have a prominent position in your head."

Pat shrugged. "Funny how memories can surface, even if you've dealt with them. He's good looking in a broody, dark, film noir way. Realistically, even if he's in the market, which seems highly unlikely, and even if he's had a personality transplant, I know him too well, and the wounds went deep. Seeing him again was a kick in the gut."

They'd arrived back at Social Services. Linda pulled the door open. "Sounds like you need a good psychologist."

Their eyes met, and both women burst into laughter. "Yeah, right," Pat choked out. "I'll keep it in mind."

They separated at their cubicles. Reports threatened to drown her, as usual, and she intended to spend a heads-down day immersed in paperwork. She anticipated the sunshiny feeling that came with being caught up for once.

Besides, intense focus kept her mind off of Alan Carmichael.

Home by mid-afternoon, Pat changed, tied on her jogging shoes, and set out to build aerobic stamina and blow off steam. The job came with a cost. She couldn't afford to become emotionally involved with the kids, but she also couldn't keep her distance. They'd had enough of distance; they needed her to be unconditionally there for them. Every form she filled out reminded her of the emotional tightrope she walked daily.

She stopped outside her front door to stretch, then set off across the street and up the narrow path that ran between her neighbors' houses to the field behind them, the future home of Alan Carmichael's new mall.

At the end of the path, she saw it.

A trailer squatted in the middle of the field, like a wart. Through the weeds she made out a gravel road leading off to Sycamore Street on the far side.

She let her feet begin their regular route, a few laps around the outside of the three-square-block field followed by a diagonal pass or two across the middle.

In the course of her first perimeter circuit she assessed the trailer from all sides, taking in its ordinariness, a little one-room number with an overgrown gas tank standing guard.

27

During her second circuit her mind constructed a virtual tow truck to haul the thing off into a locked compound where it would cost Alan Carmichael a king's ransom to get it back. Thoughts have power, so she thought hard. A woman could dream.

By the end of the third circuit she'd accepted that everyone from the current owner of the field, to the county, to Carmichael and Caine Developments, aligned against her to build the mall. When she considered the size and scale of the forces on the other side, she was forced to wonder what kind of chance her small neighborhood stood.

Still, this was her home. She wasn't giving up on it.

She decided against cutting through the middle of the field, since the invading trailer was dead center, and headed for home.

The presentation had been a sop to pacify the natives. No opposing voices allowed, no counter arguments welcome. As one of the natives, she wasn't pacified. She was insulted.

She was David against Alan Carmichael's Goliath.

Don't forget who won that one.

Well, David knew something she didn't, because for the life of her she couldn't see a win in this situation.

Pat worked in a world of compromise, of getting to 'yes' for everyone. Even if clear victory was impossible, she'd give it all she had to make sure the project didn't destroy the very values that she loved about her neighborhood. She'd use her slingshot and hurl her stones of ideas at Alan, and mold his blasted mall into something they could all live with.

Alan manipulated the display on his laptop while Brandon Caine, his partner in the Calter Creek development, leaned over him. Both men focused on the project plan on the screen.

With unruly blond hair flopping onto a brow more youthful than it should be, Brandon's was a face designed to inspire trust, open and innocent, a combination Alan was sure the man used. Nothing he'd seen so far suggested Brandon was anything but a shark with an eye on the main chance.

"I'll put pressure on the county," Brandon said. He tapped a box on the display with the end of a ballpoint pen. "We need the power supply."

"Next spring, they said. I don't like leaving it that long, but I don't see an option. At that point it's on the critical path to completion, so be prepared to play hardball if there's any more delay. You could make sure they have the contractors lined up. And ask about water. They've tossed out a few estimates, but I sense they're stonewalling."

Brandon scribbled on a pad. "What's the status on the trailer?"

"It's been towed over from Dayton, so it should be on site by now. We'll complete installation in the next few days."

"Power?"

"Generator. I've scheduled the full-sized construction trailer to come up from Louisville, should be no later than April." Alan made a note on the project plan and turned his focus from the screen to Brandon. "There'll be an investor meeting next week in Columbus, if you want to attend."

"Send me the details."

"This afternoon. I think that's it, for now."

"I'd like to review this round table you're setting up." Brandon clapped a casual hand on his shoulder, then straightened and perched on a corner of Alan's desk.

He saved the plan on his laptop before he spoke. He'd put himself in charge of the citizens' committee. Since he intended to take the credit, he wanted the control. Brandon needed to understand that.

Calling the thing a round table implied a free exchange of ideas among equals, which it wasn't, but they didn't need to know that. The committee was shaping up much the way he'd hoped. His announcement at the public presentation had spurred enough interest that he had a small pile of applications on his desk. Reading between the lines, he didn't expect any of these people to cause him much grief. The letters were polite, the qualifications they mentioned were non-technical. Concerned citizens helping design a shopping mecca.

29

He'd have to remember to add an application for Pat to the stack.

He was only a little cynical about the round table. For him, the mall wasn't just another commercial development. He was shooting for a new concept in business and retail space. The blueprints were damn good, but if he could get more input, he'd take it. Even if it meant weeks of tedium with an amateur committee composed primarily of housewives and retirees. That particular demographic would be heavy users of his mall, so he'd listen to them.

He drummed the stack of applications with his fingers. "This bunch might come up with a few good ideas, you know."

"As long as they don't get carried away. It's your job to keep them on the straight and narrow." Brandon's leg swung, and Alan wished he would get off the desk.

His work relationship with Brandon was based on expediency, because he conceded the man was a genius when it came to procuring land. The site he'd found was ripe for development, near interstates and paying lower county taxes, even before the guarantee of substantial tax breaks.

So he'd deal with Brandon as long as everyone understood he was in the driver's seat. Alan brought more to the table, in terms of both investment and expertise. Raul, the architect, worked for him, the engineering specs were his.

Despite Brandon's proven value to the project, the man really got up his nose sometimes. "Don't tell me my job," Alan shot back. "I've dealt with these committees before."

Brandon just shrugged. "If you get anything, great. It'll give them the illusion of being useful. Committees love to feel useful. But mostly we need them to sign off on the whole thing."

Alan gave a short laugh. "I have a few main areas I want them to cover. Things like what kind of exterior doors to use. Overall appearance. I'm expecting very minor stuff, easily manageable. No one could possibly fault Raul's design."

"This is my core market, so I'll attend a few of the meetings. Just don't screw it up."

Alan suppressed the surge of annoyance Caine triggered in him. "Don't worry. They can be proud of their crumbs, and I'll make sure they stay away from the bigger issues. We're not going to tolerate massive re-design at this point."

Brandon left. Alan allowed himself a break to think over the project, and especially the round table. It would be a nuisance, and he didn't expect anything earth-shattering to come from it, but it would be time well invested in terms of perceptions. He'd use the round table, and they'd be happy. This formal community involvement would be another positive for the development, another highlight on his already formidable resume.

And if Pat participated, there was a chance it would yield up a good idea or two.

Alan left it a week. When he hadn't heard from Pat about walking the site, he debated briefly whether to phone or email.

Then again, why should he make it easy for her to avoid him? He'd turn up on her doorstep. He'd walked the vacant land destined to be his mall and office complex a dozen times, but today he'd do it with more interesting company.

With the BMW's top down to appreciate the sunny and crisp late September day, he drove from Brandon Caine's office to the building site, just outside the town limits northeast of Calter Creek.

The day couldn't be better for being outdoors walking the site with Pat. Alan didn't have a romantic bone in his body, but he was happy to take advantage of whatever benefit life threw at him. He switched on a local pop station and hummed under his breath as he made his way to Maple Street.

He hadn't bothered with Maple Street, other than one very early reconnaissance drive-through with Brandon. Sycamore Street, which ran parallel to Maple to the north of their land, provided access to the construction trailer, and ultimately the mall. Sycamore was more convenient for highway traffic, people coming from Columbus, for instance.

The land comprised fourteen acres of prime undeveloped land. They would put up visual barriers, probably vegetation, to screen the houses on the north side of Maple that backed onto the site. Neither side of Sycamore had been developed, so no one would contest the plans there.

He drove along Maple Street, studying the houses. Most were small, well-maintained bungalows dating from the 1940s and 1950s. Cars parked here and there, maples towered overhead. His was the only moving vehicle.

Pat lived on the block nearest Seventh Avenue, the crossroad leading into Calter Creek, and mercifully on the south side. A brick bungalow—no more than two bedrooms, he estimated—with an old-fashioned, detached single car garage and a tidy lawn surrounded by low hedges. He parked across the street, raised the top on the roadster, and gathered a cardboard tube of plans from the trunk before following the walk to the concrete stoop fronting her door.

It took her a minute to answer his knock. The woman who stood in the doorframe reminded him of the old Pat, the ragamuffin Pat. She wore shapeless, paint-stained sweats, and she'd bundled her hair off her face in an untidy ponytail. Her freckles stood out against her pale skin. There was no reason at all to find her alluring, not today.

There it was, though. That tug, that hint of intrigue. He wanted more of Pat Fraser.

He offered her a polite nod. "Put on your work boots. We're walking the site. I want to talk you through it."

"I'm working. Go see the site yourself."

Definitely not pleased to see him. Pat's lips pinched together, as if she were trying to figure out the best way to get him off of her stoop, short of slamming the door in his face.

"I've seen it. Now I want you to."

"Won't work, Alan. Turn your charm on someone else."

He got himself into the frame before she could close the door. "You're coming with me this afternoon."

"No. Why should I?"

"Because I have the inside track on building a mall in your front yard. I'm giving you a chance to look the situation over. Who knows?" he added with a grin guaranteed to infuriate her. "I might inadvertently give you ammunition."

She scowled. "I'm busy. I can't always drop everything to traipse around a vacant lot."

"It's Friday afternoon, Pat. I'd be willing to bet that nothing you're working on is due before Monday." He locked his eyes on hers, raising an eyebrow.

33

She sighed. "Give me five minutes." Leaving him standing at the front door, she disappeared into the house.

Battle won, first engagement in the war. He wanted her out there in the field with him. As well as the definite attraction that that teased his mind, she'd be useful. Her contribution would go so much more smoothly if she bought into the idea voluntarily.

Yes, knocking on Pat's door had been a good idea. It was going to be a rewarding afternoon.

Pat kept her hands in her hoodie, her eyes alternately on the path and Alan as they crossed Maple and threaded between her neighbors' houses to the field. He provided the better view, with those chiseled cheekbones and wide, generous mouth.

Generous in terms of real estate occupied on his face, not in any more altruistic sense.

He hadn't sprouted horns. He still looked as good as he had on the stage at the public meeting. Alan must be in his late forties by now, and aging well. His blue eyes, set off by those lines at the corners, were damn sexy. Patrician nose, hairline holding, jaw firm. He'd paid his dues on construction sites; from the way he moved, he was still well muscled under his dress shirt and slacks. But then he'd always been easy on the eyes.

Doubtless, he used his looks to get what he wanted. She wondered if he was still married. She remembered pitying his wife.

She dragged her brain back to business.

The field itself supported overgrown grass and weeds, with several copses scattered around it. A small forest bordered a stream that cut through the northeast corner, feeding into Calter Creek a few miles along. Joggers like herself used the trails crisscrossing the field, and many of the older residents took walks along the paths.

Most mornings the bird watchers came out. Pat made a mental note to check with the local ornithological society. Perhaps they'd join the fight to preserve this patch of wilderness.

34

The land bore no evidence of previous occupation, and she'd never seen any sign it was serviced. Would it be possible to block water, sewer, electricity? Something else to pursue.

And where exactly was the municipal boundary? She lived in Calter Creek, but the field was county. Did the line cut right behind her neighbors' houses? She'd find out.

Explore every avenue. Who knew what might turn up?

The trees hadn't turned color yet although the wild grass had started to go brown. As they crossed the field she pulled the elastic from her hair and shook it free in the mild breeze.

"Gorgeous afternoon," Alan said.

Pat was in no mood for platitudes. "What are we doing out here, Alan? I'm not sure what you're trying to prove. Did you notice the lack of traffic on Maple? This whole end of town is older. You're disrupting things."

"If you'd give me half a chance, I'd prove to you this development isn't the beginning of hell on earth. Furthermore, are you so sure your many elderly neighbors wouldn't prefer a modern mall with lots of parking? I'd lay odds most of them go to Creekside Mall instead of into town. Don't they? Can you prove to me they don't?"

She couldn't. "Downtown isn't practical for everyday errands."

"Pat, wake up. I'd bet your elderly neighbors love to lunch, don't they? And they go to Creekside, because the parking isn't so easy in your quaint little downtown, and you might have to walk a few blocks from a parking garage or one of the lots. And as for this rot about being an older community, have you seen the demographics? People like you are moving in in droves. They're into home improvement, entertainment and recreation. They shop for clothes and prescriptions for the kids and everything else. Do you have kids, Pat?"

"No, except the foster kids I work with. You?"

"I've never had any desire for a family."

"No surprise there." Why had she even asked? Why should she care about Alan's family ties?

"To return to the subject, you can't fight me without complete and accurate information. I don't have to twist my

35

facts to prove that this location is heaven sent. It's got easy access, Calter Creek and a few other communities around it to provide a labor force, near enough to Columbus to be a destination mall, already approved for sewer and water…"

And there went that angle.

His voice grew hard. "…and I will see my development built on it. You can't win."

"I can try."

"I'll be looking forward to it. Now, do you want to see what we're planning and walk the site, or stand there fuming and throwing barbs at me? I can go either way, but I had hoped to show you the plans. Politely." His veneer had slipped. He sounded cold and impatient.

They'd reached the trailer. Alan fished a key from a pocket and let them in. She unzipped her hoodie while he spread the plans he'd carried in a tube on a card table, securing the corners with beanbags. He sat on a folding chair and gestured for her to do the same. As she sat he launched into full marketing mode.

"As you can see, Sycamore will be the main conduit for traffic, so it won't affect your sleepy neighborhood at all. It's to the north, so shade won't be a major problem. Most parking will be underground or in a parking garage, not on a lot, so visually it won't be an eyesore. The façades…" He flipped to another sheet. "We think it's tasteful. There are far too many concrete boxes out there, you and I agree on that point."

She winced to think that they agreed on anything.

"We've tried to get away from the ultra-modern. Instead we're trying for a village feel. Draw people in, not just to shop but to congregate, meet friends, sit in the atrium or on one of the outdoor terraces for their morning coffee."

He was in full sales pitch now, pointing out the wonders of his mall. "The frontage will have the feel of stand-alone buildings in a mix of styles, but none of them ultra-modern. In the atrium…," he flipped to another page, "…we plan gardens, vegetation, trees—we can let trees grow up almost to the full three stories in there."

Pat watched him as much as she watched the sheets flipping in front of her. From the presentation and the handouts she'd taken home with her, she already knew a lot of what he told her. His excitement intrigued her, against her better judgment and certainly against her wishes. She could almost bring herself to share his enthusiasm.

Much though she hated the thought, he was almost— likable.

She shrugged the thought away, putting it down to her own fatigue after an exhausting week.

He'd worked his way through all the different elevations and schematics. "Now, let's get out of here and enjoy the day. I'll walk you through the plan on the ground."

So far Pat had been mostly silent. There hadn't been much chance to interrupt his spate. Now she said, "Yes, let's."

"And you'll give me your impressions, right?"

"Right." She zipped the hoodie back up.

They began by following the gravel driveway to Sycamore. Alan pointed out the access points, producing pages illustrating what customers would see as they approached. She found herself responding, asking questions. She couldn't seem to help it.

After an hour they still hadn't left Sycamore. The time had flown, which frankly surprised her. But it had been a long day, and she'd had enough. Once, this man would have intimidated her into letting him talk until nightfall, but not anymore. "Thanks for the sales pitch, Alan, but I'm going home."

He glanced at his watch. "You're right, it's getting late." He seemed surprised by her abrupt termination of their meeting, but turned their walk back toward the trailer. "Impression?"

"It's not as bad as I expected. But remember, you caught me at the end of a workday. I'm tired, and I'm not much in the mood to analyze things." Pat took the path ahead of him, walking fast. At the graveled area surrounding the trailer, she turned toward the trail leading to Maple, tucking her hands in the pockets of her hoodie.

37

His hand gripped her arm. She stopped and spun around. "I'll say it again." He gave her a little squeeze before letting her go. He was smiling, but his voice was deadly serious. "I want this mall. For both of our sakes, I want your help to make it happen. Think, Pat. You could turn it into something you can live with. Don't reject the idea outright."

She gave a brusque nod — *the best defense is a good offence* — and headed along the path to Maple, only to find him still following her. "Sorry. I parked across from your house," he said. "You aren't rid of me yet."

On Maple Street he stopped at a fancy sports car and put a proprietorial hand on the hood. Pat noted the car, which was several steps up from the usual Maple Street vehicles, and gave it a black mark. *Show-off.*

"When can we do this again?" he asked. "One day next week? There's still a lot to cover."

"I'll be in touch. I'd rather you not invade my space like you did today." She headed for her house across the street, where she closed her door behind her with finality and one big, really big thing to think about.

Her reaction to Alan Carmichael.

The hands, the eyes, the way he'd drawn her in with his puppy-dog eagerness about the mall.

She'd nursed her grudge against him for years. Now, finding herself working with him again — no, scratch that, she was *not* working with him, she might be working alongside him, but absolutely not *with* him — she had to wonder how much of her grudge stemmed from her own youth and insecurities, nineteen years ago.

What had he seen? A kid? A woman? A competent engineer? Well, maybe not, she'd been on her first post-graduation job, after all. An easy mark? Had he bullied her, or was he right? Had it been no more than he'd dished out to the other two rookies on the team?

Impossible to know after so many years.

He was smooth as massage oil, sure. That hadn't changed. He'd coat you with his particular brand of smarm until you melted, if you let him. Cocksure, assuming the plans, and he himself, were bulletproof. Just like always.

She could tell he'd had more than his share of success. In fairness, she'd had no reason to doubt his ability, even back then. Life flowed seamlessly for some people, and Alan Carmichael seemed to be one of God's anointed.

Well, there's a switch. Not a week ago you were wondering if he'd sold his soul to the devil.

But another aspect of this whole muddle kept getting in the way of clear thinking. Something was happening between them. She'd tried to keep it buried in her subconscious, but Pat's psychological training reminded her, constantly, that she shouldn't — *couldn't* — bury it forever.

She had no doubt at all he'd been aware of her, in ways that had nothing whatsoever to do with the mall. That little squeeze he gave her arm, the undercurrent in his words — *I get what I want* — told her so.

She'd felt a draw to him. When she'd seen him at her door, there's been a response she hadn't experienced in a long time.

The sex thing was in there. No question at all.

She missed Amanda, who would be home from her honeymoon any day now. Best friends since college, there was nothing they hadn't talked about, hadn't helped each other with. She'd get her feelings about the whole mess sorted out, once Mandy was back.

Wandering around her small but up-to-date kitchen, gathering the makings for a shrimp pasta, Pat mused and struggled against her conclusions.

The mall's going through. Best you can do is make nice with Alan.

Alan's not so bad.

Yes, he is. He's a bastard.

True. But maybe not a complete bastard?

Pat abandoned her shrimp and headed out the back door. The geraniums, still blooming wildly on her south-facing patio, needed deadheading. Garden therapy helped get her mind back where it belonged.

❖

Alan made it home in plenty of time to shower, shave, and chat with Danielle while they dressed for the evening's charity fundraiser. She looked brilliant tonight in her ice-blue sheath, with the diamond pendant he'd given her a couple of years ago nestled in the hollow of her neck. Danielle was too classy to show much cleavage, not that she had much to show. Her look was classic, elegant, while he provided the suave backdrop to her looks. God knew she wore an evening gown with style.

"Tell me about your day?"

"Nothing much." Alan dealt with the buttons on his shirt. "I did some campaigning this afternoon. We have a rabble-rouser on Maple Street, so I showed her around the site. If she can be defused, it'll make things smoother."

A rabble-rouser in scruffy sweats, with untidy hair and those freckles...

What was it about Pat's freckles?

"Zipper, darling?"

He dropped a casual kiss on the soft spot under her ear, then pulled the zipper up. "You know if you mess up my makeup I'll kill you?" she said conversationally.

"I know. You've killed me before." They shared a smile as he stepped away from her to resume the button challenge. "Otherwise, not much new. Permits to shepherd through, requests for proposal to draft. The usual beginning-of-project issues. You?" The buttons conquered, he held out his arms for her to deal with his cufflinks.

She got the links attached in no time. Living with Danielle definitely had its advantages. "Good day," she said. "I booked a renewal and a bachelor suite, both fairly prestigious. The renewal's going to be interesting, it's an older home without any meaningful updates. They want me to plan kitchen and bath upgrades and flooring, as well as home décor. It'll take months, but if I pull it off I may lobby for a layout in the Saturday paper."

"You'll pull it off, no one better. Months—how many?"

40

"I'm going to ballpark eight." She balanced against his shoulder while she slipped her shoes on. "It depends on them to some extent. They spend a lot of time away, so it won't be easy getting approvals. Carte blanche would be best for me, but also riskiest." She tweaked his tie, brushed an imaginary speck from his jacket, and nodded. "Damn, we're good looking."

"Handsomest couple there. Ready?"

"Let's knock 'em dead."

And she would. When Danielle put her energy into it, she was a stunner. For events like this she wore her hair up, but even on the tennis court, when it was loose behind a headband, it swung smoothly and stayed neat. He couldn't bear to think about the probable state of Pat's hair on a tennis court.

Actually, thinking about Pat's hair was no hardship.

The charity bash featured a pedestrian dinner and a so-so band for dancing, but that wasn't the point. The point was to be seen, to be photographed, and to have their charitable donations acknowledged. To keep their names in front of the press and the public. Alan Carmichael and Danielle LaPointe, commercial developer and home stylist. Successful and beautiful, the kind of people everyone wanted to be associated with.

Their own association was cordial. There was no spark, thank heaven; that kind of attraction only led to complications, and his relationship with Danielle was uncomplicated by design. Since that early, bitterly failed marriage, Alan had avoided anything 'meaningful'. He didn't consider marriage or children even remotely desirable.

He knew better than to expect Danielle to have any serious interest in his work or life, though he sometimes wondered if other people found something more in relationships—but that wasn't a thought for a charity dance. The arrangement with Danielle fulfilled all he really needed. Their bargain pleased him.

Or at least it was no worse than many partnerships he'd been in as part of his professional life. Sometimes it felt a little incomplete, but life was about trade-offs. He'd live with it. He had for years.

He piloted her around the floor, noting with another compartment of his mind the other women he should ask to dance. When the dance ended, he kissed her hand, and they separated.

What was the alternative? Someone like Pat? Cramped house, cooking smells, worn out clothing? He shuddered, then gave his new dance partner a self-deprecating shrug. "Sorry, a totally inappropriate unpleasant thought about work. Not in the least the right place for it, wouldn't you agree?" They swung across the dance floor, chatting about the ball, the winter social season.

Pat? A problem for another day.

But thoughts about Pat didn't always stay filed in some nebulous future. He'd have to deal with that.

The phone rang around lunchtime Saturday. Pat, just in the door, muddy and winded, snatched it up. "About time you got home."

"Nice to talk to you, too," Amanda said.

"It feels like you were gone months."

"You're out of breath. What have you been doing?"

"It's called Ultimate. Kind of like touch football, only no touching, and with a Frisbee. Then I jogged home. Drinks? Coffee? I've seriously missed you."

"Me, too, so come over. Tonight? We're unpacking today."

"Time?"

"Eight? She'll love to see you." Seven-year-old Norah, Amanda's new daughter, was one of Pat's former clients. Her birth mother's death in a car accident, right before her eyes, had left her with emotional scars that had taken a couple of years to heal. Pat and Norah were pals now; best possible outcome, she figured.

"With bells on. See you later."

Thank the beneficent gods, Amanda was back. Now she stood a chance of bringing some order to her thoughts, which were as erratic as the disc she'd chased that morning. Especially after yesterday afternoon.

Alan.

The mall.

Jason.

Alan.

Could she count him twice? Well, why not? He confused her twice as much as any of the other stuff going on in her life these days.

You're overthinking. Save it till you're clean and fed.

Months ago, when she'd first told Amanda about the mall development and Alan, Amanda had very sweetly told her she was protesting too much. Was Amanda right? She didn't trust Alan as far as she could throw him, and now, to further confuse things, he was being nice to her. Or at least polite.

What's wrong with his being nice for a change?

Maybe walking the site with Alan yesterday messed up your thought processes.

You enjoyed it, worse luck.

The mall? She knew the odds there. Fate must be laughing.

And last, there was Jason. She was puzzled by her instinctive desire to bond with him. He was just another homeless kid with dirty blond hair and wary blue eyes, but one who caught her in some indefinable way. Not that she could do a thing about it without the risk of violating professional boundaries.

She stripped off her dirty clothes and headed for the shower.

Pat rang Amanda's doorbell at eight sharp. Norah answered the door and hurled herself at Pat.

"Hey, kid," she said, catching the little girl and swinging her around. "How are you doing?"

Norah glowed. "I have a jillion things to tell you. There was a boat and a tour and a hike—"

"And regular bedtimes and homework," Amanda added, coming up behind Norah. She wrapped her arm around Pat's neck. "Good to be home. Good to see you."

"You, too. I want a full account. You look great."

"I feel great. Which is just as well, with Sinclair Imports moving in a month. The timing's lousy, but I'm sure Dad's on top of it. Jacob's job hunting, so he'll have time to manage the home front. Norah, hey!" Amanda pulled her new daughter back. "You'll trip her up."

"Nah, we're good." Pat ruffled Norah's curly blond hair, an eerie match to Amanda's dark curls, given the lack of a blood relationship. "So show me the way."

"Let's start in the kitchen." They worked their way past boxes stacked in the corridor to the back of the house.

One condition of the wedding was this house. Jacob refused to live with Amanda in the house he'd chosen with his late wife, so until this place was a done deal, they'd postponed the nuptials. Now, Amanda faced a new marriage, a new home, her entire life in boxes, and a company moving to a larger warehouse.

And you're moaning about your challenges?

"There you are." Jacob, tall and blondish and looking very much like a cat with cream on his whiskers, caught up with them a few minutes later and swept Pat into a bear hug, then lingered near the door, wisely staying out of the way while his daughter and his new wife put together a tray with tea and cookies for their women-only evening. "Life going well?"

"Other than a mall on my doorstep and a few assorted aggravations, yeah. You?"

"Do you need to ask?" Jacob disrupted the tea preparations long enough to wrap his arms around Amanda from behind. "I've been told to make myself scarce, so I'll get this one into her bath...," with a nod to Norah, "...and let you get on with it. He nuzzled Amanda's neck—she turned red—then somehow herded his excited daughter upstairs, leaving quiet in the kitchen.

Amanda gave Pat a tiny shrug. "PDAs. Not used to that yet." She picked up the tray and led the way into the living room. "Okay, you can't fool me. Something's wrong. What's going on, Pat? More mall stuff?"

"You first. High level summary, at least."

Businesslike Amanda actually giggled. "Biggest drawback to marrying a man with a daughter is you can't scream in the middle of the night. He's an accountant. Who knew he had such a diabolical mind?"

45

"Thank God."

"I really, desperately have to get back to yoga. Savannah was—shall we say stimulating? Then relaxing family time at Lake Placid. That's the high level. Your turn."

Pat wasn't one to prevaricate. She dropped her tea bag into her cup while she outlined the presentation and the parking lot, her meetings with Alan, and, in his own category, her growing attachment to Jason.

"Jason first. Anything practical you can do there?"

"No, I'm just aware, and keeping an eye out. I may file an application to be a foster parent. I'll get Linda to help me, but it's tricky because I want this specific kid and no other kid, and the system doesn't work that way. I want to position myself, in case another home falls apart on him."

"The mall—you're doing all you can there. Have you considered moving?"

"Not yet. May be too late anyway, the publicity's going to destroy property values. But I like my house. I'm afraid I'm going to have to go over to the dark side and influence the plans as much as I can, to keep it from looking like the Berlin Wall across the street."

"So for two out of three, nothing more to be done. Level with me, Pat. What's going on with Alan Carmichael?"

Pat focused on fishing the tea bag from her cup. "I don't know. I wish I did."

"He's got you confused?"

"He's being civilized, even pleasant. He wanted to offer me a job."

Amanda leaned forward, the vertical line appearing between her brows. "No joke? What kind?"

"The engineering kind. He was floored when I told him what I do for a living these days. I should be ashamed to admit I haven't been pleasant to him."

"And not because of history. Or not only." Amanda was shrewd; Pat hadn't expected her to miss this, and she didn't. "When you put aside the hostility from before, what's the present situation? Any answers?"

Pat picked up a cookie. "It's not easy to sort out then and now, beyond that it's a toxic combination. He's too smooth by half. He's done well in life, on the surface anyway, and he's made it clear to me that nothing's going to stop the development. If I'm road kill, so be it."

"And you're attracted to him."

"Do I have to answer that?"

"No. I know you too well."

"I think the right word is allure. He's alluring. I can't explain why, but..." Pat shook her head and bit into the cookie. "What happened to wine?"

Amanda looked down, then back up. "We're trying—I mean, if we're going to have a child together it has to be soon. So I'm following the rules, just in case."

Pat squealed, then pulled her friend into a hug. "Mandy, for that piece of news I'll forego any amount of alcohol."

A shrug. "If it happens, it happens. It's a lot to absorb. But I'm forty, I'm not getting my hopes pinned on it."

"My logical friend, sane and sensible. But I'll be cheering for you anyway. With lots of practice—"

"Now, having dealt with that diversion..." Amanda forced them back to the main issue.

Why did Alan always end up being the dominant force in the room?

Pat settled down and sipped her tea. "I'm confused. What if he isn't as bad as I remember? What if I really was an oversensitive kid with a chip on her shoulder? On the flip side, I don't trust him and I don't think I like him. But there's something about him, sometimes. My barricades are up."

"Not too high, Pat."

"No, but high enough. I don't capitulate when someone's messing with my life. Eat your cookie, Mandy."

"And get off your back?"

Pat laughed. "Yeah. I've been pining for you to get home so I could dump this on you, but it's hard to get out."

"I know. Been there." Amanda took Pat's advice and nibbled. "When can I meet him?"

47

Pat snorted. "When hell freezes over? At the mall's grand opening? He's not the backyard barbecue type."

"That answers your unspoken question right there, doesn't it? If he doesn't fit in with the way you live your life?"

"It should. I'm not sure it does. I'm a little off balance right now."

"Coming from you, that's a major confession." Amanda tucked her feet underneath her and cradled her teacup. "I can join you in being off balance. I hope I'll get some ground under my feet when I'm back at work. It's so unreal."

"Want to give a fuller account of the honeymoon?"

"You're not getting the lurid details." Once again Amanda went pink. "I loved Savannah. We never hurried to be anywhere, we took our time and wandered and ate, but we saw so much." She giggled again. "I have a new appreciation for afternoon naps. Then going to the lake with Norah gave us a chance to be quiet together and start to forge a family."

"Photos?"

"On our phones, not downloaded yet. I'm so happy, Pat."

Tea and cookies occupied them both for a few minutes before they turned to more mundane matters, such as the new yoga session. Pat relaxed back in her chair. Yes, life had changed for Mandy, and as a result they'd see changes for the two of them. There'd be off-limits topics now, new schedules and responsibilities, but the rapport was the same as ever. Amanda would have her back, through the mall, through Jason.

And through Alan. Somehow she suspected he was where she'd lean on Mandy the most, in the weeks and months ahead.

"Tell me what you think." Pat stepped into Linda's cubicle, flicking the letter she carried with a fingernail. She handed it to Linda.

"Round table... hearings... design decisions... review. Oh, I like this part. 'Assuring the best possible integration between the development and the surrounding neighborhood entities.' Neighborhood entities? Are we talking pompous or what? But at least they've invited you to join their round table."

48

"All part of the strategy to sell the mall by convincing the world we're thrilled to be getting it. Did you read the bit about maintaining community values? Pardon me while I gag. I wonder how much of this round table thing's hand-picked."

"They want you," Linda pointed out, "and you're hardly a fan."

"I'm a little surprised he came through."

"Your nemesis?"

"Arch-enemy, more like. He did say he wanted me on the committee, though. It's unclear why. He says it's for my brilliant ideas, but I think he wants to keep an eye on me, in case I get into mischief." Pat gestured with her hand, indicating contempt for Alan Carmichael's machinations.

"And that's the only reason you can come up with? Did you see the Columbus weekend paper?"

"I don't take it. What have you got?" She sank into Linda's guest chair, her interest piqued.

"Charity bash. I brought it in for you."

Pat studied the photos on the society page. "Well, fancy that. The man can smile, even when he doesn't want something from you. I'd say our Mister Carmichael has himself a fashion-plate girlfriend."

Linda grinned. "I thought civil engineers were all about work sites and construction. This guy cleans up real well. And that's no rental tux."

"They're quite a pair. Carmichael and Caine, I mean. Dark and blond. Brandon Caine's the frat boy everyone loves, at least till you get close enough to see through the smarm. Alan's more debonair and take-no-prisoners. Both of them poised to win, and hard as nails underneath. Real charmers."

"Well, charm or no, sign up for the round table. This project's got your neighborhood on the rails, and the county's got the power. If this is the best forum to fight them, then get in there and fight them."

"I will. Can't say I'm full of anticipation." Pat spent a lot of her life on committees, so her expectations for the round table weren't high, but she'd accept the crumb.

"You're tired. Take a vacation."

"I'd rather find someone to go with."

"It's not me. The kids may be in college, but neither of them has the sense they were born with, so I stay close." Linda pulled a file from the pile on her desk. "While you're here..." The women returned to work.

Later Pat wrote a short email accepting a position on the round table, then ran downstairs to the land title office, where she made a formal request for a review of every land title and survey between Maple and Sycamore Streets, as far back as they went. Probably a waste of money, but at least she was taking action. Maybe they'd turn up long forgotten liens, or boundary questions, or title disputes... anything that might preclude the mall.

A couple of days later, Pat got back to her cubicle wishing she'd considered a different, less strenuous profession. Gym teacher or something. Seldom had her ancient office chair looked more inviting.

Maybe I'm getting too old for this?

She had spent the morning chasing after a three-year-old whose new favorite activity was biting other people. Not friendly little nips, no. This kid chomped right down. When he'd nearly taken a hunk out of his mother's leg, they'd called her in.

She'd rolled on the ground, built sand castles, studied his interactions at the park, for two long hours. She hadn't spotted a trigger. No obvious frustrations, no territorial defense, no problem communicating. She'd re-interview the parents next. A strong, physical child, it was possible he simply acted out the need for more exercise.

A dozen things were possible. Pat dropped into the welcoming chair. Bits of leaf still stuck in her hair, and soggy patches adorned her slacks, but nothing that wouldn't wash out. The child—well, he'd had a workout, too. She'd be curious to hear how the rest of his day went.

These kids. Pat picked up a file she'd borrowed from Linda. Jason Jarvis.

He'd been surlier than usual in the Wednesday circle. At one point she'd thought he might even storm out. Not all twelve-year-olds managed that kind of control, so she gave him points for staying. Disappointing though, because the previous week, the week with the brownies, he'd almost given up on the attitude.

She flipped open Jason's file. When his father had been killed in an industrial accident, his mother dumped him on the county, saying she couldn't control him and couldn't afford two. She'd taken off with his kid sister and disappeared.

Worse than being an orphan, knowing you weren't wanted.

Now Jason was in his third foster home since he'd come into the system a year and a half before. Usually a foster home lasted a year at least, so he'd been shuffled around far more than desirable.

Nothing exceptional in his file. He was an okay student and made good grades when motivated. Mostly he wasn't motivated. The topic of food consistently caught his interest. He was a skinny kid; perhaps food was the answer.

She didn't see any obvious reasons for his misbehavior in the file. She slapped it down on her desk. What was it about this one, thin boy that captured her imagination? He was far from being the neediest of the kids she dealt with. She'd started monitoring herself, to be sure she didn't give him undue attention in the circle. She saw a dozen children each week, including Jason. Just another kid.

She left the file in Linda's cubicle and headed home to review the package Alan had sent out. She'd be thoroughly prepared when the round table kicked off next Tuesday.

Cynical, Pat. There was no reason to believe they would be a rubber stamp.

There was every reason to believe they'd be a rubber stamp.

Trust the system. Or at least use it.

Alan received a phone call from the Shady Oaks Clinic Wednesday morning, asking him to come by and pick up Pete.

51

Pete? It took him a moment to remember. They'd phoned a report, so he knew that the dog was now missing a leg, but in the two weeks since the accident Pete had moved far from the upper layers of his mind. "This is a bad time. Is it possible for you to deliver him to the shelter? I'll pay, of course."

"No, sir," the receptionist said. "You'll have to come in to take custody. Also to finalize the bill. This was all explained in the documentation you received."

He almost groaned. He'd never read the papers they'd thrust at him. With the ongoing work of putting together the Calter Creek mall project and the round table launch next week, the last thing he needed to deal with was a dog.

"Could you keep him another week? It's not a good time."

The receptionist chuckled. "Animals work to their own schedule. It's not fair to Pete to keep him any longer. He's responded well to the surgery and all the treatments he's had, and he's restless. We're not a boarding hospital, and there isn't any room for him to run here."

"A dog with three legs can run? I thought he'd be crippled."

"Trust me, he can run. He's due to be checked out of here. Besides Pete's best interests, we need the space." She rattled off their location. "We'll fit him with a collar, but you'll need to pick up a leash and a crate. And food…"

"I won't need all that stuff. I'm taking him straight to the shelter."

"Oh. I see."

He could hear the disapproval in the receptionist's voice, but what was he supposed to do? It wasn't his dog.

"In that case, we can lend you a crate. Obviously, we can't let you leave with the dog loose in your vehicle."

Obviously. Alan confirmed their hours, then called the shelter and confirmed theirs, then looked at his schedule to see where he could fit in this unexpected pet intervention.

At Shady Oaks that afternoon, the vet didn't carry Pete out. The dog charged up to Alan as if they'd known each other all their lives. He was shorthair, brown and black spots on

52

white, short ears that flopped forward, and a mouth that looked like he was smiling. The animal quivered with excitement. The missing leg didn't concern him at all.

"He couldn't remember me, could he?" he asked the vet.

"Who knows what they remember? He seems to recognize you, but maybe he just senses an affinity."

Alan left ten minutes later with a bank account lighter by several thousand dollars and a plastic crate holding a dog that had no intention of either staying still or resigning himself to confinement. The animal whimpered and turned in circles in the crate. When he got the container belted into the back seat of the SUV he saw the eyes, mournfully watching him through the slats.

"Can't help it, buddy," Alan said, and immediately felt stupid talking to a dog. Those eyes carried the troubles of the world in their depths. "Where you're going they'll find you a good home. You'll see."

Pete didn't look in the least convinced, but there wasn't really any choice, was there? He checked the belt, then got himself into the SUV and drove to the local shelter.

They'd had a call from the vet and knew to expect him. He handed the dog over with a mix of relief and concern. What if they couldn't find a home for Pete?

"We try different strategies," the woman at the desk told him. "He could find himself anywhere in the state as space opens up in different shelters. Ultimately, we don't like to euthanize, but there's such a glut right now that I can't say it won't happen."

Alan surprised himself by saying, "Not to this dog. Call me before you send him anywhere else." He took Pete's new file from the woman and wrote his contact information on it, so it couldn't get lost.

Pete whimpered again as he left. The dog had whimpering down to a fine art. Alan didn't look back at those liquid eyes.

6

The next Tuesday evening, Alan's face betrayed nothing but enthusiasm and bonhomie as he eyed the men and women around the conference table. They were an unprepossessing lot, this round table committee he'd created. While he exchanged handshakes and greetings, he sized up each of the twelve people. Which side were they on? How easily swayed? Who were the hard-hitters, who were laid-back? This was familiar territory, although never structured in quite this way before.

Pat was among the last to arrive. Alan greeted her as he greeted the others, formally. He was tempted to wink at her, just to get a reaction, but decided against it. *Stay on script. Keep her where you can watch her.*

Watching Pat was going to be one of the more enjoyable aspects of this committee.

It took ten minutes of the scheduled meeting time to get the group settled with muffins and drinks, another ten to complete introductions. Tonight's meeting was to establish the ground rules and get everyone on the same page. He laid out the high-level agenda for the round table, the timeframe, what he and Brandon expected from them, and invited them to share their expectations.

She's quiet tonight.

They'd brought the packages he'd prepared, including scaled-down versions of the elevations and floor plans, some high-level budgeting information, and contact lists. Most of them had done no more than flip through the pages. *Amateurs.* He gave them five minutes to refresh their memories while he poured himself another cup of coffee. When Pat joined him at the back of the room he raised the carafe in her direction, but she shook her head.

"Caffeine. I need sleep, not a revving system."

"Is everything okay? You're not your usual self."

"Don't turn on the charm, Alan, everything's fine. It's been a long day. I may not be an engineer, but I do work for a living. Hard work, some days."

"Not checking out the package?" He nodded toward the table. The others were absorbed in the plans. He'd made them glossy and appealing, drawing the committee into his vision.

"I've reviewed it. I'm on my feet to stay awake." She glanced over at the table. "You've got them interested."

"That's the idea. I'll use every weapon I've got, Pat."

"Yeah, so you said."

Alan noted that there wasn't any fight in her tonight. Not what he expected or wanted. "You need to get some sleep. You're lined up to be my main opponent, and I'd rather have a good spar with you than bulldoze over you."

Steel glinted in her eyes, briefly. "You won't bulldoze."

"Better gird your loins, then."

The image – Pat in leather, long bare legs... Alan shook himself and checked his watch. "It's time. Shall we get back into it?"

Alan spent an hour walking them through an overview of the plans for the mall, concentrating on the street frontage and the village ambience. There were a few questions as the group tried to figure out the diagrams, but nothing to concern him.

He moved on to the next order of business. "We need a committee chair, someone to help with communication and organization, and run the meetings. I'd rather not do it myself, since obviously I'm biased. Any nominations?"

An elderly man raised his hand. "Pat Fraser. She's a good organizer, and she knows her stuff."

Pat gave the man a warm smile. Alan hadn't seen that expression on her face before, and he didn't like it.

Because she'd never directed it at him?

"Thanks, George," she said. "I'm not the best, though. My free time's limited, and I'm as biased as Mr. Carmichael is. For this group to have any credibility, the chair should be someone both strong and neutral—or at least able to work from a position of neutrality." She surveyed the table. "Anyone else?" She mentioned a couple of names, questioning.

Alan watched her eyes survey the group. Just like that, she'd taken over the round table. When her gaze brushed across him, he gave her a subtle thumbs-up, pleased that she was flexing her muscle. He wanted her active commitment.

She continued in the role without consulting him. He'd expected to have to strong-arm someone into taking on the role of chairperson, but she led them in identifying possibilities, moving them toward the one suitable person of the twelve. He suspected she'd known the outcome all along.

So he'd be dealing with a little gray-haired woman named Millicent Fielding.

He turned the meeting over to Mrs. Fielding. "Madame Chairman, I believe it's time to call this meeting to a close."

Mrs. Fielding gave him a sweet smile. "After we arrange a date for our next meeting."

With efficiency that amazed him, they set up a meeting schedule for the next month. Then Mrs. Fielding—Millicent, he corrected himself—knocked her knuckles on the table in lieu of a gavel and announced the meeting adjourned.

The committee members packed up their belongings and drifted out in twos and threes.

You didn't keep control of that one.

He and Pat were the last to leave. She turned off the coffee maker and packaged up the leftover muffins. "Surely not in your job description?" he asked, propping himself against the conference table.

"I work for the county, so I'm familiar with the drill. The Social Services office will be happy to have muffins tomorrow morning." She shrugged.

"How do you think it's going to play, Pat?"

She added the muffin container to her own pile of handouts and notes and put on her jacket. "The same as you, I expect. This group won't stop your precious development, but they know Calter Creek, especially the northeast end of town. Listen to them, you might learn something. There may be ways to make this whole thing palatable without destroying the glorious reputation you're trying to build up."

Alan laughed. "Am I that transparent?"

"It's that or money, and from the polished look of you, I doubt it's money. Is there any other possible reason? Calter Creek doesn't need it."

"Come on. I'll walk you to your car."

"I'm detouring by my office."

He followed her down one floor. She unlocked an office suite and dropped the muffins in a hole-in-the-wall break room, then locked up behind her before heading out to the parking garage adjoining the County Building.

"Rough day?"

"They frequently are. Working in the foster system takes all you've got."

"You told me it's better than engineering, but I've seen you drained and grumpy a couple of times now. Are you so sure you shouldn't change back?"

She didn't even get in his face to tell him why he was wrong. Pat truly *was* tired. "Very sure. What I do matters, Alan. These kids, they need all the support they can get. Living in a foster home has its challenges."

Doesn't it. But that part of his life had long been buried.

She was silent after that, and for different reasons, so was he. But he hoped she'd pull herself together. He wanted to take her on, not carry her dozing to his ultimate victory.

At home he found Danielle awake and reading in their bed. He took the book away and kissed her, roughly. When he broke it off she said, "It's like that, is it?"

"Yeah."

She looked him up and down. "Very well." At least she didn't sigh. Sex between them was rare and seldom tender, since frustration and need in other areas of their lives triggered

57

it. Tonight he'd take her, or she'd take him, with no finesse whatsoever, but they'd both get what they wanted.

Because tonight Danielle was his only option. During the interminable drive home, Pat had occupied his mind almost exclusively. How easily she'd commandeered his meeting, despite her obvious exhaustion.

How much he wanted her underneath him, under his control.

How much he'd always wanted her. Even all those years ago, when she was no more than a scruffy kid just out of college, she'd got to him.

Other than a Saturday night commitment, Alan saw little of Danielle that weekend. She disappeared into her world of design, scouting the warehouses and stores for the items she dealt with. She'd built a solid reputation and wasn't resting on her laurels; perhaps she too sensed the press of middle age and wanted one project to establish her at the pinnacle of her profession, make her unassailable.

That's why so much rode on the success of the mall in Calter Creek.

He met with the architect in his library Saturday morning. Raul had worked with him before, and they understood each other. The plans were solid, but like any project they expected tweaks, the little things to take it from excellent to eye-popping.

"It'll be death by a thousand cuts with the round table committee sharpening their pencils," Alan joked.

"In the eternal way of committees. They want to make their mark, and they won't love you if the whole thing's so excellent they can't find something to improve. Don't worry, we can handle it."

"If nothing else, the committee's going to play well on our resumes. Collaborative community involvement. They'll be falling all over themselves to get us to build their new shopping meccas."

"That's why I like working with you, Alan. No bullshit, eyes always on the main chance. After the dust settles, be sure to tell me how many of the changes came from your committee."

Alan put down his pencil, leaned back, and cast his mind over the mall. He wasn't a dreamer. He dealt with the concrete, the pragmatic. Comfortable office layouts. Gathering space, something much classier than a food court with Chinese and pizza. Gardens, with tables for tea... the list went on. For himself he didn't give a damn about the gardens, but they'd be a draw. Bored women would flock to his gardens.

"Are you hearing much about the office wing?" Raul asked.

"So far, no. They're starting with retail."

"You might want to push them a little. I'm not sold on the façade."

"I like the way the plainer exterior sets off the mall."

"I've played with it a little. Something like oiled wood, black trim. Harder edges, more masculine, to set off the feminine village feel of the rest."

"You don't think that would be too much contrast?"

"Have a look." Raul swung his laptop around.

He studied the mock-up and considered the mall. When it was finished, half of Columbus would make the relatively short drive to shop there. Even Pat would creep in from her dinky neighborhood to sit in his gardens for a cup of tea.

He pulled himself back. Now was not the time to think about Pat Fraser.

Think about the problem she represents.

Pat wasn't just some neighborhood activist. Her training gave her the skills to spot the flaws, and he'd rather know about them up front than have her use them against him.

Not against me. Against the development.

"Alan? Did I lose you?"

"Sorry. Long week." He returned to the work at hand.

After another hour Raul packed up his tubes and shut his laptop. The men parted at the door of Alan's home, leaving him free to follow his thoughts. Straight back to Pat.

The personal component of their opposition status bothered him. Had he really been so awful back then? He'd kept her at arm's length, because even in her scruffy, ill-fitting clothes, even though he'd been locked in his hellhole of a marriage, he'd wanted to brush his fingers over the freckles scattered across her cheekbones. He'd wanted to get rid of the overalls and hardhat. He'd wanted to do a lot with Pat Fraser that he hadn't been able to do.

So yes, he probably had been unduly harsh with her.

And now? Now he struggled to not stare at her. Not glamorous, not a conventional knockout, she had some undefinable quality that seized his imagination. Her hair shone, her clothes no longer were into round five through the second-hand store, at least most of the time. The changes in Pat, her appearance but also her self-confidence, rolled into one complicated, and potentially very frustrating, challenge.

Potentially very satisfying.

For the moment, an uneasy truce hung between them. It was time to up the ante. Tell Pat a few more rules of the game.

He wasn't sure when the notion had solidified in his brain, but he intended to bed Pat Fraser before this was over. He fully expected to enjoy the pre-game show. *His move, her move, his move...*

Something he'd prefer Danielle not know about. She wouldn't judge, but she would find the idea of his being attracted to any woman, much less a relatively unsophisticated woman like Pat, amusing. He preferred to avoid Danielle's cool scrutiny.

Committee meetings, in Pat's view, qualified as a sedative drug.

By the third round table meeting she was already bored. Of the generally mild-mannered people sitting around the conference table, a few would argue, one or two would pontificate. Some would never say a single word through the duration of the round table, and would vote tentatively with the majority.

Two or three would become involved, drafting proposals, arguing points. She'd already identified them. She'd be on a subcommittee with them to review the frontage and position of the main entrance off Sycamore.

Three meetings, and they had a three-person subcommittee to review the entrance location. Pat sighed.

Brandon Caine graced this mid-October meeting along with Alan. As the local liaison, Brandon would still be here when the Carmichael half of the partnership moved on. He showed no sign of remembering her, for which she was grateful. The older women on the round table took one look at him and melted.

Nobody raised any concerns. Alan discussed escalator speeds; they had a choice of three. Everyone looked blank.

As usual, she and Alan were the last to leave. He escorted her to her car.

Not as usual, he leaned against her car door before she could open it. His blue eyes traveled over her. She prayed she'd be able to withstand the full force of those eyes. Her stomach skittered, but she kept her surficial cool. Never, *never*, would she let him see how he got to her.

"Now what? I'm tired, I'm hungry. I want to be at home."

"Do I make you nervous, Pat?"

"Your mall, yes. You, no. Let me get to my car."

"I want to talk to you."

Pat opted for businesslike. "We talk at the meeting. We chat, and I hope you agree our chat is remarkably amiable, all the way down from the meeting room. There's nothing more to say."

"Oh, there is. Because you're an enticing woman. You must sense my attraction to you."

He was coming on to her. She hadn't expected it. Could he possibly think she'd agree to this—whatever it was he was hinting at? She let her irritation show, and took her time replying.

"That lacked subtlety, for you. Let's just say that I'm not interested. Go seduce Millicent."

He laughed. "Oh, Pat, what you trigger in me doesn't translate to Millicent. Not in a million years." He stood leaning against her car door, one ankle crossed over the other as if he had all night, every inch the debonair, successful businessman.

Pat wanted to squirm and didn't dare.

"Think about it," he continued. "We can both get what we want. Besides the modifications you think you need to preserve your neighborhood, we'll both be satisfied. You intrigue me, Pat. I want more of you."

She'd sensed his interest; heck, she secretly reciprocated it. But to act on it? The man was delusional. "Forget it."

"It could be so much more than we have now." He spoke as if he were fielding a business proposition as he straightened from the car and put his hand on her arm, stroking idly up and down her coat. He was close, in her personal space, making her aware of his height.

"Alan..."

"Don't worry, this isn't a suggestion for tonight. You'd call in the army. I'm just planting an idea in your head. When civilized adults are attracted to each other—"

"Adults, plural? I'm not attracted to you. I don't seek out your company. My heart doesn't go squishy when the phone rings, hoping it's you. I'm not sure I even like you. This is inappropriate."

"Are you sure?"

She wished he hadn't said that. He couldn't have picked up on the chemical reactions badgering her, could he?

"I'd like to be better acquainted." His voice was still businesslike, but he'd softened it. "I'm thinking of quiet dinners across the table from you, touching your fingers with mine."

His hand moved, and his fingers threaded into hers. He didn't stop her when she twisted her hand free. "Getting out in the country, hiking or skiing." His voice took on the silky, intimate tone she'd suspected he'd be master of, given the richness of his voice. "Lazy evenings doing the Times crossword puzzle together. Shows, perhaps. I doubt there's much live theater in Calter Creek, but Columbus is so close..."

Pat said nothing as she tried to figure out the best way to handle a situation that, in her experience, was utterly without precedent. This man, wanting her input on the plans for his mall and so offensively propositioning her at the same time.

He knew what he was doing, she'd bet on it.

"Alan, listen good. The answer is no. Please get out of the way."

"And afterwards," he went on as if she hadn't spoken, "Pat, you're a sensual woman. I catch myself dreaming of the texture of your skin under my hands..."

She'd used up her cool. Her heart pounding, she stepped back and pulled her phone out of a pocket. She flicked it on. He didn't stop her. "Get out of the way, Alan. Now."

In answer he smiled at her again, a far from businesslike smile. He made her feel... how *did* he make her feel?

Hot. He was melting her. This couldn't be happening. She couldn't let it.

He moved forward to brush the back of his hand over her cheek. "Think about my skin under your hands, Pat. We'll talk more later." He stepped aside and opened her car door. "Drive safely. I look forward to our... disputes?"

Pat kept her voice steady. "I expected obnoxious. I didn't realize what a total snake you are." She got in and slammed the door, hitting the lock button almost simultaneously.

As she pulled out of the parking garage she saw him in her rear view mirror, smiling at her departing car.

She puzzled over the whole encounter as she worked her way out of the downtown core. By the time she'd turned onto Seventh, the road from downtown Calter Creek to home, she'd unwillingly moved on to the thought he'd planted, the one about the feel of him... *no, dammit. Not going to happen.* The best, the safest, thing to do was to avoid Alan Carmichael like the plague.

One unfortunate fact fought through. He'd summed up the situation with an engineer's precision. Working with him on the mall was the best option for her neighborhood.

She was stuck with him. Him and his smooth-as-toffee voice.

63

Him and his insightful mind that challenged her own, making her think, analyze. His fine body and those eyes, the electricity in those hands...

She'd never let him know, but he'd tempted her tonight. If she had just a smidgen more courage, she might even have agreed.

7

"There's been another incident."

And it had been such a nice, quiet week.

Pat sensed Linda's frustration and put down her pen. "Have a seat. Tell me. Want to get out of here for a while?"

"I'd rather get out of here virtually any time, but today's not the day. Work up the yin-yang." Linda dropped into Pat's guest chair and slapped the folder down. Jason's case history had clocked serious mileage between their two desks in recent weeks. "This time he hurled a plate full of meatloaf and mashed potatoes across the room. He gave one of his fellow foster kids a face full of potato, not to mention a black eye from the plate. Seth's a little kid, six years old and non-aggressive. Scared the daylights out of him, I gather. Jason's in the penalty box for the moment. School and home, privileges suspended."

"I hadn't picked up any warning signs. Did you get a reason?"

Linda shook her head. "I'm talking to Jason in a few minutes. Seems he yelled something like he couldn't stand it another goddamned minute, but didn't say what set him off."

"Last week in the circle he was sullen as usual, except when a skanky joke got going. Mention sex and they're all hilarious. He let us see his good side as well, though, supportive when one of the newer kids spoke up."

"No sign of tension buildup?"

"No more than usual. None of the kids is exactly calm and happy, but... you know."

"Yeah. Do you want to add anything to the file before I do the interview?"

65

"Not now, but keep me in the loop."

Linda leaned back in the chair, twiddling a pencil. "What's new in your life? I'm always happy for a distraction. Mister Carmichael being his usual charming self?"

"Oh, yes." Linda knew the bare bones. The meat, she kept to herself for the moment. "Both of them at the last round table. Brandon Caine's just like on his billboards. He smiles and I get chills up my spine, like he's a vampire or a nuclear reactor leak or something."

"Some people love him, girl."

"Oh, yeah? How come I don't know any?"

She got a laugh from Linda. "You run in the wrong circles, I guess."

Pat was equally happy to break up her day with idle chat. "How are things with you? Life good?"

Linda shrugged. "Our daughter's decided she wants to be an Egyptologist. Does that qualify as the good life? Egyptology? I'm not seeing the long-term future."

"You've raised a dreamer."

Linda rolled her eyes. "Lucky us. Tomorrow morning — free for coffee? Assuming I survive today?"

Pat nodded. "But I want to hear about Jason this afternoon."

Linda gave her a curious look. "You're still drawn to him."

"I am, yes. Another one of life's mysteries. It hasn't happened before."

Linda pointed a finger. "Arm's length, right?"

"Of course."

"I'll keep you posted."

After a day of report writing and dealing with more of the biting kid situation, Pat was almost in the mood for the round table that evening. Mindless activity had its place, even if she'd require an attitude adjustment to be any use whatsoever.

As the meeting started, one of the men passed around some sheets he'd photocopied. "Now, here's how I see it. There aren't enough services in the northeast part of town, so I'm recommending a recreation center, right there in the mall. Might cost you some commercial space," he added, shooting a glance at Alan and Brandon.

Alan went a little pale. Brandon went a little red. Both looked like they'd just encountered their worst nightmare.

This could get interesting. Pat sat up straighter.

"An intriguing idea," Brandon began in his best pacify-the-natives tones. "We'll look at it for feasibility. Bear in mind, the floor space isn't unlimited, and when we consider the overall traffic flow, as well as return on investment—"

One of the quieter women interrupted him. "A library. A branch of the county library would be perfect. A place for mothers to bring their kids, access to the food court, a meeting room for story times—"

Alan winced when she mentioned the food court. The round table hadn't yet bought into his idea about gardens, food *plazas* or whatever he called them.

"A driver's license office."

"That's one of the selling points, isn't it? So older people don't have to deal with the traffic and parking in town?"

The first man was on his feet. "Perhaps we could devote one entire wing of the complex to county offices. Social needs instead of office space. Will the government pay to lease space?"

"I think we should make the development more ecologically sensitive. Rooftop gardens, one of those ecological roofs with grass and trees growing on it. A self-contained sewage treatment unit."

The talk continued. Pat liked the ideas overall, and loved that the round table was in full-fledged revolt. While Alan and Brandon both remained expressionless, Pat enjoyed the show. They'd promised amenities, but this? Commercial leasing paid much better.

Dream development, meet wrecking ball.

Brandon Caine fell silent. Pat watched him as he followed the chatter. Alan scribbled on the pad in front of him, then pulled over the floor plans from the middle of the conference table and studied them, tapping with his pen and appearing to ignore the babble swirling around him. One of the women got to her feet and leaned over him, excited, pointing.

Brandon rapped with his knuckles and called a halt. "Here's where we are." He read from Alan's notes, listing the various proposals. "We'll consult with the county and see what's possible. This is a commercial venture, remember. But these suggestions are valuable."

Pat mentally rolled her eyes at his tone. *Used car salesman. Ponzi scheme.*

"We'll report back in a week or two," Caine continued, "depending on how quickly we can get the information from the county."

Oh, smooth move. Shove responsibility off on the county before it's even open for discussion. Pat would be loving this if the stakes weren't so high.

"Adding another story to the office wing—something to consider, to increase floor space," Alan put in.

Oh, no you don't. She spoke up. "It might also make the whole thing much heavier, visually, from neighboring streets. Not to mention affecting the amount of shade."

"Thank you, Ms. Fraser," Alan said. "Now, can we move on?"

Millicent smiled at him. "As soon as we're sure everyone has had their say." Pat gave her points for putting Alan in his place.

When no one spoke up, Millicent said, with a nod in Alan's direction, "Next is the report from the team studying the entrance location."

Alan glowered. Pat sat back and didn't say a word for the rest of the meeting.

When it was over, she turned off the coffee makers and gathered up the leftover muffins at record speed. She was out the door while most of the round table members were still milling around, keeping Alan and Brandon pinned to the room. A repeat of last week's exit with Alan wasn't on her agenda. She didn't intend to go home smoldering, in any sense.

❖

Alan hadn't missed Pat's speedy departure from the committee room. He didn't mind; it meant his words from the previous meeting had found their target.

He wasn't sure where his determination to have her came from. She was far from the sexiest woman he knew. Was it rooted in her antipathy to him? The whole idea of liaisons had bored him for years. Relationships? Not going to happen. Danielle was a reliable companion, an occasional bedmate, and got cufflinks on in under twenty seconds. What more could he ask for?

He sometimes wondered, lately, if there might be something more.

At forty-seven, solidly in middle age, Alan was still handsome, and he knew it. He was fit and had a craggy, hard-edged face women seemed to like. He'd never had a problem getting what he wanted from a woman. If it had been a long time since he'd wanted anything at all, well... should he be getting back in the game, to keep his hand in?

He was home before Danielle. No meeting ever ran later than nine o'clock in Calter Creek.

Odd, unsophisticated little place. Downtown Calter Creek specialized in small town appeal, with mixed architecture, flagpoles, and flowers, but the County Building was a disaster, a model for every underfunded government building in the world, and far from the corporate boardrooms he preferred to inhabit. They might at least have one of those storybook brick courthouses that ooze heritage, but no. This one was a blocky rectangle full of cubicles with old, worn dividers and even older chairs.

And the citizenry? Innocents, with innocent enthusiasm and great faith in Carmichael and Caine's willingness to conform to their ideas. A recreation center? A library? The county's limited budget would never stretch to leasing that much space. Dreamers, all of them.

Alan wanted ideas for escalators and washroom locations, not this kind of drivel.

On second thought, he wished he'd forestalled Pat. Tonight, after the fiasco of a meeting, he'd have liked to walk her to her car, make another stab at putting himself into her mind.

Danielle got home half an hour later. By then he had settled in the library with a small fire in the fireplace and a small cognac in his hand. She leaned down for a kiss, one of those distant, formal acknowledgements they specialized in.

"How'd it go?" he asked her. Since most of Alan's musings about his current project weren't for Danielle's ears, he'd rather she talk. He could count on Danielle not boring him with details.

"I'm exhausted." She claimed the sofa, kicked off her heels, and stretched her legs out. "I've poked into every nook and cranny of the place. Hours of conversations and volumes of notes. At the moment it's all vision."

"What era? Where will you take it?"

"Oddly, given the age of the house, I'm getting a sense of something contemporary. Clean lines to contrast with the coffered ceilings and crown molding. Eclectic. I'm not sure, though. Challenging, to pull it off."

"No one better."

"Pour me one of those? It's not even ten thirty, and I'm finished."

Alan poured the drink and brought it over. "I'll be turning in early. We've hit some problems, so I need to be fresh tomorrow."

"Alan."

"Hmm?" He paused on his way to the door, still cradling the cognac.

"Is something wrong?" Her eyes locked on his.

He frowned. "No, darling, nothing. Brandon and I are finding this round table thing tiresome, plus some changes in the cost estimates. Nothing to concern me, but a lot to deal with."

"I thought I'd better check. You've seemed different lately. A little more distant, perhaps? Just an observation, not a complaint."

Nothing had changed in their relationship. Why should Danielle look for reassurance? He walked back into the room and bent to kiss her cheek. "With the issues we're facing, I guess I'm a little touchy. Would you like to join me for breakfast in the morning?"

His suggestion amused her. "Yes, let's."

"The Regency? Good food, plus visibility."

"True. Wake me an hour before you want to leave?"

He kissed Danielle's hand and left her to her cognac.

And wondered what she saw. What was different? He didn't believe Pat had seeped into his actions as well as his consciousness.

No. Not possible.

On a grim day in mid-November, one that suited his mood, Alan was at his desk at Brandon Caine Realty going through the latest cost projections when Brandon came through his door and dropped into a chair.

"We've got problems."

"Big ones?"

"Yeah. The Fraser woman on the round table? This comes down to her." Brandon was speaking calmly, but based on his voice and elevated color, he was steamed.

"What's it going to cost?"

"A bundle in terms of money, and months in terms of time. Here, read." He slapped a letter down on the desk.

The projections were tighter than he liked, so Alan wasn't in the best of moods for whatever was in the letter. He picked it up and read.

His eyes met Brandon's. "They've denied permission."

"Because *someone* dragged out the original land surveys, then somehow snagged the county surveyor for confirmation. The fucking municipal boundary's in the wrong place, and the houses on the north side of Maple benefit to the tune of fifty feet or so of our property. *Damn* her." Brandon smacked a hand down on Alan's desk.

"How do you know Pat Fraser's involved?"

"Contacts in the county office. Don't ask."

"You didn't get a survey done when you bought the land?"

"They had a recent survey. This mess dates back to the Great Depression. How could I predict a snafu like this?"

Alan spoke through the numbing effects of shock. "So this means challenging the municipal boundary location. And that means more hearings. More permissions. Money."

"Even if we could get the municipal boundary restored, the people on the north side aren't going to sit back and let it happen without compensation. A lot of compensation. There's no telling what position Calter Creek will take on this. We're going up against the street, the town, the county. We are, in short, screwed." Caine pounded the desk again, got to his feet, then sank back down.

Alan frowned at his partner with something akin to distaste. When a situation worried him, he kept it to himself. Caine shouldn't be so transparent; it was bad for business. The first burst of shock receded in favor of logic as he returned his gaze to the sheet of paper in front of him. His pen tapped on the desk; he stopped it. "Not yet," he said quietly. "There'll be a way around this, something..." However impossible it seemed at the moment, the solution had to be there.

Caine stabbed at the paper on the desk with a finger. "We need a plan of attack. We can start with the politics of the thing, and that's where I come in. I've got some leverage around here. The county wants the mall, so they'll go to bat for us, once we put the facts in front of them. We'll provide them with the best strategy — they're not the cleverest out-of-the-box thinkers over there. Cost and time estimates and our recommendation."

Alan continued running through their options. "Unfortunately, adjusting the footprint may prove to be our best bet. Live without the fifty feet, shave the floor space or build in less neighborhood buffer. But given how tight the fit is along the back boundary—"

"Get a quote from Raul, in case we have to redesign."

"According to this, the original survey was over a hundred years ago. We could insist on having the whole thing redone. But when we weigh it against the time it would take..."

72

Brandon stood. "Keep in touch. We'll add to the file as we come up with ideas."

"Wait. There's more." Alan turned his computer around and pointed with the end of his pen. "The projections are getting tight. With the increase in building costs, and the revised estimates to get power to the site, and the likelihood of a water rate hike—"

"Should've been nailed down months ago."

"They were stonewalling. Makes me wonder if they saw the water hike coming."

"We haven't defined a cut-off yet. Maybe we should."

"I want this project, Caine."

"No more than I do, but we're in trouble. I'm not going to go under to get it."

"We won't." Alan's mouth was set in a thin, grim line. "I'll fight for this one with all I've got. I'm not going to lie down and let them kick me."

When Brandon Caine left his office, Alan swung his laptop around and opened a second, heavily encrypted file, one with an overview of his personal worth. He flipped between worksheets for a few minutes, made a couple of notes, and shut the file down, frowning. He was fine, but not fine enough to invest more deeply from his personal wealth. The development was in big, big trouble.

Given her involvement, his incipient relationship with Pat was dead in its tracks. But Pat was far from being front and center in his mind at the moment.

8

Pat made her way from the parking lot to Brandon Caine Realty. She'd optimistically sketched a few alternatives for the main entrance to the mall. Her designs had promise, she thought, and she wanted Alan's opinion.

He was alone in the office, focused on his computer. He glanced up as she came through his door.

"You." Just the one word, but spoken as if she were the devil incarnate, from the hostility in his voice.

What the hell?

She'd emailed the day before to arrange this meeting, so he couldn't be surprised to see her. "Were you expecting anyone else? I've brought the drawings. I thought—"

His hand slammed down on the desk with a crack like a gun. He half rose from his chair, leaning over the desk. "Do you have any idea what you've done?"

The hostility in the room was palpable. Pat recoiled. She had never experienced this level of vitriol from Alan, not even back in her engineering days. It radiated from him in waves.

She met him head on. "Neither you nor anyone else speaks to me that way. I'm leaving. Whatever's going on, get a grip and call me."

"I'll speak to you any way I want. We're having this out. Here and now."

He stood abruptly, sending his chair back against the wall under the window behind him. Panther fast, he crossed the small office and slammed the door, then spun around, cutting off her escape. His face was livid, his hands clenched at his sides.

"You got them to pull the surveys, didn't you? You thought it would be a thrill to bring down the county's best economic opportunity in years, didn't you? And ruin me in the process, just because I wasn't polite to a snot-nosed kid twenty years ago, *didn't you?*"

She couldn't have answered if she'd wanted to. Her stomach tightened while sensation drained from her muscles. She froze, all power of movement suspended in a matrix of incredulity, tinged with fear. The papers she'd held fluttered to the floor.

"You planned it. Those old surveys. You knew what you were doing," he hissed through clenched teeth. "Well, lady, you got your wish. You'll have to live with whatever gets slapped up, but the odds are you won't have Caine and me to kick around."

He stalked across the room. From behind his desk he turned back and drilled her with his eyes. "So go ahead. Drive in the stiletto. Tell me how powerful you feel."

The bitterness in his words brought her out of her near catatonia. Pat stood still a moment to collect herself and realized she was panting, as if she'd just gone ten rounds with him. She took the time to get her breath back, never taking her eyes off him.

He leaned on his desk, his focus on the papers scattered over its surface. Her brain registered that she'd never seen any of his work surfaces, in the trailer, at the round table, here in Brandon Caine's office, or at their engineering firm nineteen years ago, less than perfectly ordered.

With the desk between them, not to mention her own rising anger, Pat narrowed her eyes and said, "It might help if you told me what you're talking about." Her cold voice cut through his fury.

"You're a liar. You've been in on it from the beginning. It wouldn't occur to anyone else to pull those old surveys."

She bent to pick up her papers, but kept her eye on Alan. "I requested a double-check of the surveys, right before the first round table. It was a long shot. I haven't heard anything since. What happened?"

He snatched a page from his desk and thrust it at her. "See for yourself."

Pat moved close enough to take the paper, stepped back, and read. "Thirty to fifty feet. That affects the buffer area, the underground parking..." She returned the letter to the desk and watched him, warily.

Her matter-of-fact tone must have reached him. Despite the palpable tension in the room, the menace faded. He leaned forward on fisted hands, his voice tight and controlled. "Try the bottom line. The time and money it'll take to straighten this out, if we even can. With what we're up against now, I doubt there'll be a groundbreaking this spring, so we lose a year. We don't have a big margin as it is, so we may not be able to do it."

"And you're saying the mall's going through, with or without you. That makes sense, I guess, the county's so enthusiastic. Another developer might ignore what we want and put up a concrete box. For you it's reputation... and a financial loss?"

"Exactly. Smile, Pat. We both lose." He yanked his chair to the desk and sat. Picked up a pen, laid it down. Rubbed the back of his neck, not a habitual gesture. Alan was rattled. Or beaten. It didn't much matter which.

"Did they send copies of the surveys, or just the letter?"

"Brandon brought this in. He didn't say anything about survey maps."

"You could double-check the county's work on this. There could have been amendments or adjustments. Surveys around here can date from the 1800s, so it's a lot of digging—"

"Give me a break. We both know the county checked their facts before they sent the letter."

The emotional temperature in the room had dropped from Hades to mid-latitudes. Pat perched on one of the guest chairs. "The people on the north side of Maple have bigger lots than they dreamed of," she said, "and the mall's pushed further from their houses. I expect the cheapest option is modifying the plan."

"In your professional opinion?" She detected fatigue under his sneer.

"I don't have a professional opinion, but I'm practical. Getting the land back? A nightmare. You'd have, what, forty households to negotiate with?"

He shook his head and smacked his pen down on the table. "And the county and the town." His mouth set in a thin line. She'd never experienced this kind of tension in Alan; he had to be stretched close to breaking.

"I get it. You've gone from potential triumph to hell on wheels." She stayed with her calm tone, hoping to give him space to cool down.

It didn't work. He stared at her. Silence joined the conversation as a third, untrustworthy participant. A shiver ran up her spine, because she couldn't read him. He'd become a man in a mask.

"No, Pat," he said quietly. "You don't get it at all."

Alan was on his feet and rounding the desk in one fluid motion. He pulled her up, his rock-hard fingers digging into her arms. She cringed, wondering if he would dare hit her, but it wasn't that.

It was worse.

He pulled her against him and kissed her, fast and hard. Then he jerked away as if she'd scalded him. Their eyes met, both of them stunned.

But his eyes flashed something else as well, just for an instant. Need, almost desperation. In his eyes she saw vulnerability, a man overwhelmed for once. And crying out for someone to understand, to fight on his side.

Not that any of that mattered. Pat twisted against his hands. The pressure on her arms lessened, but he moved his mouth to the base of her neck. She felt a sting before he released her, only to stare at her blankly, as if he'd never seen her before. He moved away and stood at the window with his back to her, staring out at the wasteland of the vacant lot.

Freed from him, gasping for air, she held her hand against the delicate, bruised skin around her lips. She heard his breath across the small room, saw his back heaving. Her voice, when she spoke, was low and bitter. "So what happens next, Alan? You take me on the desk?"

77

"No. Just wait." After a minute, the longest minute of her life, his breathing calmed. He straightened and turned to face her. "Pat," he said. Her name, nothing more. He put his hands over his face, scrubbed as if he wanted to erase the whole episode, or maybe eradicate himself.

She sat before her legs caved under her, and dredged up her earlier anger to add to her outrage now. "Build-up of pressure? Taking out your bad news on anyone who wanders in?" she taunted. "Something you've been dying to do ever since the public meeting? Just couldn't resist?"

His hands dropped. He looked toward her with shuttered eyes. "To be strictly accurate, something I've been thinking about for almost twenty years. Not that it matters."

The silence took on a weight of its own, as if the air had thickened, become glutinous. Alan heaved one last heavy breath and sank into his chair. "I can't explain. When you came in here, with everything else, it—happened. Sorry's not enough, is it?"

No, it wasn't enough. Nothing was. Her drive, her energy, drained away, leaving her a shell. Shock, she supposed. Her mind grasped a single fact, that this confrontation had nowhere to go, and she had to get away from Alan. Fast. She risked standing on her shaky legs. "I'm not staying here. Bring your plans to a coffee shop. Somewhere public."

His flat voice reflected his empty eyes. "If you'd stay, I do want to see what you've done. A good idea might help this godawful day."

"You have to be kidding." She gathered her papers and coat and walked to the door.

He got there before her. When his hand touched hers, she froze. With his other hand he brushed her neck. "One thing. Forgive me for this. I wanted to mark you. Before God, it'll never happen again. Not unless you and I—"

"Hell will freeze," she stated. "Get out of my way. Now."

His lips pinched, and his face might have been chiseled from stone, like some kind of monument to self-containment. He stepped aside and opened the door for her. Pat's long legs carried her out of Brandon Caine Realty and across the parking lot to her car. She was incapable of running, although she wanted to. She refused to cry or show any weakness whatsoever.

At home she went straight to the mirror in her ensuite bathroom. A hickey. Never mind her bruised mouth, that would fade before Monday. Now she'd be stuck with wearing high-cut shirts for the next week.

Alan. Marking her.

Her hand rubbed the mark as she stared at herself in the mirror, trying to sort out her emotions and reactions.

And, she acknowledged miserably, failing.

The tears came, from more than shock. She'd just begun to think she might even like Alan Carmichael. She'd been close to admitting that her attraction to him might grow into more.

And now this.

She gulped. *Wrong again, Pat.* She tore off her clothes and spent long minutes under the shower, then threw everything she'd worn in the laundry hamper, trusting soap and water to remove the pollution.

The coffee shop meeting was inevitable, Pat supposed, but the next morning? Alan's terse email commanded – okay, requested, but she wasn't entirely objective – her presence at the Fourth Avenue Coffee Shack at eight thirty.

Eight thirty wasn't one of her better hours.

Suck it up, Pat.

One way or another, she'd be involved in the planning for this mall. Based on what little Alan had said coherently, switching sides was no longer an option, but a necessity. Work with the enemy, or risk some other developer who'd throw up a concrete box of a mall. She'd won a battle, but fought a more dangerous war than ever. The battlefield had shifted and changed. She didn't even recognize it anymore.

She dressed in a sleeveless white shirt – with a collar – plus a jacket and jeans. To go to his office she'd worn a long sleeve knit top with a scoop neck. Not a mistake she'd make again, even when she didn't have a mark to hide.

And damn him anyway.

79

The kids in her foster circles were worldly wise beyond their years. If they saw the mark, they'd get an enormous kick out of the proof she 'did it'. Which might in fact increase her bonding with them, but at the same time decrease her authority.

The Coffee Shack had been festooned with cut-outs of turkeys and autumn leaves, and a Pilgrim couple stood on the order counter. Pat generally got a kick out of Thanksgiving, but today the whole idea of celebration felt out of place, given the man she was meeting.

Alan had already claimed a table. She stopped at the door to study him before he became aware of her. He looked pale, exhausted, and shriveled somehow, as if the confidence he wore like armor had deserted him and left him hollowed out.

She was glad to see it. Nice wasn't in Pat's vocabulary this morning.

He stood when she walked up to the table. "Coffee?"

"Pumpkin spice latte, the largest they have. You're paying."

"I intended to." She watched him cover the distance between their table and the bar. If she'd questioned their adversarial relationship before, she wasn't questioning it now. No one treated her that way. No one. The sooner Alan Carmichael got that, the better.

But watching him striding to the counter, even in his current, diminished state, she thought, *He eats up space. He makes everyone else in the place seem trivial somehow.*

She shook her head to clear it and took out her drawings. He'd left some elevations lying on his side of the table, so she studied them while she waited.

"I hope we'll be able to see enough detail in smaller copies." He put her drink beside the pile of paper, then circled the table and sat.

"Before we begin with this," he said, "we need to clear the air."

"I agree. Want to see the bruise?" She started to peel off the jacket.

He reacted instantly. "No. Please."

She froze with the jacket part way off. "Got a problem with your handiwork, Alan?"

"Thanks for taking this day from bad to appalling. Yes, I have a problem. Coming to terms with... that I'd ever... for God's sake, leave your jacket on. I'll take your word for it."

Pat's smile carried a full freight of hostility. "As long as you know it's there." She shrugged the jacket back in place.

He sighed and hunched over his coffee. "Can we talk?"

"I'd rather work."

"So would I." He put his hand on the paper, cutting off her access. His voice was quiet. "I have to say this, and I want you to listen to it. It cost me a night's sleep, so you owe me that much."

"After yesterday, I don't owe you anything." She started to pull the papers free, but backed away when her hand grazed his, as if he'd scalded her.

"No." He shifted the papers to his side of the table before taking a sip of his own coffee. "Now, will you please just listen?"

Larger than life. Commanded the room.

Pat sighed and leaned back, and allowed herself to assess him. He was telling the truth about his night's sleep, based on his slack face and red-rimmed eyes. He'd dressed as usual for a typical workday, in dress slacks and a white shirt open at the collar. The silver in his hair stood out more prominently than she'd noticed before. Alan Carmichael was getting older, and today he looked it.

Despite his command, he was silent. "Are you still married?" she asked him.

"God, no." He shot a startled look at her. "Do you think yesterday would have happened if I were?"

"Your morals are a mystery to me. It seemed likely."

"You're misreading me."

She tried to remember to be pleasant. She failed. "Lucky woman, to be free of you."

He toyed with his coffee mug. "You're at least partly right. She said I treated her like dirt, and found someone else. So

81

she cheated, but I drove her to it, I suppose. But I don't want to spend this morning rehashing ancient history."

She watched his face and calmed a little. "Alan, has it occurred to you that you need help?" She picked up her latte, keeping her eyes fixed on him.

His face reddened. In Pat's work she watched for these small tells. So it *had* occurred to him, but he'd sooner die than admit it. Alan seemed to be at a loss for words.

For once, your turn to suffer.

She watched him. The bustling around her in the Coffee Shack faded into nothing.

He swallowed and faced her squarely. "I'm sorry. I've never in my life... I horrified myself yesterday. It was wrong, and I regret it happened."

"It did happen. Nice to hear you're sorry." She refused to say she accepted his apology.

He'd looked down, away from her. "The crap I put on you all those years ago..." He sighed and ran his fingers over the handle on his coffee mug. "I've considered it. Perhaps I was harder on you. It didn't mean anything. The only woman engineer on the team? I had an audience, and you were an easy target. I can trot out plenty of excuses, first time as a supervisor, wanting to make a mark, man's world. They may not carry any weight, but that's who I was, back then."

"I told you that you almost single-handedly drove me out of engineering," Pat said mildly. "I'm not tough, and I was crying myself to sleep every night. One day I woke up and thought, okay, if this is typical of work in engineering, I'd better find something else to do. I've never regretted my decision."

"I didn't know. Your image—I figured you could take it."

"So is this in aid of convincing me you're not a full-out bastard?"

He shrugged. "Is that even possible, now? But yesterday—that was a different story. The major wrench you threw into the project plan with the survey information triggered it. I could lose something that's been my goal for over two years. Because of you. I haven't come to terms with that yet.

The frustration and rage and... desire? Toxic. But wanting you... closer."

He took a breath. "Cards on the table, Pat. I do want you, but never like yesterday."

"Well, that's blunt." Pat lounged back in her chair while she sipped the latte, telegraphing contempt. "And you get what you want, you being an alpha male and all." She sat upright. "You might be in for a shock this time."

He actually grinned, but it was predatory. If you were a lamb, this was one lion you'd do well not to lie down next to. "I know what I am. I'm not a nice person. It should be obvious to anyone I'm not material for the whole marriage-and-kids thing—wait." A flash of dismay crossed his face, disappeared. "You were married, too, weren't you?"

She gave him a smile. A full, eye-twinkling smile. "Tweaked your moral conscience? Gee, I never dreamed you had one. Yeah, I was married. Childhood mistake. I don't make those kinds of mistakes now."

"Neither do I." He took a breath. "Yesterday, you threatened me, in more ways than one. I have a lot riding on this project. I've read that men hit an age when, if they haven't made it, they never will. This one's my Rubicon. Either I'm someone, or I've failed."

She rolled her eyes. "Give me a break, Alan. You're hardly nothing, no matter what happens. What's more significant is how you handle this mess, but I doubt you see that." She frowned and drummed a finger on the table. "So you rolled this fear and aggression and lust into one pretty package and attacked me. Thanks."

"Look at me, Pat."

Reluctantly, she turned her eyes to his face.

"You can be for me or against me on this project, I don't give a damn—or I do, but I can't change it so I live with it. As for the other, I enjoy being with you, and believe me, that surprises me more than it does you. I want you, and I expect I'm going to have you, some day. But I'm dead certain you don't want anything to do with me now. So here we are."

83

"Don't mistake me for someone who gives a damn what you want, Alan."

"Where you're concerned, I get the message. But the mall—if you want it to be something you can live with, you'd better resign yourself to working with me."

"And that's our cozy little talk? Because I want to make one more point. Can you imagine the catastrophe if the survey confusion came to light six months into construction, when you'd already put your footprint on the disputed land? It's possible I did you a favor. Think about it. Now, can we get back to the plans?"

Tonight you could bake a pie. Work out your aggressions with a rolling pin.

"I did think of it. It's how I make my living." Sighing, he pushed the pile of papers back over to her. "Let's start here."

But Pat was fed up with Alan and his true confessions. She put her own papers on top of his. "No, let's start here."

Alan left the coffee shop feeling no better than he had since the confrontation with Pat. The challenge of presenting his usual self-assurance since yesterday afternoon had almost been beyond him, especially around Danielle. She'd already picked up on some undefinable change in him, and she'd have a field day with the burden of frustration he carried.

Frustration? He didn't even have the courage to put the proper name on it. Their encounter should never have happened. He'd caused it, and he'd have to pay for it.

He never put himself in a position to feel guilty about anything, much less ashamed of his actions. He was up front with Danielle, scrupulous in his business dealings.

And now this.

Pat wasn't going to forgive him any time soon, he'd bet on it. That he'd left a bruise on her... well, what did he expect? With her fair skin, she probably bruised easily. Probably got bruises all the time...

Not good enough, Carmichael.

He knew he was too tired to think straight, but he had to make some decisions about the mall, and quickly. He didn't want to go to Brandon Caine Realty, or to his office in Columbus, and he certainly didn't want to go home. His powers of dissimulation didn't stretch far enough to cope with other people this morning.

Alan entered the lot from Sycamore and parked his SUV on the gravel in front of the trailer. The day was overcast and carried a burden of damp chill, but he buttoned up his coat and set off to walk the deserted acreage, again. This time he couldn't keep his mind on the development, though.

He still couldn't sort out his thoughts, much less his feelings. He felt...

No. He didn't do emotion. He'd learned that lesson, in depth, years before. He now faced both a business problem and a personal challenge, but emotion didn't play into it. He resolved his problems with logic and action.

He kicked at a clod sticking up through the light layer of snow. The clod didn't move. It stuck there, defying him.

It was emotion that got him into this mess, after all. He'd let his fear that he might lose the project transmute into rage, and let that rage find its outlet in Pat. Yet all she'd done was what he himself would have done, in her position. He knew she'd been exploring ways to halt the project. It wasn't personal.

And why should he care if it was personal or not? Because he wanted to have sex with her?

Alan's long legs had taken him to the copse in the northeast corner of the property. The trees were skeletons now, the creek partially frozen and dusted with snow. It was probably delightful in the summer, one of those places the locals would be up in arms about saving. He stood on the edge of the small riparian forest, staring blankly into the woods.

After several minutes Alan shook off whatever mental fog he'd descended into and resumed his walk. While he'd been stewing, his brain had been working in the background, and he knew now, beyond a doubt, that the only way to save the project was to concede the boundary shift and redraw the plans. Start over. Raul would be up to it, but there would be a cost, in time and money. Still, the sooner they got on it, the better.

Feeling marginally more like himself, Alan continued his walk along the Sycamore boundary, then down the drive to the trailer. Once there, he got Raul on the phone and began the discussion. He'd deal with his reaction to Pat some other time.

9

Following an extraordinary staff meeting the Tuesday after Thanksgiving, Pat and Linda stopped at Linda's cubicle on their way out for coffee. "Here's the file," Linda said.

"Thanks." Pat took Jason's file with its bad news. They'd lost another foster family, and Jason was out on his backside. Throwing the plate was the last straw, not only for Jason but also for the other two kids in the home. The family had resigned from the foster care program, condemning three children to Christmas in a group home.

She dropped the file on her desk and grabbed her coat. "Do you mind if we go to the Madison Café? I've seen more of Coffee Shacks than I want to lately."

"Walking the extra few blocks will be good for us, I expect," Linda said doubtfully.

"Sure. Fresh air."

"It's thinking about snowing out there."

"Relax, we won't melt."

"Might freeze, though."

Once they were out of the building, Pat said, "You may think I'm crazy."

A smile from her colleague. "Could be."

"It's this tug I feel around Jason. This is the third foster home he's been in, in less than two years. That must be a record in a county this size."

"He's hit a run of rotten luck. There's been some acting out, but nothing out of the ordinary. Until the plate incident, it was just typical twelve-year-old male behavior. And now this. It's a bitch."

"Suppose I wanted to be a foster parent."

Linda stopped in the middle of the sidewalk and turned to face Pat. She didn't say a word.

"Why not?" Pat said. "I'm a mature woman, gainfully employed, and I can even arrange to be free after school."

"And with all that going for you, you want to take on Jason? You're right, I think you've lost your mind."

"Probably. But yeah. I do."

Linda took her friend's arm and started them moving again.

"Have you seriously considered what you'd be getting into?"

"Sure. I just didn't think it would happen so soon. I've been paying attention in the circle. The surliness—it's a front, defenses. Once he has stability, he'll be fine. I don't want Jason lost in the system, Linda."

"So you heard about the collapse of the foster home this morning and made a snap decision. You know I'm going to advise you to think it over."

"And Jason has until Friday to get out, which means he goes into the group home. Away from Calter Creek, change of schools, institutional gift for Christmas. You really want me to think it over?"

They reached the Madison Café. Linda didn't answer until they'd been seated and ordered their lattes.

"You're a great big bleeding heart, aren't you?"

"Nah. If I were, I'd be taking the other two kids as well. More than I could handle."

"There'll be a review process, but I don't anticipate problems. Because Jason has a prior relationship with you, we need to be sure he's okay with this. And he can't stay in your circle. The others might view it as favoritism."

"I thought of that. I'm not happy, but I see your point."

Their coffees arrived. Pat's proposal hung between them.

Linda rummaged for a notebook and pen. "Here's what we'll do. I'll talk to Jason after school today. I'll make it clear to him that he can say no, and you'd never find out—we'd call it

88

administrative. If he agrees, I'll send him to you, this afternoon because of the tight timeframe. You're north of town, right? If he stays in the same school, it'll mean driving him every day."

"In the circle he never has anything good to say about his school. He might be willing to transfer."

"Or might not. Think, Pat."

"Do you grill all your foster parents like this?"

"Worse. They—you—need to understand what they're getting into."

"Sorry. Fair enough."

"So, if he says yes, or at least he'll talk it over with you, I'll notify everyone and bring him to the office. He says no, he goes on his way."

"Why the office? Can't you take him to my house?"

"Better not. Keep it businesslike until it's resolved. It's for your protection, too."

"You're making mountains out of molehills."

"Let's do it by the book, Pat. It'll be easier in the long run." Linda wrote in her notebook.

"I'm going to make a list. What I'm willing to do and what I'm not. What he gets out of it, what I'll expect, and with a low tolerance for infractions. My sense is, Jason's a kid who'll do better with enforced rules."

"Mine, too. Where he is now, he gets empty threats. Doesn't help much."

Lattes finished, Pat and Linda walked back to the office. "Paperwork?"

Linda nodded. "I'll get you the application forms. Fill them in this morning, and I'll fast track them. Expect an interview in a few days."

The usual work of the day loomed as they approached the County Building. "You're checking on the Simpson girl soon?" Pat asked.

"Yeah. I need your follow-up on the Krahn kids."

"I'll get it done today. Wish there were something more optimistic to report."

"It is what it is."

Back at the office the women went their separate ways. Alone at her desk, Pat spent a while staring at the screen saver on her monitor. She felt the rightness of her decision, however impulsive, even if she was half convinced she'd lost her ever-loving mind.

Pat saved the report on the Krahn family and cleared her screen as Linda escorted Jason to her cubicle. Jason looked less than thrilled. His backpack dangled in his hand—suspiciously light.

"Hi, Jason. Take a seat."

He slouched in the chair next to her desk. He needed a haircut, and his T-shirt wasn't all that clean. One grubby shoe was untied, and he kicked the other one at the floor, digging his heel into the brown industrial carpet. He kept his eyes on his sneakers. Pat suspected he was as nervous as she was. He held the backpack dangling for a moment, then dropped it on the floor.

"Ms. Gonzales told you the deal?"

"Yeah." He wouldn't look at her. The sneaker gouged a rut in the carpet.

"So here's how it is. I'm totally new at this. I don't have any kids and I've never lived with a kid, but I want to try. If you're in, we'll get the paperwork going. In the meantime, I can tell you a little about my expectations, and I want to hear yours."

Jason's voice proclaimed his hostility, loud and clear. "Yeah. It's always expectations, isn't it." His voice was flat, no inflection. This wasn't a question. "Do this. Don't do that. Be a good boy or we'll kick you out. Like I care."

Pat had plenty of practice holding on to her equanimity where this particular child was concerned, although she itched to smack whatever foster parent had threatened him that way. "That's not the point. You may as well get used to people putting expectations on you, Jason. It happens to everyone."

He shot her a contemptuous look. This was a child who had taken one too many knocks, and trust was no longer in his vocabulary.

"But it's not only expectations. I want to tell you what life with me will be like. How I can support you, what I can offer. And I need to know what you expect from me. It's not automatic that we'll get along with each other. It'll be a learning process."

Jason huffed out a world weary sigh that nearly broke her heart. She hoped she had the tools in her arsenal to make it better for him.

"You don't get it, do you," he stated, his voice between hostile and contemptuous. "That's not how it works. You go into a home and you get the rules. You follow their damn rules and they feed you and they buy you a pair of sneakers, maybe from the second-hand store."

She cringed, but kept it internal.

"You break their stupid rules and they go ballistic and threaten they'll tell Social Services on you, and then they get their money and it's like you never existed and it never happened. So don't even try to kid me about your fucking *rules*."

"Rules work both ways," Pat said. "One of mine is that the money from the county will go into a savings account for your education. You might need it, down the road. If I don't live up to my rules, you have my full permission to ream me out. I expect we'll both mess up while we get used to living together."

He looked at her from under overgrown bangs. "I yell at you, you'd send me back into the system."

"No. Not for yelling because I messed up. I hope you'll learn better ways to tell me, though."

"Easy for you to say. You can sit here in your office and type into your computer or call Ms. Gonzales and I'm history."

"If I make a commitment, I keep it. I'm offering you a home, Jason. If you want it, we'll start working on how it's going to play. If not, I'll call Ms. Gonzales, and we'll forget the whole thing. Your call. But I'd like you to give us a try."

Jason studied the heel of his sneaker plowing through the carpet. Pat watched him absorb this new idea, that someone actually wanted him. Him specifically, not just any kid. Even his mother hadn't wanted him, so why should she?

91

A terrible world, where kids are afraid to hope.

She chewed on the inside of her lip and waited.

He caught her gaze on him. "What?"

"I'm waiting for your decision. Are you in, or not?"

"Yeah, I guess so." He strove for indifference, but it didn't quite work.

She smiled. "Come on. We'll tell Ms. Gonzales so she can get the paperwork started."

Jason heaved a massive, put-upon sigh. "'Kay."

The animal shelter phoned Friday just as Alan was leaving for home. Because he and Danielle were meeting friends for supper that evening and he was running late, he almost didn't answer.

Those damn eyes. The look the dog had given him when he'd left him at the shelter…

"Yes," he snapped into the phone. With his free hand he loaded his laptop and a stack of papers into his attaché case.

"Mister Carmichael? We have news about Pete for you. The note on his file said you wanted to know."

"You told me you'd found him a home." He'd comfortably put Pete out of his mind, believing the animal had people to take care of him.

"I'm sorry, it didn't work out. The child in the family, well, everyone agreed Pete would be better off if they abandoned the adoption."

Alan slowed, his hand on the lid of the case but not closing it. "Was the dog hurt?"

"Not severely, but yes. We think it was a group of young boys goading each other. He has a couple of burns, minor ones. The parents reported it and turned the dog over to us."

A dog, Alan thought. *He's just a dog.*

"I'm sorry, did you say something?"

"No, nothing." He snapped the latches on the attaché case.

"The problem is, we don't have room for him. There's space at a shelter in Toledo, so I've tentatively arranged to send him there. At that point, of course, we'll lose track of him, so we won't be able to keep you updated."

Toledo? Alan's heart skipped a beat. He thought, fast, and fought back the memories.

"If I came to get him?"

"You wouldn't regret it. He's a well-behaved dog, very friendly."

Alan recognized the futility of negotiating with the shelter. Like it or not, it was up to him to keep Pete from being shipped away.

"Hold on, I'm checking my calendar." He opened his phone.

Saturday morning was free. "You're open tomorrow? And the animal is housebroken, I assume?"

"Yes, sir. We open at ten Saturdays."

"I'll be there."

"Excellent. You'll need to get a crate for transport. We'll provide you with a starter bag of kibble. You won't be sorry, Mister Carmichael. This little guy's just longing to be someone's forever companion."

Alan cringed at the phrase. Pete wasn't going to be his forever companion, but call it a personal bias, no way was the dog ending up in Toledo.

The phone call concluded, he sank into the nearest guest chair and tried to make a coherent plan for the weekend. He needed facts. Tonight, after the charity bash, he'd spend half an hour on the computer learning what to do with a dog, and what he'd have to buy along with the crate.

Then he paused, turning the problem over. There might be another solution. He punched a number on his phone.

"Astrid?" he said when his office manager answered. "I'm sorry to bother you at home. I've got a situation here. You've had dogs in the past, haven't you?"

Within five minutes he'd arranged for her to meet him at the shelter and take the dog until something permanent could be arranged. Which, she pointed out to him caustically, was his responsibility, not hers. But at least for the moment Pete was safe.

❖

"This will be your room." Late Friday afternoon Pat and Jason stood in the doorway to her former guest room. "Once you're settled in, we'll talk about decorating."

The paperwork had taken longer than expected, but they were able to move Jason out of his last foster home just under the wire. Another twenty-four hours and he'd have had to go to the group home, even if only for a few days.

She'd gone with him to move his things, which didn't amount to much more than a limited wardrobe and a handful of personal possessions he'd been able to hang onto through the disruptions in his life. It had been heartbreaking to see how easily the foster family had let him go.

"It's okay."

She didn't comment. He'd probably never had a room to himself. Jason was between embarrassed and confused, so she gave him space. He dumped his backpack on the bed, looking around, taking it in.

She showed him the bathroom. "Unless we have company, this is yours. Good and bad. You don't have to share, but you do have to keep it clean."

"I ain't cleaning any bathroom. That's for women."

"Guess again. Lots of single men live in their own places. Someone's doing the cleaning, and I'd bet it isn't their girlfriends. You use the bathroom, you keep it clean."

"S'pose if you get company you'll boot me out onto the sofa." If there was a fly in the ointment, he'd do his best to find it.

"I don't expect visitors, but if someone turns up, either they'll stay in a motel, or they'll sleep on an inflatable mattress in the living room. Wouldn't be the first time," she added cheerfully. "The room's yours, Jason. No one's going to kick you out."

She looked straight at him and noted that he was only a couple of inches shorter than she was. He was going to be tall.

Although he avoided her eye, she thought he got it. "Come on, I'll show you around the kitchen. Steak okay for supper?"

"You kiddin' me? Sure." He followed her through the living room into the kitchen.

"Don't expect steak on the menu very often. I figured it's a special day, sort of, so we might as well enjoy it. Baked potatoes in the microwave. What vegetables do you like?" At the expression on his face she laughed. "Sorry. Veggies are part of the package."

Jason gave her a look that told her how unfair life was. "Maybe—carrots?"

"Cooked or raw?"

"Like I get a choice?"

"Like you do, yeah. I'm cooking mine, but it's no hassle to leave yours raw. Just as good for you."

"I guess I like raw better."

"I'll show you where I keep stuff in the kitchen. Can you deal with knives and forks while I get things started?"

When he'd set the table—without argument—she said, "If you want you can go start unpacking. Supper's soon. Twenty minutes okay? I'll call you."

Jason bolted from the kitchen.

Supper, she decided later as he devoured the steak, was not the best time to discuss the house rules. She'd made her list and gone over it with Linda, so she was confident it was realistic, but for the moment she'd let him eat in peace.

After she'd cleaned up the kitchen—no need to hit him with chores today—she tapped on the closed door to his room and waited until he opened it. "Sorry, but we need to go over a few things or we won't get through tomorrow. Got a few minutes?"

"Yeah, sure. Whatever." He followed her out into the living room.

"You're not a condemned man on the way to the gallows. This is practical stuff. Homework, lunches. How you're going to get to school and back."

He slouched on the sofa, sticking his hands in his pockets. "I hate it."

"School?"

Jason grunted.

"All school, or parts of school, or your school in particular?"

"The last one was better. This one—it's like they're laughing at me. Like I smell or something."

"Would you be happier transferring? You could go to Northside."

"And if I don't want to?"

"Then we need to figure out the best way to get you to school and back home. Most of the time I can drive, but that might not be cool." She'd prefer that he transfer, but wasn't going to force another disruption in his young life.

"So, about those rules," she continued. "I will expect homework to be done, and on time. If you need any school supplies, say so, or put it on the list on the bulletin board by the back door. We'll go get you a laptop this weekend—"

Jason sat up. "You'll what?"

"Get you a laptop. You can't do schoolwork without a computer, and you can't rely on using mine, because I need it for work."

She made a mental note to put a password lock on her work files. There'd be dozens of things she hadn't thought of yet.

She continued through her list. "At the same time we'll get you clothes and shoes. I can't afford designer clothes, Jason, but we can do better than what you've got."

"Are you for real? We're gonna shop for clothes and a laptop and shit?"

"I'm real, and one house rule is to clean up the language, but we'll work on it." She ignored his open-mouthed gape. "Once you have a laptop, I want you to research phones. I'll tell you what company I use, so with luck we can find a plan."

Jason's voice, when he finally spoke, was tentative. "You're gonna let me have a phone, too?"

"Not let you. Insist. I'll expect you to use it to keep me in the picture. If you're running late, whatever. You are where you say you'll be, and you let me know. Clear?"

Still reeling from the idea of the laptop and the phone, he dropped the attitude. "This isn't supposed to happen."

"Well, it is." Pat leaned back in her chair. "If you're living here with me, we're family. I've got rules and you've got rules. Among my rules are the usual. Feeding and clothing you, for instance. I'll be where I say I'll be. I'll help with homework—I used to be an engineer, so I'm good at math and science. Now, a few more things."

He sighed, put upon. A twelve-year-old boy.

She ran him through her expectations around neatness, curfews, lights out. "I'll expect help in the kitchen, too. We have a dishwasher, so cleanup isn't so awful. You'll be on dishes every night you don't cook."

"Oh, man," Jason whined, "I have to do the damn dishes? That's so lame—" The words sank in. "Cook? I can't cook."

"Twice a week, I figure. The first weeks I'll help you. You can decide the menu, I'll help you with that, too. We can do the shopping list together."

"You expect me to cook? Like, meals?"

Pat grinned. "Sure do. Consider it a life skill. You aren't that many years from being out on your own."

"I never cooked nuthin' before."

She'd already figured out Jason's language worsened when he felt threatened.

"You've eaten a lot, though." Threatened or not, she'd intrigued him. Could she use this to get through to him? "Relax. It's easy to make edible spaghetti. I'll be around to coach."

She told him about school attendance and having a key to the house. Use of the television and dropping out of the circle.

"One last thing. You have Ms. Gonzales' number, and we'll program it into your phone. If there's ever anything you don't want to talk over with me, call her. I mean it. That's what she's there for, and she's going out on a limb to get you here instead of back in the group home. She's on our side, and she'll help us figure out whatever isn't working. Got that?"

"Yeah. I guess."

"And you'll let me know what you need, right? I can't think of everything." When he nodded she went on. "We'll adapt, it's not as if you have to remember a ton of rules by tomorrow morning. For tonight, unpacking, maybe some television."

Pat watched him slouch off to his room, grateful that it was Friday and they had the weekend to start working out the kinks. A damaged kid, but smart, and with spunk. At the core, a good person. With stability in his life, they'd be okay. Pat wondered how crazy the ride would be before stability took hold.

Jason occupied most of her mind for the next couple of days. Alan and his mall might not have existed. Which was an extra bonus.

Could she be what Jason needed? Could she adapt to this new role? She didn't intend to be an arm's-length foster parent. But had her life experience taught her what she had to know to raise a twelve-year-old boy? This was going to be seat-of-the-pants, for sure. It was enough to cost her sleep, there were so many variables.

Christmas, for instance. With less than a month to go, did she have a hope of figuring out meaningful celebrations and gifts for him?

She had to. She was committed now.

A week before Christmas Alan's office manager presented him with a problem. Pete. The dog had been with Astrid since late November, and Alan had conveniently forgotten about him again, assuming the problem was solved. But Astrid planned to be away for a couple of weeks over the holidays—as, she emphasized, she'd arranged with him several months before—and Pete didn't fit into her plans.

"Don't you know anyone?"

"My job's never required me to build a database of babysitters for dogs," she shot back. Her voice could wither a cactus. "He's sweet, but he's not my responsibility. He'll be out of here within the week, or he'll be back on the street."

Astrid made Alan want to say, "Yes, ma'am," and possibly salute. Between her Viking appearance and her acid tongue, she was the only person in his world who regularly intimidated him. She was also the best office manager he'd ever found. "Give me a moment to check my schedule."

"You're free late afternoon Thursday. Meet me at my place."

"I suppose you'll add that to my calendar for me?"

"I'm not fool enough to rely on you to do it."

So Thursday afternoon he'd be in possession of a sad-eyed dog. His options were running low, but he started paging through the internet, looking for a new home for Pete.

10

By Christmas, Pat thought she might be catching her breath.

She'd had one yelling fight with Jason; she'd finally sent him off to his room to talk to Linda on his new smart phone. There'd been minor tussles over lights-out times, but the curfew issue had evaporated. She supposed it was because he'd left his old associations behind when he moved in with her.

He'd admitted he'd rather transfer to the local school. The paperwork was on her desk.

With a haircut and a decent wardrobe, he'd cleaned up well. Jason now reminded her of the teenager he'd be in a few months.

Plus, she'd discovered a reliable kitchen hand. That was big. Huge. He spent time choosing his menus, and he cooked with flair, if not accuracy. Jason in the kitchen gave her a window into the teen he would be, the man he'd grow into. She liked what she saw.

They'd evolved into a mostly comfortable daily routine, so she didn't need to keep Jason front and center in her mind anymore.

Which was unfortunate, because the alternative mind worm was Alan.

She'd met him twice, one-on-one, once at the Southside Coffee Shack and once at the downtown library. While she'd been wary, he'd countered with formality as they batted around ideas for layouts and façades.

She'd seen him three times at round table meetings. Each time he'd walked her to her car. She hadn't been able to avoid him, no matter how hastily she'd tried to get out the door. The last time he'd cut Millicent off mid-sentence to grab his coat and follow her. That time he'd hesitated as she lowered herself into her car, as if he wanted to say something, but nothing came of it.

With all that going on, taking care of Jason was a respite, if not exactly a picnic.

Pat was nothing if not courageous when it came to facing her demons, and her reaction to Alan Carmichael certainly qualified as a demon. She was in over her head. She tried to hate him, but failed, even though she was no closer to grasping the subtext of that day in his office. She'd love to throw him to the wolves, but self-interest dictated otherwise.

Besides, there had been the flash of naked honesty in his eyes after that kiss, showing her a need she couldn't explain, and he'd never admit.

That kiss.

Over the years she'd learned to rely on her intuition, and she was convinced he'd been pleading with her, but for what she didn't know.

Mentally, he challenged her. The way he took her ideas, or the ideas from the round table, and threw them at her, forcing her to study them from all perspectives, mold them into something acceptable and workable, exhilarated her as nothing else had done in a long time.

Mentally was okay. It was the other, the emotional and physical, that kept her on edge.

After that afternoon?

Yes. Emotionally, he both attracted her and repelled her, which she interpreted to mean she was afraid of the hooks he embedded in her mind.

And the physical. She wanted him. Oh, she wanted him. She hadn't responded like this to a man in years. She'd believed the desire would be easier to deny when she remembered the bruise on her arm, but it wasn't. She did her best to ignore it, because the episode in his office had shown her an edge of suppressed anger and a capacity for violence in him that she suspected even he hadn't been aware of until then.

For several excellent reasons, she'd never go anywhere near him on a personal level, but being locked in this weird non-relationship with Alan Carmichael was affecting her stress levels.

These days Pat tore into her work and her foster kid with total dedication, because it was her best hope for sidestepping the potential catastrophe named Alan.

The day after Christmas Alan had a phone call from Happy Trails Long-Term Boarding Kennel. "We wanted to let you know that Pete's settling in here really well," the man at the kennel said. "These separations can be traumatic for an animal, and he was pretty low at first, but lately he's perked up. He's quite a character."

Holding on to politeness, Alan replied noncommittally, "Yes, I'm sure he is." What made a dog a character? Didn't they mostly go for walks and chew on bones?

At Astrid's, Pete had greeted him like a long-lost father, practically dancing on his one back paw with excitement. The look the dog gave Alan when he'd dropped him off at Happy Trails was one of betrayal and profound disappointment.

"I trust you and your family had a good Christmas?"

Alan had the uneasy feeling the man was settling in for a chat. "Thanks for reporting in. You'll let me know if there's any problem? I have a great deal of work to get through today." He spoke in his most quelling voice.

"I hope you enjoy your work as much as I enjoy mine. It's always fun being with the dogs."

After another meaningless exchange or two Alan managed to extricate himself. But the phone call reminded him that he had to find the dog a home before the kennel fees bankrupted him. How? He didn't trust the shelters anymore, not with their network for shipping dogs all over the state. An advertisement? Where? He shelved the problem and returned to work.

102

Pat collapsed into her chair in the conference room, staring at the others around the table. The late afternoon meeting was a tradition of sorts on December twenty-sixth, a valuable but not a happy one. It gave them a chance to vent and get back in balance.

Last year she'd had the day off. This year, no such luck. The day after Christmas was never fun at Social Services. Christmas brought out the worst in some people, deep sadness in others. They dealt with family violence, suicide, disappointed dreams, and every other possible tragedy.

Pat had spent the afternoon at the group home, with kids who were in the system but not currently in foster care. When it was her turn to speak, she released some of the pain of the day, the wrenching confusion on little faces as the children tried to reconcile the public image of the holiday with the private heartbreak of being alone.

She'd rather be home with Jason, who was spending the afternoon at Amanda's. He hadn't been thrilled, but after almost a month with him, she was figuring out when he was serious and when he was giving her attitude. He'd help Norah construct a wonder with plastic bricks, or they'd find something to do in the kitchen.

She glanced around at her colleagues. There was a bond here, especially with her friend and work partner Linda. They got where she was coming from. They understood the hurt she'd experienced with the lost kids at the home. Yes, this debriefing was a good thing. With the emotional burden of the day unloaded, she'd be her normal self by the time she claimed Jason from Amanda's.

Following the post-Christmas meeting, Pat propped herself at the entrance to Linda's cubicle. They exchanged holiday chat, then Linda said, "Hey, your nemesis hit the news again." She handed a section of the Columbus paper to Pat.

No escape, even at work.

"Yup. That's him."

"Same chick as before, I think?"

She studied the photo and caption. Danielle LaPointe, interior designer. Her hand rested on his arm. Possessively. "Looks like it."

Linda tapped a finger on Danielle. "Aggressive. Not the sort of woman you'd invite over for morning coffee. Confident."

"Too thin."

"Catty."

"They deserve each other, I'd say."

"Tell me something."

"Sure."

"What's he really like?" Linda settled back in her chair, hands folded, eyeballing Pat.

"How do you mean? I've told you." Not everything, not about that blow-up at his office, but enough.

"You've told me he's a determined man, and he's messing up your neighborhood, and you hold a long-standing grudge against him. Personally, I'd discount anything that happened when you were in your twenties, but whatever. I mean, who is he underneath the surface stuff? You might want to think about it, Pat, because I'm picking up an attraction vibe almost as strong as the antagonism one."

Pat perched on Linda's guest chair and wished she had something to do with her hands. "Some of the antagonism's necessary self-defense. You can see for yourself that any woman under ninety would be attracted to him, but if there's depth under the suave exterior, he keeps it well hidden."

"He's hot, for a man his age."

"Between you and me, there's chemistry. He wants something to happen, or so he's implied." More than implied, but Pat hadn't shared that with anyone, not even Amanda. "I am so not going there. He's charming when he chooses to be, but it's all surface, nothing inside. He's nasty when he's frustrated, and near as I can tell he doesn't do commitment, or working on relationships, or even basic compassion. Now, with further documented proof he's not ripe for the picking..." She dropped the newspaper on Linda's desk and tapped it. "I thank the enchanting Danielle. One problem solved, and she's welcome to him."

"Keep it. Tear the picture out and stick it on your dartboard."

"No, thanks. I don't want any more reminders."

"How's Jason doing?"

"We're good." Pat grinned. Since Linda was Jason's social worker, Pat kept her well in the loop. "He enjoyed Christmas at Amanda's. Interesting—he really got into making Christmas dinner, even let go of the attitude. We talked it over, and I'm giving him cooking lessons as a late Christmas present. He's excited. Trying not to show it, of course."

Linda dug Jason's file out of the pile on her desk and made a note. "Worth recording. Whatever gets these kids interested."

"Next is to get him thrilled about math. Working out quantities when you make a two-thirds recipe?"

"Go collect your kid, Pat. You're enjoying this way more than a foster parent's supposed to."

Pat's grin left her. "I wish we knew the story on his mother. I think I want to hold on to this one."

"You mean permanently?"

"Yeah. Like, adopt."

"It's early days. Don't hop too quickly."

"I hear you. Heaven knows he adds to the workload. I've got to get the school transfer request filed first thing next week. At least if he's at the local school I won't be driving so much."

Linda yawned and stretched. "Motherhood, great institution. I have two heading back to college, and of course Josee's convinced she can't be caught dead in her autumn wardrobe. I'm pinning my hopes on second-hand, kind of a funky retro vibe."

"Try the Thrift Store on Superior. I still dress like a funky retro student sometimes, and I've scored there a few times."

"It's true, I can't see you in..." She took the newspaper back and read. "'... a taupe satin sheath with Belgian lace overlay accents at the neckline'. A waste of Belgian lace if you ask me."

Pat let out a dramatic sigh. "Yeah, too true, when it would be perfect for fixing up the frayed hems on our jeans."

Both women laughed. "The high society life not drawing you?"

Pat stood. "Just grousing. I need an attitude adjustment. Time to gather up my surly kid. If we get lucky, Amanda will send us home with leftover turkey."

"Tamales for us. Enough of turkey to last me a year."

The meeting and the chat had worked their usual magic. Pat headed to Amanda's in a much more positive frame of mind.

❖

Danielle's and his social calendar was empty Saturday night, sandwiched as it was between Christmas and New Year's Eve. Usually, the odd time it happened, Alan was fine with it, even relieved. They'd read or watch a movie, order in from the deli down the street. Drink a little too much, dredge up enough desire to have sex later.

Pat would be cooking, reading, watching television. Or taking that kid of hers somewhere. Alan didn't get the kid, but Pat was over the moon. She'd virtually babbled at the last round table before the holidays.

Lounging on the leather sofa across the library from him, Danielle's pale skin was a little flushed, her stretch was feline. He was fortunate to be living with such a stunner of a woman. She gave him what he needed, and not a drop more. No demands, no involvement.

"Alan?"

"Hmm?" He looked up from the book he'd chosen, involving Peru and native wisdom. He might need to re-think his reading material. Amazonian natives didn't resonate with his particular life circumstances.

"Want to tell me what's going on?"

We've had this conversation before. Why won't she let up?

Alan dropped the book on the side table and stood. He walked over to Danielle and took her hand. "The usual. Have I been distracted? I apologize."

"More than distracted. Pour us a scotch?"

While he went to the small drinks table in the corner of the room, she continued. "Is the mall in trouble? You're always wrapped up in your head at the beginning of a project. This is more unsettled than distracted. I think it's fair for me to know what's going on, darling."

"I've told you before, there's nothing." He placed the scotch on the table beside her. "Do you want to stay in tonight or go out for dinner? Somewhere local."

Danielle looked at him. Just looked, as if he'd acquired a third eye. An eye of wisdom opened by that sacred hallucinogen *ayahuasca*, no doubt. The Peruvian natives were getting to him.

"You're never restless, and now you are," she said. "You can talk to anyone, at length, and now you struggle to find conversation topics. I wonder if you hear a word I say. Your social skills have deserted you. Sorry, darling, something's going on. Or is it me?"

Alan sighed and leaned over to rub her shoulders. "No, it's not you. But fair enough, there's a situation. It's bothering me." He nudged her legs out of the way and settled on the sofa next to her, then templed his hands in front of his face. "There's this woman fighting the mall—I think I told you before. She's the leader of the opposition, so there's no choice but to work with her, but she disturbs me."

"Attraction?"

He shook his head. "It's complicated, because she and I have a history. Years ago, when I was starting out, I was her immediate supervisor. I gather I wasn't very nice. Chauvinistic, I guess you'd say. I barely remember it, but it's been on my mind. Most people consider me a good person to work with, but she doesn't. Our interactions are hostile. It bothers me that I trigger such an intense negative reaction. It's bad for business."

"Attraction, Alan?"

"For God's sake, Danielle. She lives in a dumpy little house in Calter Creek and takes in foster kids. She's hardly my type." Exasperated, Alan stood and returned to his chair.

Again Danielle's eyes assessed him. "Tell me this much. Is our arrangement at risk?"

Irritated, Alan wondered why this couldn't be a typical Saturday night where they'd indulge in mindless chat and flash around their phenomenal charitable sensitivity. Danielle and her probing questions forced him to places he chose not to go, especially in her presence.

But he wore his masks well. He picked up his book, using nonchalance to hide his discomfort. "You have every right to question, but she's a challenge, not a love interest. Relax and tell me what you want to do for dinner."

In the end they ordered deli lobster salad and a baguette. Alan matched Danielle scotch for scotch and fought his way through the wonders of *ayahuasca* trips in the jungles of Peru, wondering what any of it had to do with him.

There had to be a better way to spend a Saturday night.

11

The morning of New Year's Eve, Pat found herself holed up in the little construction trailer with Alan. Since The Incident back in November, they'd settled into a functional working relationship, calm and businesslike. This meeting, the first time she'd been completely alone with him since that day, was professional, as if they were colleagues, as if it were only business.

Except that no matter what her mind told her, she was on guard. Every minute. The non-stop tension wreaked havoc on her digestion, her nerves.

Not good for overall health.

The trailer looked dingy, despite being relatively new. She assumed it was the poor lighting from the single, discount-store fixture overhead and the undersized windows limiting the daylight. Or possibly it was the ancient card table and metal chairs, which nearly filled the space.

Alan filled the space, too.

He looked good, but by now Pat had plenty of experience ignoring his physical appeal. He had dressed as usual, white shirt and dark slacks. She'd never been sure if he was tanned or naturally swarthy, but the shirt accented his darker skin. He'd rolled up his sleeves, which made it impossible not to notice his strong forearms.

Her jeans were wearing on the inseam—she'd long ago given up dreaming of model-slender thighs—and risked a hole at the knee. Outclassed by Alan. But to get any decent work done, she had to be comfortable.

"You know I'm delighted you're not fighting to keep the land. It'll push the project that much farther away from Maple Street," she told him.

"We plan to use that. It'll be a good publicity point."

"I figured."

Most of their shared work in the last two months had been round table type issues, the superficial aspects of the complex such as façades, flooring, washroom color schemes, but he'd finally started showing her the new floor plans. Today they were dealing with the office wing, based on the mock-ups Raul had done. They'd been at it for over an hour when the question of the library arose.

"You can see that the recreation center idea's a total non-starter," he said. "There's not enough space. But a small library, maybe."

"Or a landmark library. A visionary library. If we could just squeeze in—"

"We can't. You know it. But something on a smaller scale..." He got busy with a pencil and gave her a minute's breathing room.

A library would be a major concession, if it happened. Had the idea garnered positive feedback? Or perhaps they'd use it to draw more locals to their development? He wasn't saying. But he was trying to figure out a way to include it in the plans.

She watched his pencil moving as his thoughts unfolded. "It's not like you to think small," she interrupted, tapping on the floor plan. "You need space, not a hole-in-the-wall. More windows, massive ones, bringing the outdoors in."

He shifted his eyes from the plan to her, a bemused expression on his face.

"A story pit. Separate rooms for meetings and activities. Computers. Good adult seating. Talk to your architect. Even I know that new libraries are winning design awards these days."

"Pat, you're a dreamer."

"I thought you were the dreamer. Your visionary mall."

He dropped his pencil on the plan and glanced at his watch. "I'm finished for today. How about you? Big plans for tonight?"

She laughed shortly. "Yeah. Trying to stay awake until midnight to keep Jason company. Not that he'll want my company, but I guess he has to get used to it. You?"

"There's a dinner and dance thing. It's valuable to be seen at these, so we go."

"You and Danielle?" As soon as the words were out of her mouth she regretted them.

His brows went up. "Yes, if you're curious."

"Not really. I had no business asking."

"It was a reasonable question, we're in the papers often enough. But it was the wrong question to ask."

"What do you mean?"

He rose and circled the card table to stand over her. Her alarm signals went nuts. Her stomach knotted, the blood fled her hands to coagulate in her chest.

"I mean there's nothing between us. It's convenient to have a partner for these things. It's part of the game."

"Alan..."

He reached down and toyed with the fingers on her right hand. "Not like last time, Pat."

"That day..."

His face flushed, but he didn't dodge. "I'm still struggling to come to terms with what happened. You were a toxic mix, but I never lose control that way. It was unprofessional."

"That scares me. It's as if everything has to be reined in, managed, so it's impossible to say what's underneath."

She sensed his discomfort in the way he tensed. She wasn't the only one to carry scars from their confrontation.

"I must have frightened you."

"Some, sure. But at least it gave me a look at who you are when the control cracks."

"What you saw that day, that's not who I am."

"Are you so sure? That much anger?" She tried to move her fingers away, but he tangled them in his, locking their hands together. "Alan, I don't want—"

"You do."

He toyed with her fingers, brushing over the tips with his thumb.

When the silence had stretched so finely it might shatter like shards of spun sugar, he put his hand under hers and guided her to her feet, for all the world as if he had asked her to dance in a formal, Jane Austen type romance. Only she'd never learned the steps to this one.

He mesmerized her.

"Alan, don't—"

"You don't need to tremble when I touch you. I swear I won't hurt you."

"You don't know…"

He didn't speak.

Oh, no.

His blue eyes held her with no escape as his mouth descended on hers. The feel of his gentle lips moving against hers sensitized her skin, wrapped around her mind, and sent desperate signals from there to every part of her, from the moment his mouth touched hers, such a contrast to the last time, nothing to fear, everything to want, to take and melt and…

He responded to her response, and what had started gentle and inquiring became primal, pushing her to the point of desperation to get more of him, merge his mouth more deeply with hers. To learn the taste of him, feel him hard against her, the leanness of him under her hands, the artistry of his body. She'd denied it for so long and now she couldn't stop it for the life of her, couldn't make it not happen, how she wanted this man, *this* man, and no, *no, she wouldn't* –

She turned her head, breaking off the kiss. He still had his arms around her, locking her to him, looking down at her.

She pushed free and turned away, but it was too late. Everything was too late. The tension of the last months burst out, and *Dammit* –

Then she was crying, and the tears refused to stop.

This could not be happening.

"Pat." His hands were on her shoulders, touching her lightly, then turning her and God help her but where was God when you needed him anyway, not here, that was for sure, because she was sobbing on his crisp, white shirt, as if he were her refuge instead of her doom.

And he let her. He stood there holding her against him and let her.

When she was able to get some semblance of control back, he put his hands on either side of her face, not even giving her time to wipe away the tears and the mucus, and kissed her cheeks, her eyes. "Want to talk about it?"

No, she didn't want to talk. "Don't be sweet. It doesn't suit you."

He laughed and wrapped her in a hug. "You're right, I don't do sweet. I leave that to you. At least I guess you're sweet with those kids of yours."

"I don't want this."

"That's not strictly accurate. But you're not willing. What I still don't understand is why not."

She turned away, but heard Alan tear a paper towel from a roll in the little kitchenette. He nudged her with it, so she accepted it to mop her face. She shook her head.

"Because you don't like me? You've said so before. It's just possible I'm not an ogre intent on destroying your neighborhood."

"I can't."

"I want to touch you again. Will you let me?"

Away from him, true north was back to where it was supposed to be, instead of bobbing around near the equator. She took a deep breath and dug her combative self out from under the quivering mess that was the rest of her. "No. Chemistry isn't enough, and that's all we have."

"Chemistry's a good place to start, I've always thought."

Wary, she backed away from him, as far as possible in the crowded trailer. "Worst possible place, if you ask me. Friendship. Shared interests. Enjoyment of each other's company. Lots of better starting places. This isn't enough." Pat fought to keep her voice calm and level, and didn't make a very good job of it.

"Even though you want me."

"And you want me. Don't put this all on my shoulders."

"Ready to fight me some more?"

"I'm going to forget this morning happened. I'll work on your mall, but nothing else."

"What's wrong with enjoying ourselves? Consenting adults?" He propped against the little kitchen counter, studying her. He looked as if she'd given him a conundrum to solve. Hadn't the man ever heard of relationships?

Obviously not.

"I'm not going to stop trying, Pat. I want to touch you."

Pat kept twelve-year-old boys under control. Her hands were shaking, but her look was steely. "We need to work together. I won't let go of any opportunity to influence this development of yours. So plan on keeping your libido under wraps, if you don't mind." She grabbed her coat from the back of the chair and shrugged into it.

"I don't think so." He reached over and touched her cheek. She jumped away as if he had claws. "We both have other places to be, but I don't want you to forget me. Not on New Year's Eve. Let's part with something to celebrate, shall we?"

His hands were inside her coat, oh why hadn't she gotten it zipped before he—

"Don't forget me, Pat."

Another gentle, seductive, safe kiss, changing in the blink of an eye to one she wouldn't forget in a lifetime. His hand caressed her breast over her sweater, his mouth was under her hair, below her ear, *in* her ear, tickling her with his tongue, blowing, murmuring, and she could no more stop him than she could stop the bulldozers coming to destroy the field and build his mall. Her only option was to cling to him while the nuclear reactor that was Alan fried her bones.

Damn Alan Carmichael.

He set her a little apart. "Go home—and don't forget." He turned her toward the door of the trailer and propelled her out.

The tears were coming again. She looked back at him once, at his thoughtful face, then fled down to the path to home...

114

...And straight into Jason.

Could this day get worse?

"Crap. What happened to you?" Trust Jason to cut to the chase.

"Nothing. Drop it, okay?"

"You were over at the trailer. With that man building the mall." Her boy stood in the front door, arms folded over his skinny chest.

Pat surged past him, heading for her room. "None of your business."

"He doesn't have any right."

She wheeled to face him. "I said drop it, Jason."

"He doesn't, Pat. He's scum if he thinks—"

"Jason." The need to stop the boy restored her focus.

He shut up.

"Get this straight. I'm upset, yes, but it's nothing to do with Mister Carmichael, so lay off. Grownup life isn't always the bed of roses you think it is, and I'm human, not superwoman."

"Jeez." Jason backed off in a hurry. "Sorry, Pat."

"We're good. I'm going to take a quick shower. Do you still have holiday homework?"

"Algebra. It's grim."

"I can do algebra. Call me if you need help. Lousy way to spend New Year's Eve, but we'll do popcorn later."

Jason bolted. She might have found a new strategy. Jason opted for algebra over a crying woman. She smiled, even if she was still on the verge of tears.

She gave him full points for loyalty. He was prepared to go toe-to-toe with Alan, a man he'd never met, rather than have her upset.

But Alan hadn't done anything, strictly speaking. He was just being Alan. She figured he was offering her the best he had to offer, which was sort of pitiful, but no reflection on her. No, her wet face and swollen eyes were every bit her own doing.

115

She and Jason muddled through the rest of New Year's Eve, until she abandoned the effort at eleven and went to bed, leaving him in possession of the television. She'd relied on a decent night's sleep to clear her fogged mind.

No such luck. New Year's Day in the morning, and she was just as hazy as she'd been the night before. She needed a quiet space to concentrate on a man she wasn't even sure she liked, and what kind of waste of a day was that?

Bottom line, if you knew what was good for you, you'd have the affair and get it out of your system.

Simple, right?

Then why wasn't she jumping his bones the minute she got the chance? She wanted to. Oh, she wanted to.

Pat wrote a note for Jason, in case he woke before she returned, and left from her back door. She circled the house and struck off in the direction of the field. The trampled snow on the paths allowed her to walk furiously, even if the footing was too treacherous for running.

It was a good morning for a walk. Cold, crisp, and everyone else in the world, including her foster son, was still fast asleep. She loved the peace and stillness of New Year's morning.

She'd circle the field, she'd get her head clear on Alan Carmichael and the embarrassing little scene she'd enacted yesterday, then she'd go home and cook up waffles for Jason.

Her plan lasted as long as it took her to cut through the path between her neighbors' houses, step into the field, and set her eyes on the construction trailer sitting smugly dead center. The site of her recent humiliation. The symbol of Alan and his bloody mall and the catastrophe facing her tidy life.

Not now, not ever. Not even for the chance to have a delicious tumble between the sheets. Because, *God*, did he do it for her.

Pat upped her pace. Suddenly, the sooner this walk was over, the better.

You're hot for him, it's not rocket science.

She pulled to a stop on Sycamore Street, half way around the loop. Looked along the driveway to the construction trailer. And sagged.

The risk was falling for him. He was everything she didn't want in a man. It was that simple. It'd be fun for a week, a month, with nothing to show at the end.

She had a job and a home she loved, a kid she was growing to love, close friends, everything she needed. She might want Alan Carmichael, but she didn't need him. Love wasn't in his vocabulary, and she'd keep it out of hers, where he was concerned. Even if it meant skipping the sex thing, because of where it could lead, much too easily.

But the ache for his body, his hands....

She short-circuited her walk and cut through the middle of the vacant lot, past the construction trailer, instead of following the trail over to the far eastern side along the frozen creek. Her brain clicked back to full functioning. Normal trumped exotic every time. She wanted home and waffles, the things that made her life rich and meaningful.

Not the edgy things, the impossible things.

At home, she found a text on her phone. And found herself agreeing to meet Alan again, at the trailer that afternoon.

Sometimes Pat amazed herself with the things she talked herself into.

12

Alan greeted Pat formally at the trailer door, not touching her, because he couldn't predict where her mind was after yesterday. "Happy New Year."

"Same to you." The repressive tone in her voice warned him to respect the distance she defined between them.

"Thanks for coming over." He stepped back to let her in.

"I'm stuffed full of waffles and cross-eyed from the Rose Bowl Parade. At the moment the mall sounds like sanity."

Not trusting. But at least she's here.

"About yesterday," she said.

She stood in the door, her head high and her eyes challenging him. He acknowledged her pride and shook his head. "I think you're about to apologize. Don't."

"I overreacted."

"I pushed you. Forget it. I think you'll be pleased with what I have to show you." He'd texted her because Raul and one of his draftsmen had worked all afternoon the previous day, and Alan was excited. He suspected she would be, too.

"In twenty-four hours? Over a holiday?" Pat skirted the table and sat on the far side, shedding her coat.

"Last time we didn't finish what we started." He gave her a moment to sort through the double entendre, then anchored them firmly in the mall project. "My team's the best. They weren't thrilled to be tackling this yesterday, but they get paid enough. They had a whole afternoon. This is good, Pat. We've incorporated some of your ideas and have others on hold until we find out what else is in the mix. It's unfortunate you left engineering. You've got an eye."

She shrugged. "I'm no architect."

"Still."

He kept the conversation on a strict business level as they studied the new front elevation. In the sketches she'd brought with her to their coffee shop meeting, she'd changed the whole shape of the main entrance, made it like walking through an arch into a town square. He knew as soon as he saw it that her idea was a winner. It was at once dominant and welcoming, phenomenal for publicity shots. Later on, people would use it as a landmark, would say, 'I'll meet you under the arch'. It was enough to make him wonder what else she'd come up with.

He yawned.

Her head went up, then down again. "Pleasant evening?" she said without looking at him.

"The usual. These things—you go to them to be seen, not so much to have a good time."

"Is that all you do? You must have friends, other than social snobs you schmooze."

"You're a bit of a snob yourself, aren't you?"

Pat narrowed her eyes at him.

Alan didn't pursue that comment. "Yes, of course we have friends. There's a ski party in a few weeks, the tennis club in the summer. In the meantime, charities love us. Can't say much for the food, though."

She might have been half listening, but mostly she was studying the sheet he'd put before her. It showed the current front façade of the main shopping wing of the mall, the view from Sycamore Street. It was one building, but from the outside it looked like an old fashioned town center, each attached building reflecting the theme of upscale, small-town comfort, but each subtly different. The arched entrance gave it variety and tied it together.

"Yes." She shoved the plans in his direction. "It works. I'm glad you think so."

"Let's move on, because I want you to cast your mind on the bigger problem."

"Let me guess. The lost fifty feet again?"

All business. He put aside the elevation and unrolled more sheets. They filled the card table. "The mall proper, retail. Raul's provided a handful of suggestions. I welcome any thoughts you might have."

Raul had sketched out three rough floor plans, ground floor only, for the newly configured mall. Alan watched Pat as she studied the revised plans, shuffling the large sheets.

The way her forehead wrinkled in concentration, her hair falling over her face...

After a few minutes she pulled one of the sheets to the top of the stack and looked up.

Before she could speak, he said, "No. Not that one."

"Why not? Alan, it's got—"

"It loses too much floor space. I should have pulled it out before I showed them to you."

Raul had designed linked pods, in octagons, the stores grouped around central plazas. The corridors connecting the pods had tiny storefronts; his notes suggested using them for the carts and corridor vendors that popped up in other malls. The atrium was still there at the east end, just before the office wing, but there were also small sitting areas in each plaza.

"Look, Alan. With a one-width central corridor, everyone loses. To give the stores adequate floor space, you'd have to be wide instead of deep, but that's boring from the shopper's point of view." Her fingers traced on the floor plan. "With these plazas, the stores facing north or south would still be small, but you could make the others as large and irregular as you want them to be."

"Will you listen for a minute? To meet revenue projections, we can't go there. It simply wouldn't be big enough."

But she didn't hear him, or was choosing not to. "I love this idea of shallow storefronts on the connectors. Love it. Independent stores, not chains. And the outer walls can mirror the octagons, so it isn't a box. With the varied façades on the outside, it'll be dynamite."

"Bottom line, we can't afford it." He kicked himself for not pulling that layout before she saw it. Even Raul had said it was probably impossible, financially.

She smacked her hand on the plan. "This is the one. You can give each plaza its own personality. It might be the kind of place I'd go. A boutique shopping complex rather than a conventional mall. If it has to be smaller, then make the size a feature. Sort of intimate. The last thing you want is for it to look truncated.

"I hate concrete and rectangles," she added, looking up at him. "If you can build something that has a good setback from Maple, and there's irregularity to the exterior walls, and it has a small-town vibe, well, I'm only one person, but it works for me."

"Raul ran some numbers already. There's no way it can happen."

"So what are you trying to create here? An ordinary place that'll be forgotten in a year, or a visionary complex? Come on, Alan, think."

He pulled the blueprint closer and traced the outer walls with a finger. She was right. He knew it, deep in his gut, but was there any way to make this layout viable? The estimates painted a different picture. The investors would scream.

He wasn't blind to the irony. His perfect project, and the vision wasn't even his anymore. He laughed out loud as he looked up. "You've shanghaied the development, you know that?"

Pat leaned back and stretched. "I won't tell if you don't."

"I'll send the pod plan back to Raul, to see if he can make it work. As it stands it's a non-starter, but the man's a genius, so maybe he'll come up with something."

"Maybe at the same time he can tweak the office plans to save the creek."

"We have to keep the project in the black, as I keep telling you."

"Trust me, the creek's marketable."

"High maintenance, though. Grounds keeping, liability issues—" As he spoke he reached for the plans and started tapping them into a neat pile.

"Turn it over to the county. If it's a proper park, and if you donate the land, it'd be more publicity, right?"

"The only hope for a library is if we sacrifice the creek."

"Sacrifice something else."

"We'll have more battles about that creek before we're done." He twisted to retrieve the storage tube from the counter and shoved the plans into it.

Pat sighed. "Should we get in touch with Millicent to put it on the round table agenda?"

Their eyes met, and to his delight she giggled. They both knew the real work wasn't done in the round table.

Alan got up and poured them each a glass of water, more as a distraction than for any other reason. His body had developed an odd tension when she was around, as if her presence tugged an invisible thread connected to his nerve endings. He should mind that, but he didn't. He wanted her close.

He sat and said, "I probably shouldn't risk destroying the mood, but yesterday… that was sort of unreal, Pat."

"Yeah, wasn't it. I've had time to think." She picked up her glass and retreated into herself.

Alan studied her while she drank. Was this the same woman who'd collapsed against him the day before? Today she faced him with no emotion at all.

She doesn't know it or care, but she's lovely.

When she looked down, her hair swung like a warm red-gold curtain in front of her face. His fingers twitched, literally twitched, with the need to push that hair back, let the silkiness of it drape across his hand.

Then she looked somewhere over his shoulder and spoke. "The first thing you need to understand is that I'm not in the least interested in a casual affair. While in theory there's no reason not to go that route, for me it's not a good option. I have more meaningful things to do with my time, to be honest.

"So the second thing is that I want to grow old with someone special, someone I love and trust. Don't laugh, I know it sounds corny."

"There are never any guarantees, though. I take enough risks in business. In my personal life, I want certainties. Nothing long-term is worth the gamble."

"That's sad, but it's what I expected." Pat shrugged. "For me, if it happens, it happens. But getting myself tangled up with you, well, it would reduce my odds. If he came along and I was having an affair with you, I might not recognize him. He might not recognize me. And I'd miss my chance."

Tangled up with you. That hurt. She must have sensed that he was about to speak, because she held up her hand. "Let me finish. The third thing... this is the one that's hard to say." She took a breath. "If I let myself get involved sexually with you, there's too much risk of falling for you. And you aren't my dream man, Alan."

She'd eliminated him categorically. Another stab, even though her dream man was the last thing on earth he wanted to be. A casual affair was the most he looked for.

Why? Because there was something he couldn't define. It had to do with Pat and him. And it was dangerous.

The silence grew palpable after she finished speaking.

He fiddled with the water. "That was a pretty cavalier rejection."

"You stated your position clearly, and it's a long way from mine."

She took a breath, then finally looked him in the eye. "The man I love will be a man who stands proud, whose personal ethics align with the values I believe in. Commitment, integrity, going the extra mile. And I doubt you know what I'm talking about. For your sake, I wish you did."

"I see." He didn't, but what else was he supposed to say? He believed in integrity. Honest, transparent business dealings had seen him through some sticky spots. Commitment, going the extra mile—she must be able to see those in him? After all their shared work on the mall? But she'd implied otherwise.

"I doubt it." She gave him a sad smile. "But perhaps you'll think about it."

It was awkward after that. He gathered up their water glasses and put them in the sink. She didn't say more, and his nimble mind came up empty.

Again that thin smile of hers. "The mall has me excited, Alan, the way it's evolving. That's one feather in your cap, anyway."

He shot back, "Do you think that's what this is about? Conquests? I'm not that depraved."

"Sorry." She stood and picked up her coat, then touched his arm. "I didn't mean to be insulting. My point is, when it comes to relationships, I don't think you even know what one is." She became brisk. "I'm going home. Jason's on his own, and I have housework to do. Good luck with the architects."

At the door she paused and looked back at him with a hint of sadness. "What's happening between us... I'm sorry, Alan. It isn't enough."

He didn't make any attempt to escort her or follow her. He'd never heard a line in the sand drawn with such cool precision. What did she want him to say? Was this psychobabble? Or what those Peruvian Indians were supposed to teach him?

What was so complicated when a man and a woman wanted each other and acted on it?

Alan hauled on his coat, snatched up the roll of plans, and left. Driving home, he mulled over Pat and her incomprehensible words. He wondered if he needed to get his hands on some of that *ayahuasca* stuff. Maybe that's what it took, to be on the same plane of existence as her.

13

"Have you seen this?" Alan thumped the back of his hand against the newspaper he held.

Brandon looked up from a real estate listing he'd been studying. "Local rag. I don't bother. It's a narrow canvas. If it affects me, I already know it."

"While in general I agree, I suggest you make an exception." He dropped the weekly Calter Creek Bugle on Brandon's desk.

Brandon read the letter he'd circled, an impassioned screed against the mall. "Rabble rouser. I'm surprised the paper published it."

"Slow news week? Not so many ads, now that the Christmas rush is done with."

Brandon frowned, reflecting Alan's reaction. "I don't get this. Other than the people on Maple, I don't see why anyone cares one way or another about the mall going in. It's derelict land bordering on farmland, for heaven's sake."

"Does that strike you as a real signature?"

"The paper's policy is not to publish letters without a name—but no, it sounds fake to me." Brandon flipped through the newspaper as they talked. He stopped abruptly. "You missed this." He slapped the paper down on his desk.

"Hadn't finished reading—oh, hell."

"Well, that explains why they published the letter."

The newspaper carried a half-page op-ed piece about the mall on the inside back page, including shots of the vacant land and a couple of the early floor plans. The article decried lack of involvement by the town of Calter Creek and lack of amenities in return for the increased traffic on the roads, an influx of unknown types of people, demands on sewer and water—none of which was true. The piece was inflammatory, attempting to dictate concessions and a suspension of progress until the demands had been worked out.

That, plus the letter which virtually promised violence if the mall weren't stopped, cast a pall over the two men.

"Recognize the name on this one?" Alan asked.

"Yeah. He tried to outbid me on the land. Sour grapes, making trouble."

"We could sue if it weren't for the negative publicity. You know the town. What's the best way to handle this?"

"I'll call the paper and book space for a riposte."

"We need to work fast if we want it in next week. I'll start an outline."

"We'll get it in." A tight restraint tinged Brandon's usually melodic voice. "You'd better believe it'll be in there."

"I'll leave this." Alan tapped the paper and went back to his own office, internally cursing. This kind of aggravation was an irritant, like a stone in a shoe. He didn't mind leaving figurative blood on the streets, but he wasn't going to tolerate any more challenges to the mall.

For Alan, the weekend was a relief, giving him a chance to shelve the Calter Creek development for a day or two. Friday night, he and Danielle met Trent and Tammy Oberlin at Richard's—accent on the second syllable, a fact that caused him to groan inwardly every time he heard it—an upscale French restaurant in downtown Columbus.

"To friends." Trent raised his glass toward them.

"Friends, darling." Danielle purred her response to the toast. The wine glasses clicked, and they drank, while surreptitiously, Alan kept an eye on Danielle.

"Do fill us in on the McCallister house." Tammy leaned forward across the table, her décolletage deepening. "Everyone's talking about you snagging the contract. Complete overhaul? You must be excited."

Danielle turned on her professional chuckle. "I'll be excited when I've got a full concept to run with. At the moment it's a lot of unconnected ideas. It's invigorating, though."

Tammy held a senior position at a finance company not far from Richard's, where they were now so busy complimenting each other on their successes. She must envy Danielle, Alan mused. An entire old mansion to renovate? Every woman's dream.

Not for the first time, Alan wondered if it was possible Danielle had another interest in the Oberlins, one involving Tammy only incidentally. Watching for signals between her and Trent might make this evening more entertaining.

Trent left the reno discussions to the women. "Flights booked?" They planned to fly to Montreal, rent a car, then drive up into the Laurentian Mountains to ski.

"Weeks ago. Routing through Philadelphia."

"Snow conditions are good. A warm front's coming through, though."

Alan shrugged. "If nothing else, it would make time to sit by a fire with a book. Give your knee a break, too."

"Might not be a bad idea. It's been bothering me lately."

"Rugby, right?" It was supposedly an old school injury, and Trent, the product of an exclusive prep school on the east coast, liked to have it acknowledged. Alan didn't believe in Trent's problem knee for a minute, but since he was the weakest skier of the four of them, it made a convenient excuse.

The appetizers arrived. Although Alan had looked forward to this dinner, now he studied the arrangement of endive, two shrimps, a pickled peppercorn, and a mayonnaise-like glop, and wondered how he'd ended up here. He could do sophisticated, but *being* sophisticated sometimes eluded him.

He hadn't gone to boarding school. He'd never had a chance to hurt his knee at rugby or any other sport. His background was a long way from the privileged one Trent and Tammy, and for that matter, Danielle, came from.

It was a miracle he'd survived his childhood. A miracle he'd made something of himself.

Even now, he didn't spend his days in high-rise offices, although he preferred them to the dump that was the County Building in Calter Creek, or Brandon Caine's strip mall office. He was an engineer, in the construction business. A man who took a vision and created it in bricks and mortar. Once the project was underway, as site supervisor he'd switch out his suit for jeans and a hardhat, and he'd be as comfortable in the hardhat as the suit.

You've come further than any of them could imagine. But Alan had built a life around not thinking about his childhood.

Danielle was purring again. "Trent, what do you think of the latest stock split?" She named a well-known tech company. "Is it a good time to jump in?"

"Not yet. I can recommend a couple of mutuals if you have cash lying around. It's a good time as long as you keep your eye on things."

"That's what you do for me, darling. Keep an eye on things. Please do send the information."

"How about you, Alan? Have any spare cash you want to get working for you?"

"Thanks, Trent, but right now most of my spare cash is tied up in the development over in Calter Creek." He put a subtle emphasis on the word 'spare' to make it clear his financial future didn't depend on the success of the mall. "We hit a technical problem, but it's resulted in exciting design modifications."

"I'm glad to hear it, since Tammy and I put money in it. We're waiting for you to make us rich."

"Oh, you don't need me for that." He kept his own financial worth private. While Danielle was comfortably off, he didn't know what that meant in actual dollars and cents. Trent and Tammy? He was sure their investment in his mall was small change to them. Their bottom line had to be healthy.

He'd eaten the shrimps and nibbled at the endive, and wondered why anyone would eat a pickled peppercorn. As the waiter cleared the plates, Alan turned to Danielle. "We need to find time in our schedules to discuss logistics, darling. Whose car to take to the airport, for instance. How much of my baggage allowance you plan to use."

She smiled at him. "Your SUV, dear, and half a bag. I can be an efficient packer when I have to be."

"So I'll get to carry your ski boots?"

"I know you won't mind." She reached for him and squeezed his hand, a move that was meant to be noticed. "You understand me so well."

"My dear, to see you contented after a day's skiing, it's worth losing half a bag."

This was getting nauseating. What were he and Danielle thinking?

The main courses appeared on the table. His steak included a sauce involving truffles. He hoped he'd be able to get at the meat without making it obvious how indifferent he was to the things.

The meal limped on. The four of them had been skiing together before, and once had chartered a yacht for a cruise in the Bahamas. In theory they were great friends who enjoyed each other's company. In practice, Alan doubted they knew each other at all. They certainly didn't know him. No one did. By the end of dessert and coffee, he longed to be at home. Getting out of his suit and having a cognac by the fire—alone—sounded like heaven.

They played the game. It was expected. His landmark mall that, to hear him tell it, couldn't fail. Danielle flaunting her home reno contracts like trophies, skipping the sweat and frustration she poured into these projects. Two beautiful couples, no storms on any horizon, because no one ever admitted to less than perfection.

All part of the routine.

As they drove home he brought up their smarmy love-fest. "Danielle, what on earth were we doing tonight?"

She shrugged. "The image, showing them who we are. Always the image." She stretched, flexing her feet in their fashionable boots.

"Do you ever get tired of it?"

"You're in a strange mood tonight, Alan. What's going on?"

"Nothing." He reached over and squeezed one of her gloved hands. "I wonder sometimes if people believe us or see right through our BS."

"I expect we're as happy together as most couples. Trent and Tammy, for instance. I don't see much love lost between them, do you?"

"Maybe not, but they have managed to produce two children. Are you sleeping with him?"

"None of your business, darling. As for the children, they hustled them out of the house as soon as the little beggars were old enough for boarding school. Not my idea of family."

He glanced over at her. "You have an idea of family?"

"Oh, not for myself. But surely, if you're going to have kids you should—you know—*have* them."

Alan's smile was sincere, but directed at the slushy road ahead. "I never suspected you had a traditional bone in your body."

"You don't sound like yourself. My guess is, it's the woman who's against your project."

"You may be guessing right. She has a way of knocking me off balance. It's disconcerting, but she's contributed a few good ideas for the mall."

"And are you sleeping with her?"

His smile widened. "Tit for tat? None of your business, darling."

Her smile answered his. "That's the Alan I know. Buck up, my dear. We both need a break, so this skiing thing will do us good."

Perhaps she was right. A chance to switch gears would give him time to sort out his mind. Pat Fraser had his thoughts far too tangled. A few days away, keeping Danielle at his beck and call—yes, he'd enjoy that, even if it drove her crazy.

Jason stared in blank dismay at the baking pan in his hand. "They're flat."

"There's an art," Pat said. She sat at her kitchen table, watching him work in her kitchen. "Not one I've ever mastered, so don't let it bug you."

Every woman in America made baking powder biscuits, or at least Pat had grown up believing it. Every woman but her. Now she'd transmitted her faulty biscuit gene to Jason.

"Do you think they'll be edible?" Jason put the pan on the stove and poked at one of the biscuits.

"Yep. Even though mine almost never rise, they're always fine. Once they've got gravy on them, you won't be able to tell the difference."

"I read every instruction. I was so careful, Pat." He was upset.

"Hey, calm down. I've been reading those instructions for thirty years, and I still end up with flat biscuits. Then a miracle happens and they come out an inch tall, and I have no idea what I did right that I messed up every other time. My theory now is, some people are born with a knack, and others — well, the biscuits hate us. But we get our revenge because we eat them anyway."

Jason abandoned the biscuits and stirred the contents of the slow cooker. "This smells good."

"Try it. Be sure." When he started to raise the stirring spoon to his mouth, she added, "Clean spoon, please."

"Yeah, sorry. I forgot." He dug out a spoon, tasted, and grinned. "I like it."

"Amanda's favorite. You notice the difference the tarragon makes? If we'd put it in with everything else, it'd be cooked flat by now. The flavor stays fresh when you add it later."

Jason's reaction to cooking fascinated Pat. Since she'd turned him loose to make his first spaghetti, using bottled sauce, he'd been hooked. He'd started the evening course in basic cooking skills she'd given him for Christmas, and had come home enthralled — and more excited than she'd ever seen him, more even than when they'd bought his computer and phone.

The cooking thing was pure chance. She'd seen his interest in food in the circle, but attributed it to the constant hunger of growing boys. Helping in the kitchen was meant to be a way to give him responsibility, not an enthusiasm that might survive his teen years.

The routes to normalcy could be so simple. And yet, in a typical, overworked foster family, this particular route might well have remained underground. He'd have grown up, struck out on his own, without ever suspecting his latent passion.

He had water going now and was washing a handful of snow peas. "Good choice," she said. "Consider sprinkling them with a herb. Mint, maybe."

"I thought mint was for sweet stuff."

"Not always. Give it a try."

Peas steamed, Jason sliced open the biscuits without cutting a finger—*mother hen*, Pat scolded herself—and served their dinner with obvious pride. She didn't comment that he forgot the slivered almonds to garnish the stew. He was twelve years old, for heaven's sake, one of the lost ones, a boy without many friends, starting in a new school, and hanging on as well as he could.

Pat praised the meal and ate, always the best test of a menu's success.

Jason's mother still hadn't been in touch. Pat hoped she'd stay missing. She'd fallen under his spell, this boy she'd singled out from her little circle of foster kids. She wanted to hang onto him, so it troubled her that with one motherly plea to get her son back, they'd take Jason away, send him off with a woman who'd been willing to abandon him to the system and disappear. Sometimes a mother ran out of choices, but to leave that way, have no contact with your son for almost two years...

"The nice part for you is, because you cooked, I do the cleaning up."

"I still don't believe that."

"Hey, I'm proving it. You're not off the hook, though, because you'll be heading for homework, right?"

"Shit," Jason said under his breath. He caught her eye. "I mean—darn?"

132

Pat laughed at the old-fashioned expletive. "It's a way of life, like all the reports Social Services expects me to write. Best to just do it, so it isn't hanging over your head."

He ambled off toward his room. It was a toss-up, whether he'd do the homework or she'd have to sit on him, but it was getting better. At least he'd clued in that since she'd been an engineer, there was no shame in asking for math help from a supposed expert.

She cleared the table, stored the leftover stew and biscuits—she'd give him toasted biscuits with butter and jam when he got home from school tomorrow—and began washing the dishes.

14

Well, that was yesterday, when she'd honestly believed everything was sorting out. Guess you never can tell with a twelve-year-old boy.

Pat approached the elementary school that afternoon with the odd mix of nerves, memory, and resolve she suspected most adults experienced when they return to the scenes of their childhood. She hadn't gone to Northside Elementary herself — she hadn't grown up in Calter Creek — but it didn't matter. The smells, the posters and artwork on the walls, the whole atmosphere of the place, were the same.

The trepidation working its way into her gut as she approached the principal's office was new, though. Pat hadn't been in trouble in school, not even once. She'd been one of the original good girls, never any concern, always making the grades.

Well, there was trouble now.

She stopped at reception, where a pleasant woman with dull brown hair and a shapeless cardigan smiled up at her. Surely she had worked at Pat's elementary school? She hadn't aged a bit. "Ms. Fraser?"

Pat agreed she was, and produced the photo ID the woman, one Mrs. Stephenson according to the nameplate on the desk, requested.

"Just a second." Mrs. Stephenson picked up her phone and pushed a button. "Mr. Oubinsky? Ms. Fraser is here." A pause. "Yes, I'll get him." She hung up the phone and gestured. "Please go on in. Coffee or tea?"

"No, thanks. Or — maybe water?"

Mrs. Stephenson grinned at her. "I get it. Trip to the principal's office. I've been there once or twice with my boys, too. Give me a minute."

Pat rapped on the door, then opened it and stepped in.

The office itself wasn't at all like the industrial school offices of her youth. Big windows let in plenty of light. The requisite family photo sat on the desk, and bookcases displayed not only books, but also a softball, a potted plant, what appeared to be a letter jacket bunched up in a corner of the shelf, and miscellaneous other souvenirs.

Mr. Oubinsky wasn't what she'd expected, either. He was young, for one thing, possibly younger than she was. Fit, blond brush cut, easy manner—and eyes that gave a lie to his relaxed posture. This was a man who controlled several hundred under-thirteens, and he was tough, no question.

She wondered if he understood that Jason wasn't tough at all, despite the attitude.

After exchanging pleasantries and sitting—he chose a chair on her side of the desk—he said, "We have a few minutes before Jason and Mr. Shaw join us, so let's review the incident."

"Please. The message I got was confusing. Someone called Jason stupid, and he lashed out?"

"No, that wasn't it. His teacher, Ron Shaw—you've met him?"

"Not yet. Jason transferred here three weeks ago."

"Good man, been on the staff here for years—well, Ron got frustrated with one of the other students, a girl who hadn't done her homework. It's endemic around here, the demographic and the age group, but he'd had enough, and he called her on it. To be honest, he said she was stupid. Jason stood up in class and told his teacher he wasn't entitled to talk to them that way."

Pat's eyes widened. "That took guts."

He conceded nothing. "Things escalated, and Ron ordered Jason out of the class. Protocol is to come to the office, but he may not have known that if he's new. Another teacher found him wandering the halls and brought him here."

135

Sitting forward in her chair, Pat studied the man, trying to figure out his position. "If that's how it unfolded, then I agree with Jason. No teacher should tell a student she's stupid."

"Nevertheless, Jason was rude and disruptive. If he expects to return to class, he has to apologize."

"We have a difference of opinion, Mr. Oubinsky. It seems to me that if anyone needs to apologize—"

"Ron." The principal stood.

The man who came in was tall, intimidatingly muscular, and impatient. So this was Jason's teacher. The one he'd stood up to.

Mr. Oubinsky made the introductions. "I caught the last part of what you said," Ron Shaw told her. "What you fail to understand is the nature of sixth grade. They're the oldest in the school, and every one of them thinks he should already be in middle school. They're starting on the hormones. Shock value is one technique to get through to them. The girl who didn't do her homework, well, she never does. She refuses to listen. I'd challenge you to keep any kind of order in that class. School's the last thing on their minds."

"That's wrong." Jason was in the room now, and talking. Wherever he'd been waiting, he hadn't cooled off. "She tried to do the homework, but she couldn't get it. This stuff is *hard*, Mr. Shaw. It's your job to teach us, not shaft us."

Mrs. Stephenson put Pat's glass of water on the desk and made a hasty exit.

"That's enough, Jason." Mr. Oubinsky was cool, but a hardness settled around his eyes. "Sit down." The four of them sat in a circle. Jason was across from her. She longed to wink at him, but figured that the alpha males on either side of her wouldn't approve.

Mr. Oubinsky led the conversation. "Jason, I've spoken to Mr. Shaw, and he's willing to let you back into his class, once you apologize."

"What for?"

Pat sighed. Jason's back was up, so manners were out the window.

"Let's start with disrupting the class, shall we?" Mr. Shaw said.

"You'd already done that," Jason mumbled.

"Rudeness, defying authority — oh, you have plenty to apologize for, young man."

Condescending. So sure of himself. He dominated the room by his sheer size. "As I understand this story," Pat said, "Jason might apologize for disruption, but not for what he said. He was right." She stared straight at Ron Shaw as she spoke. She had experience herself controlling twelve-year-olds, and she wasn't above letting her male audience know it.

The man was a rock. "No apology, he doesn't return to my class. It's that simple, Ms. Fraser."

She was negotiating for Jason now, trying to align things so they'd make sense to him later. Because Jason was right, dammit. "Limited apology, and in my opinion you should apologize to the class, or at least to the girl you were taunting."

"Everyone stop." Mr. Oubinsky knew how to control a meeting. His eyes took them in, flashing a warning. "Back off, calm down. Jason." He turned to his left and gave her boy the courtesy of complete attention. "I want you to go home and write a letter of apology to Mr. Shaw. Bring it to the office tomorrow. It'll be kept in your record, and Mr. Shaw will get a photocopy."

Jason's face had gone taut, telling her his courage was running thin. "I can't apologize if it was the truth."

"You will apologize for speaking what you *think* is the truth in front of the whole class, instead of in private. And for disrupting the class and challenging Mr. Shaw's authority. Is that clear?"

"Yeah." The heel of his shoe kicked into the beige carpet, over and over again. He tracked the motion with his eyes.

"And one week's detention."

"Whatever."

Pat kept her attention on Jason, but he wouldn't meet her eyes. The system had the power to trammel her kids, and it crushed her every time she came face to face with how easily they could be defeated. In this case it was the better part of

137

valor, but her heart went out to Jason, pale under his defiance, forced to accept a punishment he didn't believe he deserved.

Mr. Oubinsky turned to her. "We have a policy here that detentions can be served over lunch hour, to accommodate parents' schedules, provided the child brings a lunch. He'll be given assignments to do during detention period."

"We're done here. Jase, do you want to come home with me or go back to class?" She wasn't sure if he was welcome to return to his class, but wanted to snatch the decision out of the claws of the primo males ganging up on her kid.

"Home, I guess."

Pat stood, followed by the two men. Jason was the last on his feet. Her temper was barely under control. "For the record, and I expect my *professional* opinion to become part of Jason's file also, I'm a practicing child psychologist, and you, Mr. Shaw, need lessons in handling kids. We're talking twelve-year-olds here, not adults. A teacher with your experience should be able to cope with a *child* who doesn't understand introductory algebra."

Jason looked up at that and stared at her, wide-eyed. He'd probably never seen an adult challenge authority, much less on his behalf.

"When you update Jason's file, I want a copy. Or send it to Linda Gonzales, she's Jason's caseworker. Thank you for your time, gentlemen."

Before she got to the outer door, Mr. Oubinsky spoke her name, stopping her. "Jason, wait in the hall, please." When Jason, with a dejected, defeated air, was out of earshot, he said, "It's unusual for a foster parent to defend a child so vigorously."

"So call me an unusual foster parent. He's my responsibility, and what happens to him matters."

"I wish it were more common. It's a fine line, Ms. Fraser, keeping the peace and maintaining order in a school. Not all of our decisions seem logical, I suppose."

"Tell me one thing. Is it possible to assign Jason to a different class? He's defensive today, but he's a gentle kid. He doesn't function well in confrontational environments."

"On the other hand, it might be good for him to learn to deal with a person he's had a run-in with."

"Might be. I admit I'm protective where Jason's concerned. He's taken enough lumps."

"I'll consider it."

Jason was uncommunicative and went to ground in his room as soon as they got home. Pat buttered a couple of split biscuits and ran them under the broiler. She spread them with raspberry jam, poured milk for Jason and a cup of tea for herself, then called him.

He came, but sullenly. "I figure we might as well get this out of the way," she said.

"Are you gonna tell Ms. Gonzales?"

"Yes, we'll have to. The school will send her a report, but she'll have one from me, too."

"Will they make me leave? Go into one of those group home things?" She gave Jason serious points for courage; his eyes looked straight into hers.

"I'd say, not a chance. The system's flaky enough that I'm not making any promises, but first, what happened is in dispute, and second, I'll fight to keep you here. Okay?"

He nodded and took a bite of the biscuit. Almost immediately he brightened. "It's okay."

"Told you."

He wolfed down the biscuit and drank the milk. She ate her own more sedately.

"Now, let's talk."

"Nuthin' to say. He was bullying that girl."

"Do you know the girl well, Jason?"

"No, just her name."

"So this wasn't personal."

Jason gave her a typical means-nothing-to-me shrug, but said, "Pat, is it weird for you to kinda know how someone's feeling? Like you're feeling it too?"

"It's not weird. It's called empathy, and the best kind of people do it. People like Mr. Shaw—well, I don't think he's big

139

on empathy. But he might have been having a frustrating day, and she got in the way of it. You, too."

"I guess I gotta write the stupid letter."

"I guess you do. Do you want me to help with the wording?"

"I can do it. Did you get a list of the crap I have to apologize for?"

Pat nodded, fiddled with her tea. "Jason, as you grow older you'll learn that there are times when you shouldn't speak up. If you'd talked to Mr. Shaw outside of class and said your piece, you probably could have avoided the grief."

"Wouldn't have helped Ashley, though."

"Point. If you're setting out to rescue people, sometimes you're going to get caught in the crossfire."

Jason was squirming, but she thought he'd heard her. "What's for supper?"

"Hot dogs?"

"You kidding me? You don't cook hot dogs. You cook stews and shit—stuff."

"I cook hot dogs, when I'm in the mood. What would you rather have?"

"Meat loaf?"

"Baked potatoes?"

"Yeah. Can we do that?"

"I'll see if we have ground beef."

Jason swung out of his chair. She stopped him before he got to the door.

"Jase?"

"Yeah." He turned to face her, reluctantly.

"You stood up to a bully. I'm proud of you."

Her boy stared at her for a second. He said, "Thanks," his eyes back on the floor as if she'd embarrassed him, and shuffled off to his room.

Pat did a quick tidy in the kitchen, then took Jason with her to the grocery. He'd handled the upset well, but she wasn't ready to give him too much free time yet, in case he acted out, or needed her around. Equally likely possibilities, she knew.

15

The trailer was too small to accommodate three of them, so Pat, Alan, and Brandon met at the offices of Brandon Caine Realty south of town. She hadn't been there since that confrontational meeting with Alan. A lot had changed since then.

For instance, you know the shape of his mouth on yours...

Brandon's meeting room was large enough, although being in an enclosed space with Alan and Brandon at the same time reminded her of a pressurized airplane with not quite enough oxygen.

Alpha males. All you get these days.

She was still smarting from the skirmish at Northside Elementary two days before and was impatient to read their addition to Jason's Social Services file. Linda had copies of her own submission and Jason's letter.

"Pat, this is good. Very good."

That was Brandon Caine. He was a fine-looking devil—*devil* being the operative word—with that blond lock falling youthfully over his forehead, and eyes that could only be called come-hither, at least when he trained them on a woman. She still wasn't sure if he remembered her from his years with Amanda. Better if he didn't, since her negative memories didn't make for a great working relationship. Too smooth by half, and that was saying something, given her entanglement with Alan. Alan was smoothness personified.

The way Brandon had treated Amanda, as if she were an arm decoration without a mind of her own, much less ability...

141

Shake it off, Pat. Today she was dealing with Brandon Caine, professional to professional, like it or not.

But if Alan had said, 'This is good, Pat. Very good', she wouldn't be fighting an urge to go wash her hands.

"If you go for a diagonal wall here, you'll add architectural interest, and you'll save the creek," she said.

"And mess up traffic flow. The creek's off the table, Pat," Brandon said. He made his words sound intimate, caressing, as if his presence alone were enough to... *Ugh!* "With the loss of the strip along Maple, we need the space."

Alan got into the discussion, pointing with the eraser end of a pencil. "Raul suggests building out here more than we'd planned. Push the layout into more of a shallow 'L'."

Alan was arguing for the creek?

Pat spoke up. "If you put big windows on the ground floor along here, and turn the creek into a park, you'd create a highly desirable library space, and—"

"Where the library's concerned, don't hold your breath, Pat," Brandon said.

The way Brandon repeats your name. Patronizing.

Get a grip.

Alan said, "We're still negotiating to see if we can fit something in, but the bottom line is, the county can't afford much. They haven't even budgeted for a new branch library."

"The county's ability to afford it depends on how much you push for it."

"We're losing marketable space to the redesign," Brandon elaborated, as if she didn't have the sense to figure it out herself. "We have to consider return on investment."

Explaining it to the little woman.

Keep your cool, Pat. She detected a quick brush of her hand under the table. Alan—but what message? I'm with you? Keep it businesslike?

Interesting.

They worked, hunched over the table, for over an hour, lobbing ideas off each other, factoring in the absent Raul's thoughts. Pat began to understand the rhythm of the men, how they functioned as a team. What they were doing was purely conceptual, and she wished she could meet Alan's architect to learn more about how he translated their suggestions into reality.

In fact, she'd already won what she'd hoped to. The greater buffer between the building and Maple Street, plus more irregularity in the outer wall along the back, meant her street was spared the worst of the impact. Visually, the thing wasn't anywhere near the concrete hulk she'd feared.

She straightened and put her hands on her lower back as she stretched.

"Feeling your age, Pat?" Brandon asked, a little too jovially.

It was his first misstep.

"Yeah. You have a few years on me, though. How are you holding up?" Her voice was silky.

"Wonderfully. It's a delight to work with you. Alan should have brought you around sooner. No telling how much further along we'd be."

"I'm sure Alan's shared anything of value." Pat gathered up her purse and her notes and headed for the door.

Alan followed her, leaving Brandon to pack up the plans. He spoke quietly, for her ears alone. "You've added a lot. I'd like to take you to dinner, to thank you. Do you have a free evening soon?"

She cocked her head, frowning. "I'm never free. Twelve-year-old boy, remember."

"Lunch, then. Day after tomorrow?"

She hesitated, then said, "I'll let you know. I don't have time to check my calendar now. There's been an issue, I need to be home for Jason."

"Call me."

"I'll be in touch." She'd been inching her way out the door as they spoke, in a hurry to get home. Jason was coping well, all things considered, but she wasn't letting him out of her crosshairs yet.

143

When she'd gone, Alan found himself waylaid by Brandon. "Getting anywhere?"

"You think I'm trying to?"

Caine made a derisive noise. "Little hand touches under the table? Transparent."

"Enough to warn you off. I believe you're between women at the moment?"

Brandon's mouth twisted into something resembling contempt. "You're safe from me. I made the mistake of getting involved with a friend of hers, a few years back. Bitches, both of them. Watch yourself, she's a ball buster."

"I find that hard to believe. She's a social worker. Spends her days with kids."

"Trust me. Play with her, but get out before it gets serious. She can be nasty. Did everything she could to break up Amanda and me."

He'd seen that in her, but he'd call it determined, not nasty. He'd seen the other side, too.

He locked eyes with Caine. "I'm telling you, stay away from her. She's not your type, and she's not a playtoy. Could be that's where you went wrong with her friend."

Brandon's bark of laughter echoed off the walls. "They're all playtoys. Some more serious than others, but isn't that the point? Find one you can play with for a long time."

Alan was noncommittal. "Bit of a bastard, aren't you?"

"I get what I want, they get what they want. I'm good at it. You and Danielle free for supper in the next week or so?"

I get what I want.

"I'll check."

He had turned to go to his office when Pat crashed through the outer door. "Alan!"

He wheeled and almost collided with her.

"Trouble. Come see." She bolted back outside.

Brandon overtook him, following her across the parking lot, dodging the mounds of dirty snow left by the plow. When he pulled to a halt, he saw what had sent her flying back to the office.

All three cars had been tagged with spray paint.

Pat's was the nearest, marked with the word *Turncoat.* He walked around her car; on the other side it said *Bitch.*

The graffiti on his car read *Get out of town,* along with a couple of run-of-the-mill cuss words. On Brandon's, *Capitalist.* That last one was pathetic, as if the vandal had run out of invective and failed to come up with a fresh insult.

Pat stood in the lot, thumbing her phone. She spoke, hung up, and dialed again. Listened for a moment, talked quietly, then closed the phone and came over to where he and Brandon studied the damage. "I've called the police. They'll be here in ten minutes or so." To Alan she added, "I checked in with Jason. He'll be okay."

"Right under our noses," Brandon said, almost admiringly. "I didn't need this. I don't have time to run around to auto body places."

"Not much choice." He got busy with his own phone, taking pictures of the cars, a distance shot positioning them in the lot.

"You know anything about this, Pat?" Brandon asked.

The urge to punch the other man caught Alan by the throat. Pat rolled with it, though. "Not a thing. Funny question, Brandon."

They stood there, stewing. After a minute Alan said, "Come on, I'm freezing. We may as well wait inside." He took Pat's arm and started them back toward the office.

When the county sheriff's deputy turned up twenty minutes later, the picture taking happened again, and they were questioned, but to what point? They'd been huddled in the windowless conference room. There wasn't a hope of finding the vandals unless they got lucky.

When the excitement was over, he and Pat left together. She didn't resist when he took her arm. As they walked across the lot, he said, "Are you okay?"

"I'm mostly irritated. Like Brandon, I don't have time for this, but I have to get the car in today. I don't want Jason to see it."

"I expect he's seen worse."

"I'm sure he has. He's having a rough time right now. I'm trying to avoid exacerbating it."

"You'd be a fabulous mother," he heard himself saying, out of the blue.

"I am a fabulous mother, just not legally. I'll let you know about lunch."

She hadn't forgotten. Or used the incident as an excuse to forget.

"I'll meet you at the auto body place. You may need a ride home." He gave her arm a squeeze through her thick coat, then climbed into his car to follow her out of the parking lot.

I get what I want, they get what they want. Brandon's words, but they could have been his.

What separated him from Brandon Caine? They didn't exactly line up where principles were concerned, but Caine's flat statement was unnervingly close to what he'd told Pat, more than once.

Pat was at her desk when the buzzer sounded at the entrance to the Social Services office, fifteen minutes before the next round table session. She'd extracted a promise concerning algebra from Jason and was trying to get a few reports done before going upstairs for the meeting. The story of her life, those reports.

Funny how you always know when he's around. She knew before she left her cubicle that she'd find him on the other side of the door.

"Alan?"

He gave her a terse nod. She locked up behind them and led the way back to her desk. Among interruptions she could have done without, he pretty much topped the list. His silence set off warning signals. She didn't welcome him with open arms, but what did he expect? Was *he* going to write the blasted reports?

"Problem?"

He sat. "I guess you got your car back?"

"They're efficient. Thanks again for the lift home."

"The county police paid me a visit today."

Okay. This was big. She hit a sequence of buttons and closed her laptop. "Not speeding tickets, I presume. The spray paint?"

A short nod. "Listen, Pat, you need to hear this. You're involved in the plans, and you're visible."

"You're freaking me. Spit it out, please. We have to be upstairs in ten minutes."

"Things are escalating. The police received an anonymous tip, and they believe it's credible. Someone wants to stop the development more than you do. I didn't get any details, but they're talking violence."

"Oh, come on. This is Calter Creek. No one would go to those kinds of extremes to fight the mall."

"You saw the local paper? The letter and the op-ed piece? Then the paint job on our cars? Be careful. A lot of people know you've been working with me—the whole round table, for instance. I don't want you to get hurt."

What? But he wasn't laughing.

"You can't be serious. What kind of violence?"

"They didn't tell me."

Unusually, Alan was a little disheveled. His hair had the tousled look of a man who'd been...

Get a grip, woman.

She snapped back to attention. "The police are taking it seriously?"

"After the cars and the stuff in the paper, yes. We have to get upstairs, Pat."

She slotted the laptop into its case, grabbed her binder, and headed toward the door. "Are you going to tell the round table?"

"Is there a reason to?"

"Possibly. You could ask them to keep their eyes and ears open. No need to cause a panic, most of the committee's mild to a fault."

"True. Makes me wonder why they volunteered."

She locked the outer door to the Social Services offices. "Mostly because they care. They want to be happy with it. Two of them live in the immediate neighborhood, so they have a vested interest. There may be one or two into architectural or design aspects. Not one size fits all, by any means."

He took the stairs up to the next floor two at a time. She trailed behind, watching his obvious comfort with his body. This wasn't a man who needed the muscular babying of an elevator. These days she fought a compulsion to fill her memory banks with little facts like that about him.

At the door to the conference room, Alan stopped for a short word with Millicent. Pat worked her way to the foot of the table and found a seat.

And scrutinized the other committee members.

Alan had a lot to answer for, putting suspicions into her head. These were her neighbors, friends, colleagues. The idea that any of these reasonable—well, mostly reasonable—people would spray-paint their cars because of a mall project was ludicrous. But then, if someone was out to sabotage the development, it made sense they'd use the round table to gather information.

As her gaze swept the room, tuning out Millicent's welcome and Alan's opening remarks about the possible risk, she created categories in her mind and dropped her fellow members into them. By her reckoning, of the other eleven round table members, she counted four milquetoasts, two architecturally curious, three perennial committee members, joining up for the fun of it, and two unclassifiable. Not that either had raised any warning bells.

The talk moved on to the new front elevation. Alan gave her full credit. He described the concept of shopping pods and said Raul was investigating it. Someone suggested more use of stone, less of brick.

A subcommittee to study parking and access to the mall for the infirm and elderly reported. Subcommittees popped up and disappeared like figments of the imagination. This report was a rubber-stamp; she sensed the subcommittee wanted to propose something new and unusual, or at least a modification of what Alan's team had laid out, but they'd come up empty. No one got that having no criticism was arguably a good thing.

Another round table meeting.

Afterwards, she didn't object when Alan walked back to Social Services with her. Pastries dropped off, they went to the parking garage together, and she told him her conclusions.

"The unclassifiables—they both must be sixty years old and overweight. They don't strike me as being terrorists, Pat."

"Me either. Some people simply love being on committees."

Alan had thrown off his serious mood. "Should we mount surveillance?"

She laughed—and mused, in the tangled recesses of her mind, that it was good to laugh with him. "Ward's a bookkeeper with a roster of small businesses as clients. Ingrid takes in kids. You could sign up for bookkeeping services, or loiter in Ingrid's back yard, but she might phone the police and say there's a stalker after the kids. Sounds tenuous if you ask me."

"It made you laugh, though."

Instantly the cheerful mood deserted her. Another nail in her coffin? "Yeah, it felt good. Good night, Alan." They'd reached her car, and she got herself settled at the wheel.

He leaned on the door. "Watch yourself. I meant it earlier. I want to know you're safe."

"Same to you. Want me to give you a ride to your car, in case there's a mall terrorist lurking?"

This time it was his turn to laugh. "Brat. See the security guy over there? He'll protect me."

She glanced to her right and saw the security guy. At the same time she spotted Alan's car, parked a dozen stalls away from hers. She grinned, closed the door, and left him standing there.

Alan stood in the nearly deserted parking garage and watched Pat drive away.

And remembered, with annoyance, the reaction he'd had after the police spoke to him. His gut had clenched as his thoughts fled straight to Pat.

Not to mention the reaction he was fighting now, triggered by that saucy grin she'd shot at him before she drove off. An unexpected echo of his response to her New Year's Eve, which she had to have noticed when they'd clung to each other as if they might fuse together.

He couldn't explain that day, his need to hold and comfort the same hardly-his-type woman while she soaked his shirt, sobbing because she wanted him as badly as he wanted her, and she'd be damned if she'd have him. How could he ever make sense of that?

Tonight she'd been frazzled. That hadn't gone one inch toward making him want her less. *Damn*, he wanted her, half an hour, an hour, get it out of his system.

Now she was in danger because of her association with him. The police had mentioned Brandon and Pat by name as being possible targets.

Turncoat, the guy had sprayed on her car. Like it or not, she was making a serious contribution to the development. Quietly, outside of committees. He considered her a part of his team, and had come to respect her ideas, even relish them. She pushed him to make the complex unique. That's what he wanted. A landmark project.

And to get her clothes off.

At the moment it was a toss-up, which he wanted more.

16

By the end of January, Pat had reached the point of never wanting to see snow again. Or slippery sidewalks, or hazardous driving, or heavy sweaters. Call her unreasonable, she hated winter. Which may have contributed to her agreeing to meet Alan for lunch.

Monet's Garden had been open for a year in downtown Calter Creek, and it promised summer. At the moment she'd take whatever she could get. If the town had a Tiki lounge with Polynesian décor and drinks with umbrellas, she'd be there with a grass skirt on.

He stood up and held her chair when she arrived — *smooth*. Pat was ultra-sensitive to smooth these days, the aftereffect of an afternoon with both Alan and Brandon Caine.

The last time or two they'd been together had been... nice. After she'd made a fool of herself that day in the trailer, he'd backed off and appeared content to be merely pleasant, in a formal, polite sort of way.

Pleasant, and the most intriguing man you've ever known.

Who needed summer? The notion of getting his clothes off gave her a hot flash. Hoping the heat didn't show, she smiled her way into small talk after they'd studied the menus. "Nice place. I'm not good with this time of year. I need warmth and sun."

"We could go away. Barbados, Jamaica."

She rolled her eyes. "Sure, we could."

"Why not?"

Why not?

"Well, there's Jason."

151

He shrugged. "Bring him along. We'll get him a separate room."

"I'm not sleeping with you, Alan. I thought we were clear on that."

"We're also clear that I fully intend to keep trying." He turned a happy, innocent smile on her. The kind that sent far too many of her cells to wild Polynesian drums and Tahitian hula. "A chance to be somewhere warm strikes me as a reasonable gambit."

He kept his eyes on her face. She wished he'd fasten them on something else. Between his eyes and the lingering effects of the hot flash, rational conversation became a challenge. "Don't mess up a perfectly good lunch, okay? Life is stressful enough."

A waitress arrived at their table, dropped off two water glasses, and took their orders.

He waited until she left, then smiled. These days he smiled more frequently, despite the tension she picked up around his eyes. "Right. Strategic change of subject. Want to tell me what's going on with your kid?"

Why did he keep doing this to her? Knock her so far off base she'd be tagged out the next time she moved, then sit back, throw a completely normal comment at her, and give her a chance to recover, for all the world as if the off-base hadn't happened. And smile while he did it.

Pat took a breath. For whatever reason, she believed she could trust him to keep the story confidential, and she was still in the grip of moral outrage, so she gave him a summary of the meeting at Northside Elementary. "He's confused, and rightly so. As far as he's concerned, he didn't do anything wrong. I got into a sparring match with the principal and told the teacher he needed lessons in anger management. I wish I knew if the man apologized to the little girl, but I'd be willing to bet he didn't."

"Once upon a time it was a trip to the principal's office for a thrashing and notify the parents later. At least you were called in early."

"Personal experience?"

He shrugged and looked down for a moment, but didn't answer. Pat thought she saw a flicker of pain cross his face, but wasn't sure.

"I'm beleaguered, between this and your mall."

Whatever she saw was gone. He grinned. "The mall's meant to amuse you, not put pressure on you."

"Oh? You started this project for my amusement?"

"No, but your amusement figures in its completion these days."

This made no sense to her. She knew what Alan wanted from her, and it had more to do with him than with her own pleasure. "You're an enigma. I don't see any way my amusement intersects with your development."

"Complicated vectors. You know I value your ideas. Then, when you laugh and relax, it helps me unwind." He reached over and brushed a finger across the back of her hand. "That's an intersection I could encourage, if you'd let me."

Her hand jerked. She speared him with a look. "Relaxing around you is not an option."

His grin turned into a full-fledged laugh. "Pat, you're so brave. You're fighting our attraction with everything you've got, and you can still look me in the eye and say that."

Why had she imagined a delightful lunch in a summer garden, even for a few minutes? "Hilarious, isn't it?"

She played with her water glass, tracing tracks with her finger in the condensation. "I've been working this out in my mind. As you've so helpfully pointed out, I can't afford not to be around. I want my hand all over the look and feel of your development, because you'll move on, and I'll be sitting here with the result for a long time. When it's like this..." She gestured with her free hand "...I enjoy your company, and I never *dreamed* I'd say that. But that's all. The end, finito, no more. And don't be too charming, okay?" she added, pointing at him. "I got enough of oily from your partner."

"Not a fan of Brandon's, are you." It was more a statement than a question.

"You catch on quickly."

"Will you tell me why? He's both my business associate and our main conduit into the business community around Calter Creek. While the mall will serve a much larger catchment, it's still important to stay in touch with local perceptions. I go to the Chamber of Commerce meetings, but I'd value a more personal assessment."

"You can't expect to be popular. The town's going to take a hit, and you know it. It's a struggle to keep downtown vibrant, with Creekside Mall and its easy, free parking. And now another major mall? You'll steal business from Creekside or from downtown, or a nefarious combination of both. It's bound to happen."

"I'm sorry, Pat."

She glared at him. Hard. "I'm sure you considered it before you started, so I don't understand sorry, in this context."

The skin around his eyes tightened, and the finger that had brushed her hand wasn't anywhere near her now. He studied the cloth napkin he'd unfolded, then crumbled on the table "You understand well enough, you just don't want to. I'm a businessman. I have complete analyses of the impacts of the developments I build. The costs, and the rewards — to me, to the businesses that move to the mall, the governments that get the taxes, the companies involved in designing and building and maintaining. I do my homework. I'd never risk going out on a limb with a project otherwise. The bottom line is, Calter Creek's a minor economic center. It'll live or it'll die. I'm sorry if the hard realities of capitalism upset you."

She'd been sucker punched. Wordless, she stared at him.

He met her eyes. "Calter Creek matters because it's local to the mall, but your town won't even be the primary market. Columbus's bedroom communities are as close as ten minutes from here via interstate. Some local businesses will flourish once construction starts. The only other reason Calter Creek's important to me is that you live here. I acknowledge the impact on you."

The waitress returned and put their plates in front of them. Omelet for her, Ruben sandwich for him. When she'd left, Pat studied his face. "You're a cold man."

"A pragmatic one. It's not a touchy-feely world, and I intend to be on top of it. I'll fight anyone who tries to stop me. That's why I need to hear your opinion of Brandon. If he's a liability, I have to find ways to mitigate it."

She didn't answer. The omelet held less appeal than when she'd ordered it, but Pat wasn't the kind of person who couldn't eat when she was unhappy. Rather the opposite. She suffered a perverse envy of women who shed pounds when they were upset. But she'd never be in that clan, so she'd eat the thing.

As she took a bite, she acknowledged why she felt wounded. Not that what he'd said surprised her in any way, but that he'd throw it in her face. If she'd wondered before, now she was sure. Her fine speech New Year's Day about being proud of his life had gone right over his head. That realization settled like dead weight in her stomach.

And you were looking forward to the omelet, worse luck.

Alan also had fallen silent, whether to tackle his sandwich or because he sensed her disquiet, she wasn't sure. After a minute he said, "I've upset you?"

"Confirmed what I already knew."

"No point in pursuing Barbados, I suppose."

"None whatsoever."

Another silence.

"Tell me your impressions of Brandon."

She shrugged and swallowed a bite of home fries. "He doesn't treat women well. As if we're objects to be used, then discarded. I don't know about his business ethics, but if they're the same as his personal ones, he's a man I'd prefer to avoid. He's successful, by all accounts, and I've never heard him associated with any scandal, personal or professional."

"There was something yesterday, his tone when he spoke to you."

"I knew him once, not well. That colors my reaction to him. I doubt he remembers."

"He does."

"Not favorably, I take it."

155

"A certain kind of woman appeals to a man like Brandon, and you're not it."

"Funny." Pat set her fork on her plate and took a drink from her water glass. "I'd assumed you shared a taste in women."

Their eyes met and locked. His gave nothing away. She'd never felt the distance between them so acutely.

"We don't. There haven't been that many women in my life, but they've all had a brain in their heads. That's why I enjoy being with you, even when we don't see eye-to-eye. You're refreshing. You give me a run for my money."

"You only find me refreshing because I refuse to fall for your charms. No room for love in your equation, is there?"

"None."

"Well, that puts it squarely on the table."

"Yes, I guess it does."

It also brought the final curtain down on any pleasure Pat experienced in lunch at Monet's Garden. For a woman who loved food and craved summer, that was no small deprivation.

They ate in silence for a few minutes.

"So, what's next, speaking of the mall?"

He'd almost finished the Reuben. "I want to walk the land with you again, this afternoon if possible. To get a feel for the new footprint."

Pat looked at her watch. "I have to be home in an hour for Jason. Not enough time."

"Bring him, why don't you? Give him something new to do."

Don't do this. Do not do this.

"Might be an interesting idea. He's smart, and it's impossible to tell, at his age, what's going to catch his interest."

"I'll meet you at the trailer at—three thirty?"

"Enough daylight left for a short look around."

Alan signaled for the check. She sighed, wishing he hadn't turned a lunch in summertime into an Arctic winter meal that lingered on her palate like whale blubber.

And what did you honestly expect?

156

Pat introduced Jason, and Alan ushered them both into the trailer. She kept an eye on her boy, but today he seemed to be on his best behavior, politely shaking Alan's hand, saying little. Just for a moment she saw Jason as Alan must see him, a skinny kid in the middle of a growth spurt, his arms too long for his coat sleeves. A little wary, not giving much away.

"Let's review the blueprints," Alan said. "It'll give us a better idea what we're seeing."

He spread the sheets on the table and outlined the plan for the development, glancing at Jason periodically as he did so. When it came to the office block, he took time to explain why the creek had to be sacrificed. Not that they hadn't been over the whole thing the day before. She wondered if he was doing this refresher for Jason's benefit or to drive the point home with her.

They put coats, hats, and gloves back on, and he shepherded them out the door.

Their starting place was the new boundary line the surveyors had marked. Alan paced to show them roughly the size of each of the pods, the impact on the sight lines and the setback from the houses on Maple Street. Approximate, but Pat could see how the plan was evolving. She approved. The outer wall indented to echo the outline of the pods, so it wouldn't be a plain, flat wall resembling a prison. She blessed Raul for making it happen.

Jason was okay, maybe even interested. He seemed to be hanging onto Alan's words, frowning occasionally at a new architectural term but taking it in and grasping the concepts. Alan made an effort to draw Jason into their discussion, which surprised her. She'd expected him to consider Jason a not particularly welcome tag-along. Instead, Alan was taking Jason seriously.

Another facet of the man, showing regard for the boy.

Why, and what it meant, she had no idea, but she was grateful.

The building's footprint at the east end, site of the future office complex, had been marked out with stakes. "You can see why we can't save the creek." Alan said. "With the need for lobbies, elevators and stairwells—there's simply too much loss of leasable floor space. The pod idea is brilliant in the commercial area, but it's not going to work here."

"So, that's the creek over there?" Jason asked.

"The line of trees." Pat pointed. "Birds all year round, ducks in the summer. I believe it's an amenity they can't afford to lose. If it were turned into parkland…"

Jason was frowning. "So, you need to stick the building where the creek is, or you can't fit in the elevators and all."

"That's the situation," Alan said.

"But the creek's a good thing… I think it'd be good. I get kinda sick in malls, with fluorescent lights and stuff."

"We'll be minimizing the use of fluorescents."

They began the walk back along the new property line to the path leading to the trailer.

At the junction with the trail back to Maple Street, Jason spoke up. "So, couldn't it kind of stick out over the creek?"

Stick out over the creek?

Jason's point flashed into her mind. A cantilevered building. The second floor jutting toward the creek, expanding Alan's precious commercial space. The ground floor library with a park setting, a garden or a picnic area under the shelter of the second story. It came alive for her the instant Jason stopped talking. "Windows everywhere," she said as she envisioned it. "Shelter, shade, verdant. Views from the library windows—"

"Every idea you have costs me money," Alan said mildly. "The pod construction's sending the estimates into the stratosphere. Where a cantilever's concerned, Raul's played around with it, but when you consider redesign, structural and materials, the reduced commercial value of ground floor space…"

"Where the library could be."

"Pat—"

"A mall that will make your name."

"It still has to be affordable."

158

Jason listened to the back and forth and shrugged. "It was just an idea."

"Conceptually, a very good one," Alan said. "If appearance were the only challenge, you'd be onto a winner here."

"We have to go. Think about it, Alan."

"I will. Thanks for coming out today."

She gave him a nod. Alan again shook hands with Jason, respectfully. They separated, and she and Jason headed along the path for home.

A few days later Pat stopped in at Morrison Books in downtown Calter Creek, a heritage building full of derelict tomes and bookshelves dating from a century ago. Stacks of books cluttered the aisles and were shelved two or three deep. Dust swam in the faint sunlight streaming through the grubby windows, giving the whole place an otherworldly ambience.

It's our bookstore. Worth hanging onto. Pat had become possessive of Calter Creek in the last four months.

The rickety bookstore stayed in business year after year. She'd heard that they did a brisk online trade.

She was restless and tangled up in her mind.

Dreams. Like the three of them together, as they'd been the day before, she and Alan and Jason, as if they belonged that way... dreaming the impossible dream.

A book might help, she'd thought. Focus her errant mind on something more rewarding, get her out of her funk.

New books were shelved near the front, and that's where she headed, with half an hour to kill before going home to meet Jason. To her annoyance, she found herself gravitating toward the shelf of romance novels.

Not that Pat had a problem with romances. But she didn't need the reminder of eyes to drown in, muscular torsos. And other male attributes, like the one she'd forced herself to ignore, that horrible day of the tears. So she hoped to find something more educational. Meditation, perhaps? Herbs? A biography?

You need to have the affair. Badly.

159

She spotted a friend from the Ultimate Saturdays in the cookbook aisle and waved absentmindedly.

But romance? *Lusty sex and happily-ever-after?*

Suppose the prince hadn't turned up with the slipper. Suppose the prince was a real dog. Where would Cinderella be then?

So, she thought as she moved over to the literature section. Dreams.

The dream of having it all—that's what Alan was chasing, wasn't it? Except his *all* didn't line up with hers. She remembered the shape of her long-ago imaginings. The career, the loving marriage, the home, the kids... how innocent she once was.

So what did she have? More university credentials than she could afford to frame and put on a wall. Two careers, psychologist and social worker, not that either paid that well. A cozy home facing a shopping mall. A mercifully failed marriage, a kid whose first twelve years were closed to her.

And a dream for now?

Grim, gritty tomes filled the literature shelves. No tome for her today.

Alan wasn't the dream. She'd told him so—he'd never be her dream man.

You dream about Alan.

That's sex.

Are you sure?

Of course she was sure. She knew her own dreams, didn't she?

She wandered over to biographies and found a new release on the Brontes. Well, why not? She could explore the Yorkshire moors for an evening. Better than obsessing about Alan. That prospect sent her rummaging in the second-hand section, where she unearthed an old copy of *Jane Eyre*.

At the cashier's desk she checked her watch. Time to head home. She hadn't realized, pre-Jason, that being at home by three o'clock, every day, meant a lifestyle change.

But she was learning. Jason was the most concrete part of the dream at the moment. Milk and cookies with him after school was no hardship at all.

She paid for both books and headed for the parking garage.

❖

The next day Alan tossed the wrapper from his sandwich in the trash and slapped his pencil on the table in frustration. He'd hosted a breakfast meeting with major investors in the mall, and there'd been too many unhappy faces in the group. Alan wasn't about to try to gloss over the financial challenges, although Brandon had suggested they do just that—a conversation that left him uneasy. He needed these investors, so he'd used all the techniques in his considerable arsenal to make the whole thing palatable.

Now, facing Pat, the trailer could barely contain the simmering emotions ricocheting off the walls. "You're out to bankrupt me. You honestly think you can do whatever you please to the plans and it'll happen."

"I'm trying to give you what you want," Pat retorted. "Something to make your name. Our interests mesh on that point, so stop being such a jerk."

"Someone has to pay attention to the bottom line. A fact you're conveniently forgetting."

"Don't snarl at me. I'm sure you can dig up another investor or two."

She had to be the most frustrating female on the planet.

Frustrating or not, Pat's ideas were good. But the investors' meeting painted a different picture. He had to keep these people happy.

She was speaking again. "You'd planned on mixed façades in the shopping arcades. So what's wrong with continuing that theme into the business wing? At least the ground floor, around the library..."

"Pat, stop. Can't you get it through your head that the library isn't going to happen? This is premium business space, and the county won't be able to afford it."

"So make the premium part start on the second floor. Your ideas conflict with each other, Alan. You're dreaming gourmet, but you're designing for ordinary. A dollar store isn't visionary."

He winced. "I'm designing the best it can be *within the budget*. Remember the budget?"

"Remember that I have to live with the damn thing?"

"Do I need to remind you that some of the best architectural minds in the country put these plans together?"

"Are you kidding? You've told me and the round table and everyone within shouting distance often enough. I'm going home."

"Oh, gee," Alan heard himself say. "Just when we were having so much fun together."

That earned another glare. "Grow up."

He stood when she did and let her struggle into her coat on her own. He wasn't in the mood to help her this time. Instead he rolled up the plans and shoved them in their tube, more impatiently than they deserved. He spoke to her back. "Want to tell me what brought on this bad mood?"

"Want to tell me what brought on yours?"

"Sure, it might give you perspective. I met with the investors this morning. They're not happy with the numbers, and then I get you riding me to increase the costs and cut the revenues. You're not in my shoes. You don't know what I'm juggling here." He picked up his coat, put it on.

She stood still for a moment, her hat and gloves dangling in her hand. "That's too bad," she said without much sincerity. "But you're forgetting my side of the story. Your mall's going to sit in my front yard for the rest of my life, so I'll wring any concessions I can out of you. That library could make your name, and Raul's, too, and you're too stubborn to see it." She skirted the table and made the two steps to the door.

He got there at the same time. When her hand touched the knob, his arrived on top of hers, pulling it away. He wrapped his fingers around her hand. "Let's part friends, shall we?"

"Okay, we're friends." Her voice didn't reflect the words, though. She tried to pull her hand away, but his was stronger. After a short struggle she gave up.

"Pat?"

His chance to do what had been teasing his mind all afternoon. As his mouth descended on hers he heard her mutter, "Con man." But she didn't pull away, and that riposte bought him time to get the kiss going. She responded, even though her hand went rigid, battling herself and him all the way.

He didn't push the kiss, but he did smile at her when he ended it. "Fighting not to wrap your arms around me, are you?" He released her hand and brushed a finger over her cheek. Her eyes stared at him, enormous and, he thought, confused. "Don't worry. You'll have plenty more chances."

He killed the lights, gathered up the roll of plans, and followed her out the door. He guessed Pat was pretending the kiss hadn't happened.

"Where did you park today?" she asked.

"Maple. I'll walk you home."

"I can't tell you how thrilled I am."

Pat and Alan headed over the trampled snow along the path back to her neighborhood. The day matched her mood, still and gray. He hadn't said a word since they'd left the trailer. As for her, she'd have to reflect on that kiss, why she had let it happen and what it meant and why this man was cluttering up her neat mind with these random landmines of needs and feelings.

So it was safer to maintain a good separation between them. She wrenched her imaginings away from Alan, pictured the pleasure of getting home and kicking back with a beer. He walked with his head down, studying the weeds and dirty snow as if expecting to find gold.

From a raw field to his ground-breaking development. His name, his fortune.

They were well along the trail to Maple when she sensed a change in the air behind her and turned.

Flames, in the window of the trailer.

Alan had turned, too, and for a moment they were frozen in place, as frozen as the ground under them, as fragile as the dry grasses sticking up through the snow.

163

He woke up first. "Jesus," he said. "Gas tank." He wheeled around and grabbed Pat's hand, yanking her into a run.

She fought to keep her footing. "It might not..." she gasped.

"It might."

She felt more than heard the explosion. It picked her up and hurled her across the lot, to land heavily and awkwardly with her face ground into the frozen earth. She was aware of a flash of pain, then of nothing.

17

Alan couldn't move. He'd had the breath knocked out of him, so he lay very still for a small eternity, waiting for his lungs and diaphragm to catch up. He should hurt, with every front part of him in brutal contact with the rough, icy surface of the vacant lot. But he was numb.

Once his breath returned he carefully started to test his body. They'd almost made it to the fences separating the houses on Maple Street from the field. It wasn't until he was able to pull himself semi-upright that he saw Pat, sprawled face down and motionless across the frozen ground next to one of the back yard fences. Her head was turned slightly, so that a tiny part of the left side of her face was visible.

He tried to stand and couldn't; his legs refused to take his weight. Fighting panic, he dragged himself over to her and positioned his fingers on her wrist.

He'd never know if he picked up her pulse or if it was his own shock and wishful thinking. At any rate, he managed to get his phone out of his pocket—by a miracle it had survived the explosion—and called 911.

He was aware of people around him, probably from a house on Maple, before his mind shut down and he collapsed.

❖

Alan knew two things above all others, as he waited, not patiently, in an examining room in the emergency department of Sunnybrook Hospital. First was that the numbness had gone, and he hurt like hell. He hadn't landed lightly, and every single sharp stone had taken a chunk of his skin. Shrapnel from the exploding trailer had peppered his back, including something that had left a foot-long gash. He moved cautiously, because even breathing was agonizing. In fact, any movement sent shafts of pain lancing through his body. His muscles were tightening against the insult. At least nothing was broken, and the pain, while universal, was exterior.

Second was that however rough things were for him, for Pat they had to be ten times worse. Once she woke up.

Because she *would* wake up. She must have taken a nasty blow to her head, but soon she'd be back, fighting fit, to go another round or two with him.

But she wasn't awake yet. And they weren't telling him anything.

A harried doctor appeared. "X-rays are clean, Mr. Carmichael. We've finished with the abrasions and cuts, and you're free to check out." He scribbled on his pad. "Here are prescriptions for pain killers and a muscle relaxant; moving's going to be a challenge for a day or two. Plan to come here or go to a clinic to have the dressing on your back changed, daily if you can manage it. The stitches can come out in ten days." He tore off the paper and handed it to Alan.

"Pat—Ms. Fraser—how is she?"

"We've moved her upstairs. She's coming around. Probably feels terrible, to be honest. Generally the same injuries as you, other than the impact to her head, a couple of cracked ribs, and a sprained wrist. That'll give her grief for a while yet."

"Can I see her?"

"No, no visitors. Perhaps later. Do you have contact information for her? Family, friends?"

He didn't. He was beginning to realize how little he really knew Pat Fraser. "Parents, a brother out west. I'm sorry, I don't know how to reach them. There's one thing, though. She has a kid, I mean not her own, she's got a foster kid. Is there any chance I could get her keys so I can check on him? He knows me."

The doctor shook his head. "Thanks for the offer, but we'll contact Social Services. Usually when something like this happens, the child goes into a group home. We'll see to it. I don't suppose you know the name of his social worker?"

"Linda somebody."

"Linda Gonzales. We get to know them. I'll give her a call."

Alan glanced at the clock on the wall. "But look—it's after four. The kid'll be home by now. She was heading there to meet him when..." He waved a hand, since he didn't have the words yet to describe the explosion. "If I could have the keys—"

"No, Mr. Carmichael. I'm sorry, but we have protocols we have to follow. I'll notify the police and get in touch with Mrs. Gonzales. Now if you'll excuse me..." The doctor left, leaving Alan with a prescription slip, pain throughout his body, Pat lying helpless and out of reach...

... and a realization. An urgency gripped him that might seem irrational to anyone else and even took him by surprise. He had to get to her house. No way was the kid going to their group home. He'd kidnap him first.

He fed the small bag of his personal possessions back into his pockets, grabbed his cell phone, and called a cab.

Outside the hospital there were reporters. Alan was exhausted, hurt, shaken, and desperate to get to Pat's, so he threw down the gauntlet when one of them got a microphone in his face. "Yes," he said, not masking the fury in his voice. "I have a statement. Tell whoever did this that development is the most important thing in my life. No punk with a fire starter's going to stop it." He shoved the microphone out of his way and stormed toward a waiting cab.

He beat officialdom to Pat's door, where he rapped, wincing at the pain from his grazed knuckles, then tried the knob. The door was unlocked, so he let himself in and shouted, "Anybody home?"

The kid appeared from the kitchen with a piece of cake in his hand and a milk mustache. "Mr. Carmichael. Where's Pat? What are you doing here?" Then Alan's face and clothes sank in, because he added, "Shit, man. You get caught in that?" He waved toward the lot. Fire hoses still ran from the hydrants on Maple Street, while in the field there were numerous fire trucks and police vehicles. The stench from the fire hovered over the neighborhood.

"I wasn't far enough away from the trailer when it blew." Some of the tension in Alan released. The kid was fine, and for the moment was okay where he was.

The kid's eyes got wide. "It, like, exploded?"

"Yeah. Your name's Jason, right? What's your last name?"

"Pat wouldn't want you here."

"She'd like it better than everyone else who's about to descend on you. Your name, kid. Now."

The boy looked defiant. "You're not very bright, are you? You might have remembered."

"I might have. I should have. I don't, so give."

Defiant changed to defeated. The change passed over his face, then through his body, like a tidal wave. Alan recognized that change; he'd lived through it himself, in another lifetime.

"Jarvis," Jason mumbled.

Alan attempted to stride toward Pat's kitchen, but his legs weren't moving as well as they should, and the rest of him was in training for the agony he knew was coming later. He managed an amble. "Okay, Jason Jarvis. Does Pat have any painkillers around here?"

"Dunno."

"Don't go sullen on me. We've got a problem. I'll get you through it if I can, but if we don't work together you're the one who's screwed, not me. Got it?"

The defiance was back. "What going on? Where's Pat? And how soon before you get your smart ass out of our house?"

Alan sighed and sank onto a chair. In the cab he'd learned not to risk leaning back. "Look, kid. I just got out of the hospital, I hurt all over, my trailer got blown up a minute after I left it, and given a choice I'd go home and pour a scotch and forget this whole screw-up. But for the record, the police and Social Services are presumably on their way here right now to take you away. So work with me, okay?"

That reached him. "Take me away?" His voice was frantic. "Where's Pat? She'll fix it, where is she?" The panic was real. Alan sighed and got up, put his hands on the boy's skinny arms, and looked at him, man to man.

"Pat's in the hospital. She was with me when the trailer blew. She's in the same state I'm in, but worse. They say she'll be fine but she's not coming home for a few days. So, are you going to cooperate, or do you want to go off to that group home thing? Those are the facts. Your call." Alan let the boy go and sank back into the chair, suddenly aware that his strength wasn't a match for the pains assaulting his body.

The kid wasn't processing. "She can't... I mean, she's supposed to be here. She can't be hurt."

"Sit. Or even better, would you get me one of those?" Alan nodded at the cake the kid still held, forgotten, in his hand.

That brought things back to earth. The kid—Jason, he corrected himself—gave himself a shake and turned to the counter.

With a piece of chocolate cake in front of him and Jason settled into a chair, Alan felt marginally better. He picked the square up and took a bite. "Good. Pat made this?"

"No, I did." He caught the pride in the boy's voice.

"You did a good job. Now, listen a minute," he said around another bite of the cake. "You know this Linda person?"

He nodded. "Ms. Gonzales. She's okay."

"Well, I expect she's on her way right now, and maybe the police. If you want to stay here while Pat's in the hospital, I'll help you. But you have to help me, too. Between us we have to convince your Ms. Gonzales that I can take care of you until Pat's back, and that you won't be any trouble. Assuming it'll only be a couple of days," he added. He could handle the weekend, but it abruptly hit him—what if Pat *wasn't* home by Monday? Was he saddling himself with this kid and her dumpy little house for any longer than that?

The kid was wary. "You wanna move in here?"

"No, not much. But I will."

"Why?"

"Because Pat's a friend. I doubt she'd want to see you in some other foster place."

The kid's eyes narrowed. "You fucking her?"

169

Alan choked. When he got his breath back he put the cake down, slowly, and nailed the kid with a menacing look. "Listen good, because you're old enough to understand this. *Fucking* is what you say when you're talking about a prostitute. When it's someone good, someone who matters, that's the wrong word. It's insulting and degrading, to the woman and to you. You can say having sex. Or if it's deeper, making love. But you do *not* talk about fucking. Not with a woman like Pat. Got that?"

"But are you?"

Alan sighed. "No."

"But you want to."

"What is it with you, kid? Some things are frankly none of your business."

The boy returned his attention to the cake.

"Now, once we've dealt with officialdom, I'll take you to see Pat, if she can have visitors."

He looked up. "You mean, like, in your car?"

"Easier than walking." The roads were bare, so he'd driven the roadster.

"Cool."

"But." Alan came down hard on the word. "I'll do this for Pat, but I don't want any crap out of you. You be where you're supposed to be, got it? And no lip."

"Whatever." The kid shrugged, but his face betrayed his enthusiasm; the car had done it.

The phone rang. Alan let the boy answer and talk a minute, then took the receiver when he handed it over. It was Linda Gonzales. The next ten minutes were an interrogation, taking up what was left of his reserves. But the timing was good; he was able to pass the phone to the police officer who turned up. The woman talked to Ms. Gonzales and went away again.

In the end there was a plan. Linda Gonzales would attempt to talk to Pat. They'd meet at the hospital so she could *assess* him, see if she approved of his staying with a smart-aleck kid for a weekend.

Then, his whole body stiffening, the kid a mix of worry about Pat and excitement about getting into his car, he drove them to the hospital.

❖

Linda Gonzales got there before them and met them outside Pat's room. It was very formal. "Mr. Carmichael?" She extended a hand.

"Ms. Gonzales." They exchanged a brief shake.

Pat was conscious, she told them, although not by much. Alan hadn't spared a glance at himself in a mirror before he and the kid left for the hospital, but based on the pain coming from his face, he realized suddenly how he must look, and by extension what kind of shape Pat must be in. He wondered if bringing the kid to see her had been such a great idea.

"We're not staying long. The hospital's having a fit with so much activity. They get that we need to resolve this, though. Hi, Jason. How're you doing?" She put a hand on Jason's shoulder; the boy leaned into her for a moment. Alan felt a small, totally unexpected, stab of jealousy.

"She okay?" Jason said.

"Sort of okay. The doctors say you can see her for a minute, but I need to talk to Mr. Carmichael alone first. Could you wait over there?" She gestured at a row of hard chairs against the wall.

"Yeah, sure." The kid seemed to accept this as part of the routine. Alan wondered how many times he'd been shuffled to 'over there' while the adults in his life discussed his future.

Linda took his arm and turned them down the corridor, walking mercifully slowly. "I've talked to Pat. She says it's okay if you stay with Jason. I have my reservations, but she knows you and I don't. Can you tell me again why you want to do this?"

"That's hard to define." They'd covered this territory on the phone, and Alan would give a year's investment income at that moment for a painkiller, a scotch, maybe a hot tub. Instead he had to say the right things and convince Ms. Gonzales he was the soul of responsible moderation. "Out of respect for Pat? There's something about the kid—Jason—Pat thinks he's great.

171

From what she's said, he's had a rotten run of luck. I doubt he needs any more shuffling around."

"And your own family?" She consulted her file. "The police report says you live with Danielle LaPointe. Can you afford to take a few days off to stay with Jason?"

"Yes. Danielle—I mean, we're not—it's hard to explain." Was it ever hard to explain, when faced with a social worker. His life with Danielle made perfect sense, in its own context. But explaining it? "I don't have family. Danielle shares my house. We're colleagues."

"Colleagues," Linda repeated, more to herself than to him. Then she looked up at him. "Okay, I'm going with Pat on this one. We'll give it three days, with these terms. I'll be talking to Jason daily and most likely calling or dropping in on you to see how things are. He knows he can reach me any time. Sorry, but this is irregular, so you're under a microscope. That's how it is."

"That shouldn't be a problem. It was my trailer that blew up, so I'll be around the neighborhood. I'll be there when he gets home, make sure he eats, the usual."

"It says here that you know the system, Mr. Carmichael." At his narrow-eyed look she added, "Of course I've been checking on you. No choice."

"I understand." He left it at that.

They'd returned to the chairs where Jason waited, staring at his sneaker while he repeatedly kicked the flooring.

"Jason?" He must have known they were coming, but he didn't spring to his feet until Ms. Gonzales spoke. "You can see Pat now. The nurse said you could stay for a minute or two. I have to tell you, she looks worse than he does." She nodded at Alan. "She's hurting. But she'll be glad you're here. Remember, your job is to make her feel better, not give her more to worry about. Okay?"

"Yeah, sure." The lecture had embarrassed the kid. He supposed these things had to be said, but it bugged him anyway. Jason was no idiot, he would have figured it out.

172

"Okay, go." Linda gave Jason a quick shoulder hug, then sat in one of the chairs outside Pat's room. "I'll wait here until you're done."

Watched. He remembered that feeling. But there wasn't any help for it. He put a hand on Jason's shoulder and steered him into Pat's room.

She looked so small. Diminished. Her face purple and swollen with bruises and cuts. Her left wrist bandaged. Tubes everywhere, part of her hair at her right temple shaved away and another bandage covering the side of her head. Her eyes closed.

Alan stood by the bed, Jason beside him. The room was silent other than the faint ticking of a monitor. Suddenly ungrounded, he looked at her, at the bandages, the abrasions.

At her sandy lashes against her cheeks. The flash of pain that crossed her face and went away.

She's so fragile.

Time stopped. The ticking receded into the far background. He stared, stunned.

So this is it. This is what it feels like.

He hardly dared to breathe.

Pat half opened her eyes and twisted her mouth into what should have been a grin. Her voice was faint and slurred. "Hi, Jase."

"Hi. You were gonna take me shopping."

"I guess something came up. You okay?"

"Course I am. You're the one got beat up."

"Boy, am I. Hi, Alan. You look like hell."

"So do you. Perhaps I shouldn't say that."

She barely shook her head. "Not good to laugh."

Keep it to business. "I'll be at your house while you get back on your feet. Do you have a spare key?"

A tiny nod. "Jase, in my dresser, second drawer. There's a baggie with a bunch of keys and other junk."

"I'll find it. We came over here in his car, Pat. It's unreal."

Her smile was recognizable this time. "Make him take you to the grocery. The list's in the usual place."

173

"Okay. Pat?"

"Hmm?"

"I'm, like, real sorry." That embarrassed Jason. Any admission of emotion would embarrass him.

And that rang bells for Alan, too.

Again the little wince, quickly gone.

To touch her face, smooth away the traces of tears on her cheeks. To hold her while she heals…

Alan spoke as if the universe hadn't changed course. "We're going downstairs to get prescriptions filled, then I'm taking Jason home. I'll bunk on the sofa, and we'll come tomorrow afternoon."

He wanted to touch her battered face, but her eyes sagged closed. He again put his hand on Jason's shoulder. They left her sleeping.

That night Alan was awake late. Getting comfortable on the sofa was impossible given the bruises and cuts and trauma to his muscles, the gash on his back. But he'd taken more painkillers than he was supposed to, so for the moment at least, it could be worse. As it was for Pat, he was sure.

But now he had this new, and unwanted, realization to deal with.

It wasn't ever supposed to happen. Not to him.

She's wounded. Hurting. Because of you.

And he couldn't do a damn thing about it.

He found Pat's limited supply of alcohol and poured himself a glass of wine. Then he remembered the painkillers and dumped it out.

He pulled the curtains aside and rearranged a chair, and sat in the dark, watching the flurries against the nighttime sky. Because he suspected it wasn't going to go away, he had to come to terms with that flash of awareness, there in her hospital room. It carried the same inevitability as the moment when time had hung suspended before the explosion.

What it feels like.

He'd said he'd have her. The whole idea was ludicrous now. What he needed from Pat was so much more.

She wanted someone to be proud of. That didn't include him. He had to understand why not, so he could fix it. Once, her rejection was a game. An unfair one, since it had caused her tears, but a game nonetheless, and going nowhere. Now it threatened to destroy the underpinnings of his life.

Alan didn't put words around the turmoil in his head, never mind the dull ache in his heart. The man who would drag himself off that sofa in the morning wouldn't be the same man who'd stepped out of the trailer a few short hours ago. When he wasn't paying attention, when he was obsessed with his usual priorities, like having his name on the perfect commercial project, his own rules had changed.

He sat in the window, suffering every bruise and abrasion, and stared out on the bleak night.

18

The next morning, a Saturday, gave Alan a whole new perspective on agony. Insufficient sleep had done nothing to soothe the muscles that had seized up following the outrage they'd suffered the day before. From his bed on the sofa he surveyed Pat's living room in the daylight. It looked a little battered, a little the worse for wear, but welcoming. He wasn't sure why he should have a positive reaction to Pat's home, but at the moment he was grateful for any sense of shelter and safety.

It took him minutes to lever himself off the sofa. A hot shower, carefully avoiding the gash on his back, soothed the muscles, but not the cuts on his face, hands, knees, and torso. After the shower he frowned at his shredded shirt and torn, filthy slacks. Ruined, but with no options he resigned himself to looking like a bum off the street for another couple of hours.

As he dressed he mentally reviewed his plans for the coming weeks. He'd have to reschedule. He needed time to see to his body, fallout from the explosion, the kid.

In two weeks he was supposed to be skiing. Not going to happen. The idea didn't distress him.

He found Jason in the kitchen cooking bacon. Pat's kitchen was nothing like the living room. It was small but sleek, with granite counters and dark wood cabinetry against neutral walls. "Thought you might be hungry. I can do eggs, too," Jason said nonchalantly, making sure Alan knew it was no big deal.

He could relate. Made it easier to hide the hurt if your offering was rejected.

"I'm impressed. Any coffee around?"

"Yeah. Up there." The kid nodded at a cabinet and went back to turning the bacon.

He limped to the counter, located the coffee maker, and started a brew. Resigned to wait for his coffee, he asked, "Do you have any plans for today?"

"Naw. Pat'll make me do homework. We were gonna go shopping for a winter coat, but I guess that's not gonna happen."

"I want you to come to Columbus with me this morning. I have to pick up some clothes and change cars." He had no intention of leaving Jason alone with a whole morning to kill. He remembered well enough what it was like to be Jason's age with too much time on his hands.

The kid caught fire again. "You have another car?"

"SUV. You'll like it. It has its share of bells and whistles."

"Cool."

"Keep an eye on that bacon, please."

A few minutes later the boy put a plate of bacon and scrambled eggs in front of him. He'd forgotten toast, but the rest was surprisingly good. Alan said so, and watched the kid glow and pretend he didn't care.

When the coffee was ready, Alan struggled to his feet again and poured a mugful. His body relaxed marginally as the caffeine hit his system. "We'll go to the hospital this afternoon. Pat can give us advice on shopping for a coat. And I may need to call in at the clinic. My knee wasn't so bad yesterday, but it's swollen this morning. Then we'll see if there's any football on. Make popcorn."

"Never watched football."

But Alan sensed eagerness. Probably the kid hadn't had much chance to do things like watch sports—or spend time with a man. From what Pat had said, there hadn't been a father figure in his life.

Not that he'd ever, in any alternate universe, be anyone's father figure. But he was grasping in the dark for ways to keep Jason entertained. He'd never watched a football game, either, but his body had become his own personal torture chamber, and he needed something to both occupy the boy and give himself a break.

"Half an hour. Don't forget to brush your teeth." Alan put his plate in the sink and started to walk away.

Jason looked from the plate to him. "Pat'd kill you."

"Pat's not here. This is a guy weekend. We'll wash the dishes later."

A winner, based on Jason's grin. He disappeared. Alan popped pills, rummaged until he found a bag of frozen corn, and retreated to the living room with a refill of coffee. Settled on the sofa with his improvised ice pack on his knee, he tapped his phone.

Astrid, at home, answered on the fourth ring. "Figured you'd survive."

"Disappointed?" He'd known not to expect sympathy from his acerbic office manager.

"Nah. You pay too well."

"Gives me the right to call you on the weekend. I need you to reschedule my week. Clear the calendar. I'm going to be stuck in Calter Creek, there's a lot to deal with."

"Reschedule everything?"

"Everything."

"Heard anything about that dog of yours?"

Pete? The animal's hopeful eyes and smiling face popped into his mind. Right now, the noncritical affection of the animal sounded good.

Give me a break. Dogs don't smile.

With everything else going on, the last thing he needed was a dog to take care of. Pete was best where he was, at whatever that kennel was called.

He ignored her question. "Thanks, Astrid. You're a peach."

She grumbled something he didn't catch and hung up on him. Calling that Brunhilde of a woman a peach proved to be a great retaliation. He'd have to remember it.

❖

The dusting of snow during the night had barely covered the main roads. He took his time driving, paying only superficial attention to Jason's commentary; he had no desire to risk the roadster on a stupid move. He looked forward to having the SUV, a big Nissan, under him, given the weather.

Jason chattered through the forty-minute drive. His wrists sticking out of his beaten-up coat, he explored the controls on the dashboard, turned on the radio and surfed until he found a station he liked — surprisingly, not loud metal or hip-hop, but mellow pop. He asked about the basics of football, so he'd have a better idea of what they'd be watching this afternoon. Told Alan he'd put popcorn on the list, so they had to go to the grocery. Offered to make spaghetti for supper, explaining that Pat expected him to cook twice a week.

Alan relaxed into the chatter and surprised himself by not minding it. He was amused to note that Jason's use of English improved when he wasn't paying attention.

Attitude. The kid had it in spades. Keep them out, where they can't see the hurt.

Jason went bug-eyed when they pulled up the circular driveway to his home, then again when Alan installed him in the oversized, never used kitchen with a TV remote, while he changed clothes and packed a bag. Shaving was impossible with the nest of abrasions on his face, but he optimistically added the shaver to his suitcase. With today's list of unusual tasks, especially the throbbing knee, he didn't linger.

Interesting. Home, sanctuary, and you're rushing to get out of it.

He wanted to see Pat. Before the game, after the game, he didn't care as long as he saw her today.

He left a note for Danielle. He'd sent her a text last night, so she knew he was all right; her reply had been in their usual, unemotional shorthand.

Then he grabbed a book out of his library and some work he'd been doing from home, rounded up the kid, and they hit the road.

Back to a tiny 1940s era house in unsophisticated, boring Calter Creek. How ironic is that?

179

As he piloted the SUV along Sycamore toward the turn onto Seventh, Alan said, "Once we've dropped off my stuff, I have to call in at the clinic, then lunch."

"Can I just stay at home? 'Cause you'll end up waiting forever at the clinic. Lots of kids with runny noses."

"You're going to keep out of trouble for a couple of hours?"

Wrong question. He felt the boy tense. Jason turned away and stared out the window.

"Look, kid, sorry I asked. It's my job, and we can't afford to mess up here."

"I ain't gonna mess up." Jason's voice was surly, his body hunched in that godawful coat.

Alan sighed. "Okay, listen up. You think I don't have a clue, right?"

"You kidding? That fancy house and car and shit?"

He turned onto Maple. "You're wrong. I spent a couple of years in foster care when I was your age. It sucks."

Jason looked at him. "Like I believe that."

"Ask Ms. Gonzales, she's checked up on me." He turned into Pat's driveway and put the SUV in Park, then carefully shifted to face the kid.

"I bet that's why, then."

"Why what?"

"Why you've got all that stuff and you're not happy. Nuthin' makes you happy when your folks don't want you around." Jason's voice broke on the last words. He kept his gaze out the window.

His speech hit Alan like a bucket of ice water. *Not happy?*

"What gives you that idea? Foster care doesn't have to be the end of the line."

The kid looked at him, with hard eyes and contempt on his face. "Yeah, I saw Pat, that day. You got her cryin', didn't you? Happy people don't do that."

"You think I want Pat to cry? You're wrong. Get that through your head right now." His lips tight, he faced the kid down.

The memories. The bruises, the rejection, the hunger.

What the hell was he doing, locking himself into this babysitting arrangement?

"You sure ain't provin' it."

"I'm here with you. Mainly for Pat. You're growing on me, though, no matter how hard you try to be unlikable."

"Bull."

"Truth. Now, I expect you to stay put while I go to the clinic. I'll pick up subs on the way home, then we can hit the grocery and watch that football. While you wait, why not do your homework?"

Jason had tuned out, becoming the obnoxious, remote pre-teen that—yeah, face it, that he remembered being.

"Why don't you call the hospital? I don't know if Pat can talk or not, but it's worth a try. At least get us a status report."

Those skeptical blue eyes turned on him. "They'd take a call from a kid? Yeah, right."

"They don't care how old you are, Jason. Try it."

Jason shot a withering glance at him, then shouldered his way out of the SUV, slamming the car door before disappearing around the back of the house.

Alan sighed and backed the vehicle down the driveway. Yes, he had more than an inkling of what was going on in Jason's mind.

He was a success, he'd accomplished everything he'd planned. How could he not be happy?

Except there was this new thing. He'd file it under miscellaneous for a while, since factoring it into his life was impossible.

It was past noon by the time he got back to Pat's, subs and potato chips in hand. He found the boy in the kitchen with a book, which he put away as soon as Alan came through the door.

"What are you reading?" He set the bag on the counter and rummaged for plates.

"Pat called 'em graphic novels. It's mostly pictures. It's good, though."

"Did you talk to Pat?"

"They said she was asleep. They prob'ly didn't want me talkin' to her."

"More likely she was asleep. You saw what a mess she's in."

"Yeah."

"If Pat agrees, we can go coat shopping tomorrow."

"It's a stupid coat." He'd tossed it over a chair instead of putting it away. It was a stupid coat. Besides Jason's wrists sticking out, it looked as if it had been through multiple previous owners. He was surprised Pat hadn't replaced it before now.

Jason fingered it. "It was okay once. But it's kinda falling apart, especially inside. She made me put it in the wash, and it shredded."

"And shrank, I'd guess. We can do better."

Alan put the sandwiches on the plates and watched Jason with amusement as the boy confronted a meatball sub. He hardly noticed the lettuce and tomato as he wolfed it down. Alan wondered if he'd ever had one before. He let Jason's chatter float over him, eating because he was supposed to, replying when he had to, and coping as best he could.

She still looked tiny, but at least her bed was at an angle so she wasn't flat on her back. Alan got the impression that staying awake was a challenge.

Jason hit Pat's hospital room at mach speed, talking before he had fully arrived. The day had been a hit with the kid, especially the meatball sub and the game. Neither of them had known that football was over for the year except for the Super Bowl, but they'd found a hockey game, picked sides, and more or less figured out the rules. That had been kind of fun, and for him a brand new experience. At no time had his life involved wasting an afternoon watching pro hockey with popcorn and cans of pop.

Pop. A scotch would have been orders of magnitude better, but Alan was heavily enough into painkillers that he wasn't risking alcohol. Not with Jason to keep an eye on.

Pat's eyes stayed on the kid while he talked, without any of the poor grammar or language he used when he felt threatened. It had been the same over hockey. Jason was proving himself to be fully capable of functioning at a level above that of a moron.

As the onslaught tapered off, Pat managed a smile and shifted her gaze from Jason to him. "It sounds as if you've taken better care of things than I could have," she said.

"Ribs hurting?"

"Along with everything else. I'm doped up, taped up."

"I guess that means you don't want any hugs or anything," Jason said.

"I need them, but they might do more harm than good at the moment." Stress lines of pain and weariness added to the scrapes and bruises on her face.

"Any idea when they'll let you go home?" Alan asked.

A gentle shake of her head. "Ask out there."

"I will. You don't need to worry, we've got things covered."

"I wasn't worried."

His eyes met hers. He'd hoped to avoid that, because he wasn't sure what she'd see in his. He did his best to school his face into its usual mask. Whatever he was feeling for her — and he wasn't willing or able to name it, not yet — he chose to keep it to himself. He didn't believe in revealing his hand too soon.

Then she turned her attention back to Jason. "There's chicken stew in the freezer."

"I know where it is. I can make rice."

The careful smile again. "After that — hamburgers?"

"I made eggs and bacon this morning."

Alan added, "It was good."

"Jase, you're amazing."

183

The boy blushed and changed the subject. "Alan says we can go shopping for a coat tomorrow. Only we don't know what kind."

Sometime during the day he'd become 'Alan' instead of 'Mr. Carmichael'. He found he didn't mind.

Pat tried to shrug, but mostly failed. "Whatever you want, within a reasonable budget. Warm enough and big enough to get you through the next three months, please."

"You're fading, aren't you?" Alan said. "We'll go and let you rest."

Pat nodded, looking at Jason. "See you tomorrow? I mean, if Alan..."

He noticed Jason's hand resting on top of hers. "We'll be here. Get better, Pat. We'll be fine."

She smiled at him, and he risked touching her other hand where it lay limp on the covers, sticking out of the bandage on her wrist. A barely-there touch, but she registered it, he saw it on her face, a subtle twitch around her mouth. What that meant, he had no idea.

But then her eyes drifted closed, so he made a gesture to Jason, and the two of them left.

An odd notion flashed through his mind as he glanced back at her from the door. *We're your men. We'll take care of things, until you come home.*

Alan visited Pat Tuesday afternoon while Jason was in school. He wanted time alone with her, and he didn't want to bring up the explosion in front of the kid. He doubted Jason knew how close they had been to going up with the trailer.

She'd cranked the bed up to a sitting position and looked more alert. He stood next to her bed and studied her. After four days the bruises were starting to go green, which gave her a sickly look. Seeing her like that... it got to him. He'd be glad when Pat was back in her house and he could put distance between himself and whatever it was that gripped . him whenever he was with her.

She was ready to talk. "They came to see you, too, huh?"

"The investigators. Yes, this morning. I went over the site with them. Nothing left of the trailer, of course. We're fortunate that we didn't store anything valuable there."

Neither of them mentioned how narrow their own escape had been. For him it was still too close, too raw. He suspected it was for her, too.

"You're better," he said.

Pat nodded. "Going home tomorrow. They tell me I have to keep swallowing pills or I risk pneumonia from not breathing properly or some other dread effect. I don't like suffering, but I hate taking pills."

"So do I, and take them. I've been living on them. I'm just starting to phase them out."

She snorted. "How are you, apart from what I can see? You obviously didn't end up in the hospital."

He shot a grin in her direction that he expected was lopsided, since an abrasion pulled on the skin of his left cheek close to his mouth. "Bruising and cuts everywhere. Left knee took a beating. I hadn't done up my coat, so I was wide open to every rock and frozen clod. There's a gash on my back, probably from a piece of the trailer. Ruined my coat."

"Yeah, mine too. And pretty much everything else."

He wanted to sit, because of the knee. He gambled and perched on the edge of her bed.

She didn't object. He found himself relieved out of all proportion to the situation.

"Jason's happy with his new coat," he said.

"Hope so. He's had little enough of his own. Tell him I'll be home tomorrow, okay?"

"It's good you're getting out of here."

"They've only kept me this long because of the shock and concussion and because my muscles won't work. Not everyone gets a chance to fly through the air with the greatest of ease, even though I missed the 'greatest of ease' part. What's the worst for you?"

"My knee, but it's improving. They say there's nothing seriously wrong, it just needs ice and more ice. That first night on your sofa—I wanted to crawl out of my body."

He watched her hands. They knotted together, came apart to twist in the sheet covering her, knotted again. Was Pat as on edge as he was? Hard to believe, she seemed so patient and... peaceful.

Did she know?

He doubted he was that transparent, but where Pat was concerned, all bets were off. He didn't begin to understand what she knew, or how.

"I got lucky," she said. "Nice comfortable bed, people dancing attendance."

"You stiff?"

"Rigid. It's getting better."

"Same here."

"I couldn't tell the investigators anything. I turned around and saw the fire, then you said something about the gas tank and started dragging me, then I don't even remember the flying through the air. I'd hoped to create a story out of it for my kids."

"Make it up?"

"Better than the real thing."

"Besides the trailer, some fencing collapsed and a window was blown out. Your neighbors are more worried about you than annoyed about the destruction. We've already started repairs."

"A delegation came by yesterday. It's a good neighborhood, we take care of each other."

And she'll do all she can to preserve it.

"About the investigation," she said. "I can't believe it was deliberate. But what could have caused it otherwise? It doesn't make sense."

"They've found traces of accelerant and the probable start location. They figure there must have been a timer, but they haven't got it yet."

"Deliberate, then." Pat surely saw the underbelly of life through her work, but this was an evil he wished he could have protected her from. She looked at him, and he looked back, steadily.

186

"You could help me."

"I'd be happy to. What can I do?"

"An arm for support. I'm supposed to be up and walking, and the best place to walk is to a fridge down the hall. They have juices, so it helps vary the menu around here. Would you mind?" Pat shoved the sheet off with a foot and swung her legs over the side. Her movements were guarded, as if waiting for the next assault from her body, as she rose from her pillows and held out a hand.

He took it and gave her enough support for her to get her balance as she slipped her feet into a pair of slippers he'd brought her along with a change of clothes. She shifted to grip his arm, then stopped. "Is this okay? Are your arms beaten up, too?"

"Yes, but don't worry, it's fine."

Pat wasn't even remotely seductive in her hospital gown and robe, but he wanted her close. Alan pinched his lips together, watching her as she walked. Her hand closed more firmly around his arm; she was well aware of him beside her.

The bruises and abrasions would keep for later. He could pace these halls with her for hours.

19

Okay, people can change. But Alan?

She hadn't needed him to walk down the hall. She'd been doing it all day, getting stronger by the hour as long as she didn't get too tired. So why had she asked him for help?

What game are you playing?

Why had he given it, without any digs or innuendo?

Amanda had dropped by after work, and Linda had promised to drive her home tomorrow. She had a nice collection of cards and flowers to take with her. She'd worn herself out, though, and hadn't been disappointed when Jason phoned to say they couldn't come that night. Cooking class; lying there losing track of time, she'd forgotten. Now, provided she didn't fall asleep—and that was a way of life these days—she had space to let her bruised body rest. And think.

Or maybe not. Thinking was too confusing.

There was Alan, and the sabotage. She hoped the police and fire departments figured it out soon, because everyone was going to be jumpy until it was resolved. She imagined the next round table meeting, the whispers and gossip. Could anyone on the round table be responsible? Surely not. Right from the first they'd impressed her with being anything but activists. And thank heaven for that.

Her home. Oh, she was ready to be home. Her own bed. Her own bathtub. She sent a silent blessing to her freezer, well laden with dinner options.

Jason. Her boy. With Alan, and not complaining. She suspected that Jason was torn between wanting to exert his authority as the man of the house and wanting a man around to show him how to do it. That was a dynamic she wished she'd had a chance to observe, a fly on the wall.

Was Alan still on her sofa? She supposed so. He hadn't mentioned shifting to a more comfortable place to sleep, although she certainly wouldn't have blamed him. Her bed, for instance. If she'd known she was going to get blown up, she'd have changed the sheets for him.

Laughing was *so* not a good idea, even at her own feeble jokes. Her ribs hurt if she so much as breathed.

Alan. Enough wool gathering. Focus on the main confusion.

Had things changed? Had Alan changed? What on earth prompted him to move into her house and hang out with Jason? Because he *was* hanging out with Jason, not just there for meals and homework, but actually spending time with her boy. She'd been amazed by everything Alan had done. Watching hockey? Shopping for a coat? But he wouldn't last. He must be miles out of his comfort zone.

On top of that, his visits to the hospital, especially the last one, when she'd been coherent, had been—enjoyable.

It was possible that she *liked* Alan Carmichael.

Wash your mouth out with soap.

If she was completely honest, she'd admit that his arm under her hand had made her feel safe and protected. She wished she could fall asleep in his arms. Nothing more—she hurt too much to even *imagine* more. But yeah, she'd like that.

And he'd laugh, because it would mean he'd won.

Wouldn't he?

Alone for the moment, she called Amanda.

"Hi. Are you okay?"

"No serious change since earlier. I'm tired, but I'm moving."

"So, what's up?"

"I have a problem. I need to talk it through."

"Do you want me to come?"

"Telephone works."

"So talk."

Pat took a deep breath. "I'm afraid I'm falling for Alan."

"Since supper?" Amanda quipped.

"Yeah. Or since this afternoon."

There was a pause. A long one. Then Amanda said, "Are you waiting for me to say you're out of your ever-loving mind?"

"Am I?"

"From what you've told me, how he's been with Jason, I don't think so. Can't be sure, since I haven't met him, but I don't think so."

"Something's changed. I don't know if it's because of the explosion. The look in his eyes—"

"You're studying what's in his eyes? You're not falling, girlfriend. You've fallen."

"That's what worries me. That you may be right."

"Pat, this isn't a negative."

"Don't be so sure. You're sitting there with your nice, middle-of-the-road accountant—no offence to Jacob, you know I adore him. Alan's alpha. He takes what he wants. I'm not sure I can live with that."

"Could be he still has a few things to learn?"

"Come on, Mandy, you're supposed to talk me out of this."

"Okay, I'm simplifying. But from what you've said, he's not introspective. Is it possible he's started to look at himself, and that's why you're sensing a change? Almost getting killed can do that to a person. Don't panic, Pat. Assess."

"What if I don't have the reserves? After everything that's happened between us, and then the explosion and his staying with Jason, it'd take more energy than I'm going to have for a while to sort this out."

Amanda laughed. "You sound like me, sorting it out. Then I finally stopped sorting, and guess what?"

"You found yourself with the man of the century. For all I know, Alan's the man of the millennium, but I can't quite trust him enough to find out."

"Oh, Pat." In her mind she pictured Amanda shaking her head and quietly sighing. "We need wine. We need a dissipated evening."

"Not going to happen any time soon. I'll be on painkillers forever and you're doing the practice-to-be-pregnant thing."

"When you go home, will Alan be there?"

"We haven't discussed it. What I'll find…" Pat shrugged. It felt good to be able to shrug, even gently, without wanting to run for the bottle of acetaminophen. "I suppose it's manners to invite Alan for supper, but I expect he'll want to go back to wherever he goes to. Back to Danielle the not-girlfriend."

"Mm hmm. Ignoring the Danielle complication, it's always good karma to practice one's manners."

"Stop that." Pat very nearly laughed.

Amanda must have caught her groan. "I'm sorry. I forgot."

"You're allowed to forget. Text me tomorrow and tell me what I'm supposed to do. Falling for Alan Carmichael is *not* on my life plan."

"I can't say that Jacob and Norah were on mine. Live large, Pat."

"I'll live small until my ribs heal. Then we'll see."

Mid-morning Wednesday, after Linda left, Pat stood in her kitchen and surveyed the disaster.

She hoped and prayed that they'd intended to clean up before she came home. Because no way was she going to do the dishes for them.

In the living room she found a stack of folded bedding and a small suitcase. There was no sign of the inflatable mattress. Alan had said if he got that low to the floor he'd never get back up again. But the sofa? It sounded like self-imposed torture, given that he wasn't any more comfortable in his skin than she was in hers.

She concluded that they'd shared the main bath rather than using hers. It wasn't too bad. No whiskers in the sink, but

191

then Alan hadn't shaved since the explosion. The graying five-day stubble gave him a slightly devilish appearance.

Her own room was inviolate. On the whole, she was glad. Alan in her bed was one image she didn't need cluttering her mind.

She'd put away the few groceries she'd picked up with Linda, so there was little to do but make coffee and relax. Which she needed; getting out of the hospital and a small grocery shop had cost her a day's reserves of energy.

As she settled on the sofa, mug in hand, a key turned in the front door lock. The options were limited to those with keys: Amanda, Jason, Alan.

Hoping it's Alan?

He walked in and hesitated when he saw her, then got out of his coat and crossed the room, looking sheepish. "I came back to finish cleaning up. You're home sooner than I expected."

Everyday business. Easy. "For two bachelors, the place looks okay, kitchen excepted. Grab a coffee if you want."

He did, and shoved aside the bedding to sit next to her.

"I'm sorry about the mess in the kitchen."

"I'm surprised. Don't you believe in washing dishes?"

He grinned. "It's a man thing. The kid thought it was the coolest ever, to leave them. The idea was we'd clean everything up before you got here, but you beat us. Last night—have you noticed you get tired easily? You're going along fine, and the next minute you're on the verge of collapse?"

"Yeah, I have. The shock, perhaps?"

"Well, it hit me last night. Then, when I went to find Jason, I figured he'd keep me awake, but he'd conked out. I didn't have the heart to wake him up."

"You're fortunate you had the good sense to come back. I'm not nice to people who mess up my kitchen."

He looked at her. She looked back at him. Before she knew it they were both laughing. Or he was, and she was doing her best not to. "When you can't afford to laugh, everything's a joke."

"Thanks for the coffee. Don't worry about the kitchen."

The silence felt companionable. As if sitting on a sofa with Alan, mugs in hand, on a snowy February morning was an everyday thing to do, not unusual, not dangerous.

It's the company that makes it dangerous.

"Glad to be home?"

She nodded and put her mug on the side table. "I love this place. It's me."

"I can see that." Alan took one last swallow, then carefully stood. "Kitchen. Give me ten minutes."

"I'll time you. I make it twenty, minimum. Stay for dinner?" She wanted to see for herself how the dynamic with Jason worked. And she believed it would matter to her boy if Alan was there.

He touched her cheek with a finger, a bare hint against the bruising. A look flew between them, a look she couldn't interpret. Alan hesitated, as if there were something he wanted to say, but his words, when he finally spoke them, were mundane. "I can't stay now, but I'd like to come back." He disappeared into her kitchen.

When she woke up a couple of hours later he'd tucked her in on the sofa, a soft blanket from the pile of bedding snug around her. She stayed there for a minute, luxuriating in the feeling of being taken care of.

By Alan.

She eased herself up, lunch on her mind. The kitchen sparkled and a pot of miniature iris bloomed on the table, with a note: "See you for supper. Call me if you need anything." The card was signed in Alan's handwriting, but he'd included Jason's name next to his own.

Pat looked around her sunny kitchen, soaking in the normality of it. Because in two hours, hours she'd slept through, Alan had shifted her thoughts, her feelings, her axis, everything. With flowers and a blanket, he'd changed her world.

When Alan got to Pat's, his head still buzzing with the simple delight of laughing with Pat that morning — when was the last time he'd spontaneously laughed at anything? — he found Jason busy with noodles and tins of tuna, while Pat sat at the table. The kid seemed happy and settled; this thing with Pat was working for him. He reflected back on his own childhood and wished he'd experienced the same welcome and warmth when he was a kid.

He'd learned very early that wishing got you precisely nowhere.

"Hey, man," Jason said, his attention on the tuna.

Alan hadn't bargained on tuna casserole, but at the moment he felt he was up for anything. Maybe Pat knew a secret ingredient that would make it edible.

She smiled at him. The same tug he'd felt that day, staring down at her in her hospital bed, came back, as if a spring had connected his chest to this woman. He suspected it was there permanently. "You've lost weight."

"I doubt it. I don't lose weight that easily, worse luck." Her mouth quirked.

"What's with you women, always wanting to be so skinny?" Jason piped up. He slotted the casserole into the oven and straightened, frowning at Pat.

She grimaced. "Ask the advertisers or the fashion designers. I can't say it matters to me anymore."

"Personally," Alan said, "I agree with Jason."

He could see her catch his meaning, although it went right over Jason's head.

"Oh."

An eye lock. Hers were puzzled. He wondered what she saw in his.

He wondered about a lot of things.

Her house was special, and she had to be at the root of whatever caused it to be so. It was perfect for her, and it was hard to imagine anything negative entering it. He'd bet she baked cakes in here on snowy days, stirred thick stews.

The place wraps you up, enfolds you.

It was a feeling of... belonging. For him it was an illusion, he understood that. He could never belong here. But looking back over the last four days, he recognized how rich Pat and Jason were in the things he'd never had.

The conversation meandered lazily from topic to topic. He relied on his cocktail party skills, since interacting with Pat had become a whole new experience, and it was going to require practice to get it right.

Later, supper eaten and the kitchen cleaned up, a shared male experience, Jason disappeared into his room. Alan helped Pat settle on the sofa and sank down next to her. "I wish the two of us weren't so beaten up."

"Thanks again for the flowers. They brightened my day." They sat on the coffee table now; she reached toward them but didn't risk leaning forward to touch them.

"My pleasure." Idly he brushed a gentle finger over the bandage at her temple, where they'd shaved her hair off, then ran his arm along the back of the sofa. He registered the twitch in his nerves when Pat leaned her head against him. She'd washed her hair, and it felt silken against his hand.

"We lived, Pat. With no permanent harm done." His fingers touched the elastic support on her left wrist. "It's nothing short of a miracle."

She tried to flex the wrist, winced. "We could have been in the trailer. I'm still having aftershocks, like jumping at strange noises, bad dreams. I'm beyond grateful to be alive. And, Alan..." She turned to look at him, shifting not just her head but her whole body. "It means more to me than I can tell you that you've been here for Jason. Reading between the lines, he's liked having you around. I never expected that."

"It surprises me, but I like the kid. He reminds me of myself at his age, I guess. And he's a heck of a cook. Better than either Danielle or me, come to that. It gets boring, eating out or phoning in."

She was still sideways on the sofa, looking at him. "Alan... what's Danielle to you?"

He flushed, and mentally cursed himself for mentioning her. "There's nothing to say. I've told you before, it's beneficial for both of us to be seen together." He shrugged. "That's it."

"I think it has to be more than that."

A cramp seized his biceps; he moved his arm from the back of the sofa and rubbed the muscle. It was going to be a while before his body accepted his normal movements and postures.

Pat's eyes skewered him but revealed nothing beyond mild curiosity. That funny twinge in his chest pinged at him. He sought the right words, then said, "It's not a conventional relationship. She shares my house. We appear in public together. We look good, so it's promotion for each of us. It's convenient."

Her eyes narrowed at the word 'convenient'. But the word was accurate, the most succinct way to describe his relationship with Danielle.

"Does she share your bed, too?"

Alan looked away. "She has," he said. He couldn't bring himself to admit that she still did. "There's no love between us, Pat. Not even very much friendship. It's pragmatic. It's always worked."

"You get what you want."

He studied a picture on the wall for a moment before facing her. "I'm not as sure as I was. I'm questioning myself these days."

"So am I."

Three words, but they resonated like a gong inside him, setting up reverberations right to his toes. But mostly in the region of his heart. Simultaneously, he felt a clench low in his belly.

Fear?

An emotion he avoided, or disguised. He wrapped his hand around her good one and raised it briefly to his lips.

She didn't pull away; in fact, she gripped his hand.

"I'm not sure what to say," Alan told her.

She shook her head. "Nothing needed."

"Can I offer you a painkiller or two?"

She almost laughed. It came out closer to a snort. "Don't. It hurts."

"I'm serious, though."

"No. I'll be fine for another hour or so. I'll take my pills before I go to bed."

"Don't get mad, but I'd like to stick around until then. I still get lightheaded occasionally. I want you to be safe."

"I'm fine, Alan. I'm just less mobile than I'm used to. Jason's here."

"Which will keep me out of the shower with you." She flushed; he shouldn't be surprised. "Just an idea. My staying, I mean. Not the shower."

She shook her head. "I'm sure you're ready to get home."

But she didn't release his hand. And he didn't dare move so much as a muscle in his little finger, holding hers.

The next morning Pat sent a text to Amanda. *"Consider it official."*

Of course Amanda was already at work. The reply was immediate. *"Courage, friend."*

"Couldn't you manage a cyberspace cartwheel or a hip-hooray?"

"Not until you do."

Amanda knew her too well. Recognizing her state—she refused to dignify falling in love with Alan Carmichael by any other term than *state*—didn't mean it was going to drive her to rhythmic gymnastics around the back yard any time soon. Pat let Amanda have the last word, left the phone on her desk, and started the coffee.

20

"You're fretting," Linda said.

"I know." Pat couldn't sit still, couldn't stay on her feet for very long, couldn't settle her mind. "I'm scattered."

The day was a sun-drenched wonder. Light poured into Pat's living room where the two women were sharing morning coffee, bouncing off the snow in the front yard.

"I hope work's not worrying you," Linda said. "We've got it covered until you're back on your feet."

"It may be a while. Every muscle in my body's got a vendetta against me. I tell myself it's getting better," Pat moaned. "Sometimes I even believe it. Not usually, but sometimes." She glared at the ice pack on her left wrist, resting on the arm of the sofa.

"You are. The bruises are this greenish color that goes so well with your hair."

Pat threw a sofa pillow at her friend.

Linda caught it in mid-air. "Good to see you coming back to life."

"So many things have me messed up right now. I just flop here and get in my head, and that's dangerous."

"Like Alan Carmichael?"

"Yeah. Worse luck to me."

"I talked to Jason yesterday at school. He likes the man."

"The man has a snazzy car."

"The man apparently gave Jason plenty of attention while you were down for the count. Praised his cooking, too."

Pat grinned at that. "Jason has a flair for it, for sure. Alan got him to his cooking class Tuesday."

"He did more than that. Found the argument to convince Jason to do his homework, for instance."

"Took him to Columbus—I got an earful about Alan's house yesterday."

"Cars, houses—man toys. Plus they bonded over hockey."

"Which neither of them knows a thing about, as far as I can tell."

"In short, Pat, he made a good job of his temporary foster father role. The kind I wish we saw more often."

"It's a conundrum."

"Another thing. It's in Jason's file, so I'm not breaking any confidences here. Alan was in foster care himself for a while, when he was around Jason's age."

And doesn't that explain a few things. The rough edges under his sleek exterior, for instance.

"Did you find out why?"

"Abandoned. There may have been violence. It's an old file, I was lucky to dig up that much. It doesn't say what happened to him when he left the system. I assume he went back to the family home, but I can't be sure."

"So that explains the rapport with Jason. The willingness to help him—that's been a mystery to me. They barely knew each other. Why did he step in that way?"

Linda was easy to be around. They thought alike on most points, did similar work, and enjoyed the same recreations. Now she reached over for another doughnut before saying, "And you're in love with him."

She didn't bother denying it. "And what am I supposed to do with that? We have such different values, our lives are on wildly different trajectories. But he can be… what should I say? Intriguing? And the whole thing with Jason."

"Kinda bad luck?"

"In a nutshell. At least with the pain it's easy to keep the hormones at bay."

"So you've got another week or thereabouts before the pain goes, except for the ribs."

"I hate looming deadlines."

"You want me to bring you a stack of reports to work on?"

"With this?" She raised the wrist, balancing the ice pack, then lowered it again. "I can type for three minutes before it reminds me how much it hates me. But it'd be better than sitting around mooning. Keep my mind off the disaster on the horizon."

"Tell me about the trajectories."

"Well." Pat settled in for the reveal. "He wants sex. He doesn't want involvement. He'll build his mall and disappear. He apparently has a mini-mansion in Columbus, plus the dynamite Danielle, of indeterminate status. In short, he's rich, he has no use for Calter Creek, he's looking for a temporary hook-up, and none of that appeals to me. This is where I live my middle class life. I won't be a playmate, even though I admit the idea's tempting."

"Yeah, nice ass."

Pat laughed. She was learning to regulate her laughter, so she managed not to wince. "You're no help. So however intrigued I am, I'm not going there. The risk's too great. I love my little home, my domestic routines, my work—isn't that boring? I'm not interested in chasing the big win. Fortune might be nice, at least enough to pay off the mortgage, but fame leaves me cold. Our paths through life couldn't be more different. They intersect at the mall—I wish they'd give the thing a name."

"They'll probably sell the name. You'll end up with it named after a hardware store."

"How charming. But once it's done and he moves on, the lines shift, and there won't be any common ground."

Linda got up to cross the room and sit on the sofa next to Pat. She squeezed her good hand. "You've drawn a bum deal this time. I'm here, if it gets bad."

"Thanks. When I need a light on the horizon, first I remember that I'm alive, which isn't much short of a miracle, I mean we escaped by seconds. Then I remember Jason. I'd adopt him, Linda, if the opportunity ever arose. He's a great kid."

"It's not always going to be so wonderful. Teenage boys can be hell on wheels, and this one's had more disruption than most."

"Doesn't matter."

Linda stood. "I've got to go. Guess what I'm doing for the rest of the morning?"

Pat put on her most innocent face. "Reports?"

The women laughed, Pat with a hand firmly on her side. She stood to see her friend out. "You coming by—it's made my day. Thanks."

"Always good to visit. Oh, hey, I almost forgot." Linda fished in a pocket and handed a USB flash drive to her. "Arguably my husband has too much free time. He thought you might want a look at the news reports from when you were in the hospital."

"That's sweet. Give him a hug for me."

Alone again, she dropped the flash drive on her desk, then stretched and settled back on the sofa, content. Alan's history gave her a different perspective on the way he related to Jason. Most important, though, she'd had an hour with a friend, and that mattered.

The sun reflecting on the snow lit her little home in a way that nothing else could. Pat luxuriated in the clear light and warmth, and found herself dozing off.

Can't ask for more.

The explosion wasn't ancient history yet, but life was getting back to normal. Pat had returned to work a week ago, after a full week off. Her movements were far from smooth, and she tired easily, but each day she tried to be useful before she collapsed and had to go home. Too much still hurt, and too much scared her. Once the memory faded and her ribs and wrist stopped throbbing, she might be less skittish. She could hardly wait to look in a mirror and see her usual face instead of this greenish one with scabs and a temporarily changed hairline.

No matter what Linda says, bruises are not good colors on you.

Overall, it was a miracle she hadn't been hurt more seriously. The persistent, low-level pain wore her down, though, and then she wasn't very nice to be around. She'd laid it out for Jason, and so far he tolerated her rotten moods.

At least it was a simpler tension to understand and cope with than the one that had plagued her before the explosion. The Alan-based tension. Which had morphed into the start of a friendship that only accentuated the old familiar desire. He'd proven something about himself to her, without even knowing it, and she wasn't as troubled by what was happening between them as she had been.

She'd hosted her Wednesday circle. It went okay, the kids acting as if the whole thing was an action thriller. The bruises and scabs caused open-eyed wonder. Mostly though, it had been a quiet week.

Work at least provided her with an interruption from the turmoil in her mind, where Alan was concerned.

Well, so much for that.

Monday afternoon her peaceful environment evaporated, because he stood in her cubicle door. She took in the scabs and faint bruises, the way he favored his left leg. He'd shaved, at long last.

"This is where I work," she said. "Not where I socialize."

"This isn't a social call. Is there somewhere private around here?" Alan's voice sounded stiff and rehearsed.

She studied him. He was ill at ease, toying with his gloves. "Can it wait?"

"No. It can't."

She saved a file and closed her laptop. "If nothing else, you're good at being mysterious. Come with me." She stood, a little embarrassed by the uncomfortable way she still moved, and led him to the conference room, where she rapped twice and opened the door. Empty.

"This'll do. The chairs aren't the best, but nothing's comfortable these days."

"I know. Same for me."

She sat, hands folded on the table. He closed the door and stood by it, unmoving.

"Mall news?"

"Yes, in fact. It's got a name. Landmark Center."

Pat considered it and nodded. "That's good. You want it to be a landmark. But you don't need me for that."

"No. I don't."

"Will you please sit down? You're making me nuts."

He circled the entire table before settling into the chair to her left. "I have to say this."

She sighed. "You're scaring me, Alan. What's wrong? Not another bombing?"

He shook his head.

She gave up prodding him, since this little meeting obviously was going to be run according to his timetable, not hers, and waited, studying his face while he stared at the door as if it were his only portal to safety, if he could only find the combination to the lock. His color was up, which was unusual. He *was* nervous.

When he spoke, it was formally, as if he were delivering a business proposal. "The thing is, I realized when you were lying in that hospital bed. I love you."

At her work, in a conference room. Only Alan would choose this venue to tell you he loves you.

If she felt anything at all, it was stunned. She certainly couldn't put words around the numbness in her mind, or the way her energy drained out of her muscles. She stared at him.

The silence that descended between them was so heavy, it was like molasses filling the room, thick and sticky, blocking her breath.

She'd swear she could hear his heart, but it was probably her own.

"Say something, Pat. Anything. Just say something."

She hesitated. This was dangerous.

This was miraculous.

How was she supposed to react? Her less practical side heard heavenly hosts singing alleluias in the background. Her more practical side, now fighting for dominance, dredged up a memory from nineteen years before and gave more than a passing acknowledgment to the irritating, self-assured man she'd let invade her peace. Miracles hardly mattered, in light of every other obstacle.

She regulated her voice to cool and calm, with difficulty. "I'm not only speechless, I'm breathless. You must be mistaken. I must have looked pathetic in the hospital. I don't need pity."

Alan continued in full business mode, clipping out his words. "I'm not mistaken. And I didn't say pity. I said..." He'd managed it once, but then the word seemed to have stuck in his throat.

"From you?" Then immediately she added, "I'm sorry, that was rude. But it's hard to credit. What you want from me, besides taking me on your bed or desk or whatever's handy, is my ideas for the mall so you can sit on your pinnacle and look out at the peons. Or so I've been led to believe."

"And that's your opinion of me."

"That's what you've shown me. Even your determination to seduce me—isn't this just the latest move? Should I see it differently?"

A flash that could have been pain crossed his face, and his eyes slipped from hers to his hands, resting on the conference table. "That was before. Before this happened." He looked back up. The tension she read in his posture forced her to pause and rebalance her wayward thoughts. She was going to have to take him more seriously. Alan was hurting, and hating every moment of this strange conversation.

She studied him, sensing that it took all his willpower to meet her eyes steadily. "You're serious."

"I am. Very."

"Is there a business decision needed here? What do you want me to say? I'm at a loss."

Relief washed over his face. "That's it—a business decision. That's within my terms of reference, because frankly, I don't understand much else right now. I was hoping you'd be able to help us wade through this. I don't know what happens next."

"Us? Is there an 'us' in this?"

"Of course there is. You wouldn't be sitting here taking time out of your day if there weren't. You wouldn't have agreed to my staying with Jason."

She didn't confirm or deny. "You want a road map. A project plan."

"Not only want. Need. Nothing like this ever happened to me before. I'm trying to figure out how to get to where you might..." He swallowed and let silence hang for a beat. "Might care about me. I understand that you don't now. I'm asking for your help, Pat."

She met his eyes but didn't reply, although she was afraid he'd crawl out of his skin if she didn't organize her brain cells into a coherent speech soon.

He laughed shortly. "More fool I, right? It doesn't mean a thing, does it, my finding the courage to come talk to you. Fair enough, I guess. I haven't given you much reason to risk getting close to me." There wasn't a trace of humor on his face.

"Oh, it means something." She sighed, looked away to stare into space at nothing. "But I don't know what. The signals I get from you don't add up into a logical whole. Sorry to be so blunt."

"I expect you're right. I've been working through a lot the last few days. I can see where you're coming from."

"You did take care of Jason."

"You did let me kiss you, before the explosion."

"Alan, I can't process. Can we do this some other time?"

"Tonight?"

Please God, no, I'd collapse in his arms.

Like you will any minute if you don't get him out of here.

"No. Too soon."

"Tomorrow. Morning, afternoon, evening. Any time."

"Last I heard, you have meetings with the county tomorrow."

"I'll cancel them."

"You'll do no such thing. That library's important."

"This is more important."

205

"In the big scheme of things, no it isn't."

"Evening, then. Can you get away from Jason for an hour?"

"As a matter of fact, yes. It's cooking night, remember? He'll be out. This doesn't make me happy," she added, "but I don't intend to discuss our relationship—if there is one—in a coffee shop or Brandon Caine Realty."

"What time?"

"You know the drill. I drop him off at seven, so half past works."

"Good." He took out his phone and began typing, presumably entering their—date? Brainstorming session?—into his calendar.

"It is a business decision, isn't it? This is beyond weird, Alan."

"More for me than for you, I expect. Feel free to laugh."

She shook her head. "It's no laughing matter."

"See you tomorrow." He stood, offered her a hand. Which she was grateful for; that rib made movement difficult. Besides, the muscles that still functioned had decided to take a temporary hiatus under the onslaught of his words. He'd left her limp, as if she were coming down from an adrenalin high.

She watched him until he disappeared around a corner, then returned to her cubicle. But it was a while before she fired up her laptop to resume work.

He hadn't touched her, except to offer his hand to help her stand. Pat felt as if she'd been ravished, taken so thoroughly she couldn't think straight, by the man of her dreams.

Drivel.

Only it wasn't. It was real. It was happening.

Leaving you with what, exactly?

And what are you going to do with it?

21

Alan and Danielle had settled in side-by-side leather chairs in the library. They each held a scotch, which was just as well. Alan, for one, was not looking forward to saying what he had to say, but after baring himself to Pat that afternoon, he no longer saw an alternative.

"The ski trip—have you considered going on your own?"

She shot him a cool look, as if to say he should know better. "Appearances, darling. It wouldn't look good."

"I can't do it."

"Clearly not. I'll talk to Trent, if you'll cancel the reservations."

"I'll see to it tonight." A pause. He caught his lower lip between his teeth for a moment. "Danielle..."

"Alan," she said with a sigh that approached boredom, "you're so transparent. It's the woman in Calter Creek, isn't it? Ever since you started this project it's been different, and we both know it."

So she knew. He didn't have to spell it out. Relief flooded him, warming his hands. He hadn't realized how cold they were before now. "I feel bad about this."

"Maybe I don't." She studied him over the rim of her glass. "Maybe we've derived all we can from what we've had, and it's time for us to move on."

"Perhaps. I wasn't aware you'd see it that way." He returned her scrutiny, although he could read nothing in her eyes and kept his own masked.

Danielle had been the most significant person in his life for seven years. The society pages in the Columbus paper linked them; their shared address linked them. They understood each other, right to the bone. He suspected she'd had lovers, which he hadn't, in their years as a couple. It wasn't a betrayal, because it wasn't a marriage. It was a relationship based on convenience, and a verbal contract they'd both agreed to, back at the beginning. It was business, and she'd played her role as his partner remarkably well.

Losing her, cutting himself free from their arrangement, the way they lived together — it felt dangerous, the loss of a solid foundation, leaving everything else unstable. He knew they'd be the subject of speculation, but they both had the skills to weather, even take advantage of, whatever the gossips brought out.

She interrupted his musings. "What happens next?"

"There's no rush. I may sell the house, I don't know yet. Do you have plans?"

"You remember that development east of Columbus, where I staged the model suite? In fact I bought one of the units. I'd expected to lease it out, but I believe it will suit me."

He smiled at her. "You're amazing. You're not like anyone I've ever known. Successful on your own terms, logical to a fault with no heavy emotion. Possibly that's why it's worked so well for so long."

She sipped her drink, studied it and sipped again. "The two of us are vultures. We know what we want and we take it. Plus, we're a handsome couple, and you've provided a perfect setting." She gestured around her. Yes, his home — their home — was perfect for what they'd both wanted. "A winning partnership."

"If there's any way I can help, Danielle..."

"There isn't, thank you. I've done very nicely."

"You always will." He paused. "The house — you chose so many of the furnishings. I thought you might want to—"

"I've been thinking about that."

He raised an eyebrow and let his mouth quirk in amusement. "Have you? You saw this coming?"

She laughed, which could have been dismissive but actually seemed to have warmth to it. "As I said, you're transparent, to me at least. I've started a list, I'll get it to you in a day or two."

He looked at her, then laughed, too. "I wish I could love you. We'd have been the perfect couple."

"We have been. But we both know love and marriage aren't for people like us. Be careful, Alan."

He raised his glass. "To you, Danielle. You're tough and you intend to stay that way. I hope you never get broken."

"To you." She skewered him with her eyes as she raised her glass. "I hope you find that breaking doesn't hurt too much."

He tapped her glass with his own, then sipped. "One more thing. Do we need to agree on a story?"

"Oh, we can fall back on growing apart, differing goals. The usual. It's always best to stick to the truth, as far as possible."

He nodded. "Timeline?"

"It'll take a couple of months, I expect." She nonchalantly stood and left the room.

Not so much as a brush of hands, and it was over.

She saw him as broken. He'd kept his face frozen when she said it, but offhand, he couldn't come up with a more apt description.

Alan wasn't ready for his evening with Pat, but then, would he ever be?

He'd put his cards on the table, which he never did. He'd learned through years of experience, back to his boyhood, that the first thing you *never* do is show your hand, leave yourself at your opponent's mercy. There wasn't a person out there he trusted fully, not even Danielle.

But he'd told Pat, flat out, how he felt. He didn't know how far he'd gambled, playing it the way he had. Worse, he had no idea where she was in this.

The criteria she'd outlined for him, New Year's Day— surely he met them. He'd been successful in every area of his life up to this point. He was wealthy, popular in his own sphere.

Unusual though it was, he had maintained his partnership with Danielle for seven years. He gave generously to charity. He'd spent five nights of physical torture on Pat's couch, to be sure Jason was okay. He was a sensitive man, he gathered beautiful things around him, making up for the squalor of his youth.

So what was wrong with him? What did she see that he didn't?

Yesterday had been its own kind of hell. First, telling Pat, then ending his relationship with Danielle. Standing on Pat's front stoop Tuesday evening, a major part of him wanted to turn around and never be seen in Calter Creek again, Landmark or no Landmark.

He had to laugh at himself. Landmark Center had been his obsession for a couple of years now, and so close to seeing it happen, could he even remotely imagine letting this chase him away?

Not likely.

So he rang Pat's doorbell and waited. He waited for over a minute before she finally opened the door.

She gave him a wan smile. "Sorry to take so long. I was wondering if I should pretend to not be home. Or if I should throw up."

"You're not well?" He stepped into her foyer, brushing against her and fisting his hands to avoid pulling her against him.

She shook her head. "Scared."

That hung in the air before he said, "Do you want me to go away again?"

Again a shake of her head. "I'm making chamomile tea."

"Could I have a glass of water?" He took off his coat and followed her into the kitchen. "Smells good in here."

"Jason made fried chicken for supper."

The kitchen was too small. The *house* was too small. Feeling caged, he paced, wandering into the living room, then back again, while she fussed with the tea things.

She touched his arm to bring him to a halt, pointed to a chair, and said, "Sit."

He sat. Fiddled with the water glass.

"I hope you're not expecting me to lead this conversation, Alan."

"It would help. I'm floundering."

Silence.

How could he love this woman so much that it challenged every reflex he had not to touch her—not for sex, or not only, but just to make the connection? How could he ignore the belt that tightened around his chest when he saw her, thought of her? What the *hell* was he doing?

"How have you been?" she said, once he'd demonstrated that he was incapable of speech.

You can do this.

He rallied. "It's been an interesting twenty-four hours. Danielle and I agreed last night to break things off."

"Why?"

Why?

He felt the first heat of anger. "Did you hear anything I said? Do you believe I could go on living with her, after telling you?"

She put a hand on his arm, just for a moment, stilling him. "No, I guess not. You'd expressed it as a business arrangement, so I didn't realize—"

"Have a look at the society pages, Pat. Whatever does or doesn't happen behind the scenes, in public we've been a couple. I couldn't let that continue. Danielle's fine with it, incidentally. The social fallout's going to take a month or so to settle, but it's over."

"Regrets?" He read sympathy in her gaze, which surprised him.

"Yes, some. We understand each other. You can't live with a person for seven years and not have a connection, even if it's more like a partnership. To tell you the truth, I've never been sure how to define it."

"I'm sorry."

"So am I, in a way. I don't like losing my direction."

"No, me either."

211

Again the silence. Pat kept her gaze on her tea, but having revealed his hand, he let his eyes stay on her.

On the scruffy kid on his engineering team, years ago.

On the sleek woman he'd seen in the audience at the public hearing.

On the woman in sweat pants with her hair in a messy ponytail, when she didn't expect company.

On the pale, diminished Pat in that hospital bed, scraped, bruised, in pain. Those sandy lashes on her cheeks.

And now on this lovely but not composed woman sitting at her kitchen table. A woman who, underneath the calm veneer, was as scared as he was. Because of him.

"I can't stand this," he said, and stood. "Let's walk."

"Good idea. I can't stand it, either."

Outdoors, on the sidewalk, he touched her arm, then went with instinct and claimed her hand.

She turned their conversation to the explosion. "Alan, have you talked to Brandon? Could he be at the root of this? You don't have a history here, so that leaves the mall or Brandon. Had you considered that?"

"It crossed my mind. But it's hard to imagine that level of destruction because someone's house deal went sour."

"True. Stranger things have happened, though."

A slow walk suited him, and Pat fell in with his pace. They went to the end of her block and turned left onto Seventh Avenue, the road that led into Calter Creek. The night was crisp; he was grateful for the air on his face.

Echoing his thoughts, Pat said, "The cold feels good. Everything's healing, but there's enough residual bruising in there, it soothes it." She tipped her head up, as if to get more of the fresh air.

Watching her giving herself over to the night and the weather put an end to his tenuous control. He drew her to a stop, turned so they were facing, and kissed her.

This time there were no tears mixed in with her response. Her coat padded her ribs, but in the moment he hated the thing, keeping her apart from him. At least she was there, and he clung to her every bit as much as she clung to him. When he broke off the kiss, he buried his face in her knitted hat. "I want your hair, not wool," he muttered.

And the tension snapped. Her body quivered as she tried not to laugh. He managed a reasonable smile himself, and hand in hand they continued to walk.

He said, "What it boils down to is that I've never felt this before."

"Odd. I guess I haven't, either."

"Are you saying you — care — for me, Pat?"

She glanced at him, then away. "Hard word to say, isn't it?"

"Yes. It is."

She made a short, derisive sound. "Wasn't it blatantly obvious, after I sniveled all over your shirt front? But I didn't know it, then."

"When did you know?"

"The day I got home from the hospital."

"The flowers?"

She shook her head. "Waking up to find you'd tucked the blanket around me. But mostly the way you took care of Jason."

"I told you a long time ago I wasn't going to stop. But now..."

"That particular game's over?" She didn't smile, but he heard a lightness in her voice.

"I think you won."

"Which doesn't go anywhere near answering your question, what happens next?"

He turned them onto Buckeye, the street south of Maple. "What do you want, Pat?"

"This is the hard part." She said that much and no more, leaving him suspended in uncertainty while he waited her out.

When she finally spoke her voice was thin as a thread. "We lead different lives. Calter Creek is my home, and I won't leave it. Your lifestyle is alien to me, Alan. When I try to imagine doing the things you do, I cringe. My world is backyard barbecues, not sophisticated soirees and charity balls."

He still waited.

213

She walked carefully, clutching his hand, studying the sidewalk. She took a breath, let it out, took another. Her exhales fogged the cold air. "What's harder to come to terms with, though, is that we have different values. The things that matter to you don't resonate with me, and vice versa. And I don't see a common meeting ground."

He forced the words out. "So different that it's not worth trying?"

"I don't know. But probably not. If I can't imagine a future…"

He felt compelled to argue with her. "Jason—Didn't I stay here with him? Didn't I take him shopping and eat his meals and even help with his homework?"

She looked at him. "And then you disappeared. He'll bring you up, in that ultra-casual way, as if it doesn't matter. He misses you."

Get out before you're abandoned. He'd learned that very well, a long time ago.

But he was no longer the boy he'd been. He'd proven himself, over and over again, since then.

"Speaking of Jason, I have to get back. I have to go pick him up."

Bewildered, he said, "That's all? I don't understand."

They turned into the next cross street, heading toward her home. "That's it, isn't it?" she said gently. "You don't understand."

They walked the rest of the way in silence. At her doorstep she gazed at him. The sadness on her face pierced a part of him he hadn't known he had—or perhaps it was his heart? He'd never had cause to find out, before.

She let him know, without words, that they had nowhere to go.

Standing on the stoop one step above him, she cupped his face in her mittened hands and kissed him, leaning forward so their bodies didn't touch. A gentle kiss, a sad kiss. "Good night," she said. Then she turned, unlocked her door, and disappeared inside.

❖

214

"It could be better, could be worse," Pat said. "How do you feel about it?"

'It' was the March report, and Jason's grades, while nowhere near failing, weren't brilliant, either. The teacher comments concerned her more. Inattentive, not reaching his potential, things like that. His teachers believed, to a person, that he could do better.

"Dunno."

"Uh huh. Want cookies?"

Hanging on by a thread here…

Jason frowned at her, but at least he looked up. "Aren't you gonna yell at me or ground me or something?"

"No." She was on her feet, pouring milk. "The grades aren't brilliant, but not all kids are scholars, so that doesn't worry me too much. Does it bother you?" She set the milk and a plate of homemade peanut butter cookies on the table, then sat back down.

"Nah."

"It's okay to take a cookie, Jason."

He didn't move.

"Well, if you aren't going to have one, I am." Pat helped herself to a cookie and bit into it. "So, level with me. What's with the attitude? I'm not seeing it much around here, but it seems to be your prevailing style at school."

He squirmed. "Whaddaya expect, anyway? I go all prissy-pants and I'll get beat up. Like before."

"Before you transferred?"

"Yeah."

Pat left it. Jason was off balance, and that wasn't what she wanted. Hoping to convince him to relax, she picked up a cookie and handed it to him, then sent out a prayer for wisdom and waited.

Out of the blue he spoke up. "I'm not gettin' into trouble or nuthin'."

"Good. That's important. You know what's at stake."

"I ain't leavin'."

"I sincerely hope not."

"So I'm not grounded?"

Pat shook her head. "How are things with the other kids? Are you starting to make friends?"

"It's tough in a new school."

"I get that."

Jason sat up straighter, took a bite of the cookie and swallowed a gulp of milk. "When you got blown up, I got popular real quick. Everyone wanted to hear about it. And when Alan was here—they were curious about that."

She noted, as she had before, that Alan was no longer Mr. Carmichael to Jason.

"You know," she said, picking up the report and tapping it on the table, "Given what you've gone through in the last couple of years, this isn't bad. But what I want is for you to be able to say, 'I did my best, this is my best work.' I'm not sensing that right now. So let's get from here to there. I'll help, but you have to tell me what you need."

"Yeah, okay. Can I go?"

"Go."

Pat watched as he gulped the last of the milk, grabbed another cookie, and bolted. What kid liked the report card conversation? None, in her experience, not even the good students. But she'd been honest, she wasn't disappointed, except that clearly he was.

She didn't have it all figured out, and neither did he, but she hoped he was less lost, after being with her the last three months.

Best she could do.

And working her way through the morass of conflicts, peaks and troughs that was Jason kept her mind off her other problem. Three weeks since she'd seen or heard from Alan. Her whole body ached, and not with residual pain from the explosion. Even loving her, he couldn't grasp the level of openness and commitment she needed from him. She'd have given him time, if she thought it would do any good. But in her heart she didn't believe either of them could breach his walls. He probably didn't even realize it, but he had neither the strength of character nor the temperament to stick with a relationship—the kind of relationship that included emotional involvement—for the long haul. Where Alan was concerned, she was out of options.

Which did nothing to assuage the ache.

22

The county police were at her cubicle at 10:00 the next morning, with a photo.

Pat studied it, then shook her head. "Sorry, I don't know him. Is this about the explosion?"

"Yes, ma'am. His name's Dirk Farndon. Mean anything to you?"

"No. You're not going to tell me any more, are you?"

The constable at her cubicle door crinkled his eyes in a smile. Social Services' dealings with the police were a mix of the official and the personal, which made a good working relationship.

"No, ma'am. But Pat—watch out, okay?"

"Thanks, George. I will."

The day settled into routine until mid-afternoon, when Alan turned up.

Which kicked normal off into the nether reaches of space.

He held himself stiffly, standing outside her cubicle without entering.

Speechless, she closed the file she'd been working with and picked up her mug of tea.

Before she could sort out her disordered thoughts, he spoke tersely, without preliminary. "They got the guy."

Something to hang onto. A conversational hook.

Why, oh why, did she have to be so glad to see him?

"I met the police this morning. Dirk Farndon?"

"Once we had the name, we did some digging. He bought into one of Brandon's developments three or four years ago, as an investor. They lost money, and the man was furious, to hear Brandon tell it."

"So it was Brandon Caine Realty all along." Pat traced a finger around the rim of her mug. She wasn't willing to meet his eyes, so for safety she looked down, following her finger. "Why are you here, Alan? What's so important that you couldn't have told me by phone or email?"

She didn't see his eyes leave her face, but she felt the let-up in energy connection between them. She was glad, sort of.

And how pathetic is that? A glare's better than nothing?

"I just—I wanted to be sure you knew. The explosion was supposed to go off at night. The guy couldn't even get a.m. and p.m. straight. Seems he feels bad about what happened to us."

"I'm too resentful to care, to be honest."

"I have to go."

She stood. "So do I, in fact. I have an after school kids' circle."

He turned abruptly and strode down the corridor without another word or backward glance.

She followed him as far as the meeting room, much more slowly, lost in thought.

He'd shut her out. She couldn't blame him, after the way she'd reinforced those walls he used to protect himself. Yet he'd come to see her. What was going on with Alan?

Whatever, she couldn't let it mess up her afternoon. With the kids in the circle, she had to be on top of her game, always. Even if there was a crack inside, where heartbreak found its way in.

Danielle proved her efficiency yet again. Within a couple of weeks she'd organized the move to her new, up-market condo. As he'd offered and she'd itemized, she took a selection of the furnishings from the house they'd shared. Alan was acutely aware of what was missing.

To his surprise, Danielle's absence was a presence in itself. No trace remained of her energy, her faint fragrance.

Nothing lingered of what they'd had for so many years together.

The social fallout had begun. There'd been one or two phone calls as their friends tried to manage long-standing invitations. Alan was happy enough to bow out and concede the space to Danielle. His appetite for their gatherings had ebbed, and he'd as soon be at home.

Not that home held much appeal, either. He found himself pacing, one Saturday afternoon in mid-March, looking out at the snow-covered gardens and wondering what to do with himself.

The latest set of blueprints for Landmark was spread out on the desk in his library, and he'd looked at them long enough to know he was pleased with them, but he couldn't focus on finding the minute faults, the small-scale changes that comprised the final planning stage.

The boundary issue had been resolved, and in any event was moot, since they'd moved the footprint of the building complex north on the lot. The elevations were attractive and dynamic; no one, looking at it, would immediately say, *oh, another mall.* But no one would fail to identify the building's purpose, either. Cutting back the size had brought it to life.

He'd been a month without Pat, other than that absurd visit to her office after they'd identified Dirk Farndon as their near murderer. Not seeing her was driving him out of his mind. She'd never know how hopeless she'd made him feel, as if he were beyond redemption, not worth her trying.

Which was why he didn't do emotion, especially love. He could never handle the vulnerability.

Could that be at the root of what she found lacking in him? Vulnerability?

His pacing took him back to his desk, where he ran his finger across the floor plans for the office complex at the east end. His gift to Pat.

Raul had designed the library to be bright and open, and to look out over her creek. There were meeting rooms, open floor space for story circles, plenty of space for stacks and reading areas. And the county was on board, not only with the library but also with the park. It was one of the best ideas in the whole package, and he hadn't seen it.

He'd had to fight for it. Prove to the investors that it would be a draw, that it was worth the sacrifice of more profitable floor space. He'd found other malls that had done similar things, and presented their facts and figures. Even Brandon had told him he was out of his mind.

Well, that's what he'd thought, too, at first. Until it became obvious that it was the making of Landmark Center. Business, shopping, dining, amenities; between the library and a small county office on the ground floor, he rounded out what he'd hoped to accomplish.

But on this snowy Saturday, he wasn't in the mood for Landmark, or much of anything else for that matter. A whole afternoon stretched in front of him. He yanked open the fridge and pulled out a chunk of Cheddar, then added crackers and sat at the breakfast bar, treating himself to a dull, uninspired lunch.

What had he done, other Saturdays? There was always work. Coordinating preparations, the rare time he and Danielle had entertained. What else? The day loomed empty and, as a result, intimidating, before him.

Sometimes he'd gone over to Calter Creek, to walk the site, look around, check the survey posts, imagine the complex when it was complete. He couldn't do that anymore. The land was too close to a dumpy house on Maple Street.

He wouldn't call her. It wouldn't do any good.

She'd be busy with Jason. He wondered how the kid was doing, and had faith life was better for him because he was with Pat.

His house—it was the symbol of his success. It had always revitalized him, driving up the circular driveway to the portico, reveling in the luxury in every room. It had been balm when things went wrong, the proof that overall he'd been a success. Now, it might as well be a shack.

Should he sell it? And then do what?

What did she want of him?

When he'd had enough crackers and cheese to last a lifetime, he chose a book from his library and settled in a chair by one of the windows. Watched the snow, tried to pay attention to the book, and waited for the interminable weekend to end.

Her sunny living room, a friend, and a cup of tea. Hard to get much better on a snowy Saturday, Pat thought. She and Amanda had settled in on her sofa, taking it easy.

Jason had gone to Creekside Mall, courtesy of a friend's mother. This was a new development, Jason having friends with mothers who drove the boys places. She was keeping her fingers crossed; the presence of other mothers had to be good.

Other mothers?

"How's Jason?" Amanda asked.

"Doing okay. We went grocery shopping this morning. It's kind of fun. Jason spots things on the shelves I've never even noticed." Pat sighed. "Today he made a point of telling me how much he enjoyed having Alan here. Just what I needed," she added glumly.

"What happened, Pat? I know something did. It's been a month, and you're not talking."

This was Amanda, so Pat talked. She gave a full run-down on his declaration, their walk. The abrupt, pointless meeting when he stopped at her office.

"Maybe if he hadn't said what he did…"

"When? What did he say?"

"Listen." She'd finally watched the news reports on the flash drive Linda had given her. Pat's laptop was on the coffee table. She fired it up and plugged in the drive. "I only saw this last week." She double clicked, adjusted the pointer to thirty-seven seconds in—obvious to anyone that she'd listened to it more than once, memorized the location in the clip—and Alan's voice began speaking. Alan saying in no uncertain terms that Landmark was the most important thing in his life.

And he'd said it right after the explosion. Right after they'd both almost been killed.

He finished speaking. She disconnected the flash drive, then dropped against the back of the sofa. "I'm so screwed up, Mandy."

"I can see why."

"He doesn't get it. I don't see how I can let myself love someone whose values are so different from mine. Shallow, materialistic."

Amanda watched her, her eyes soft. Then shrewd. "You're hurting yourself."

"I know. No options." Pat took a vicious bite out of a scone, bit her tongue, and felt tears spring to her eyes. She put a hand to her mouth.

She wasn't sure if Amanda understood that the tears were from pain, or if she believed they were because of Alan and the mess her life was in. "You're hurting yourself," Amanda repeated. "There has to be another way to look at this."

When the pain in her tongue subsided, Pat finished chewing, swallowed, and faced her friend. "So what do you recommend?" She reached over for the teapot and refilled their cups, watching as Amanda traced a finger over the rose pattern.

"I need a new tea service. Deb had one, and it's lovely." Deb, her husband's late wife. "But Jacob's — well, he's convinced it'll upset me if we use her things. Like the house. I could have lived in the old house, but he had this fixed idea that it was Deb's, so we had to move. Not that I'm complaining," she added with a laugh. "It's the male mind."

"You're driving me round the bend," Pat said. "If you have advice, spill it."

Amanda raised her cup but cradled it in two hands rather than drinking. "Consider this. A year and a half ago, if you'd asked me what the most important thing in my life was, I'd have said Sinclair Imports. We both know it's true. It wasn't until I found room to let Jacob in that things started shifting. He'd say Norah and me, without a moment's hesitation. And I'd say Norah and him, now. Sinclair's still in the mix, but the weighting's different."

"But first you had to let him in." Pat turned it over in her mind. "First you had to make the shift inside yourself..."

Amanda nodded at the laptop. "When Alan said that, he was in shock, and he might not have known that things were shifting for him. His project had been the most important thing,

223

and the explosion was a direct hit at the project, so what else was there to say? If he'd figured out his feelings at that point they'd still be too new. And too private."

"It cost him several lives to tell me how he feels. He's bewildered. But I can't trust it. In his mind his worth is tied up in Landmark Center."

"Except for Jason. Did you have any idea Alan would step up there? He certainly didn't have to. Not to mention the extras. I mean, executive men taking unrelated kids coat shopping? Come on, Pat."

Pat groaned and put her head in her hands.

Amanda went on. "How many times did you have to tell me to let go?"

She didn't answer. Every normal, needy cell in her body was screaming, *Call him. Give him a chance.*

Every specialized, logical cell said, *Don't be a dope.*

Mandy hadn't stopped smiling since that night she finally kicked her logical mind into the back bleachers and let her feelings take over the cheering section.

"Think about it," Amanda said. "And pass the scones. One more, then I'm heading home."

Alan almost didn't bother to answer the phone.

"I need to see you," Pat said.

The nerves and the urgency in her voice perplexed him, but he kept his reaction calm. "I could meet you at Brandon's office."

"No. Not the office."

He felt himself frowning. "The trailer?"

There was a pause. "No. I thought…" He heard her take a deep breath before she plunged on. "The Madison Café—it's in the Madison Inn."

"All right. What is it? What's wrong?"

Now she sounded agitated. "Nothing. I don't know. An hour? No—say five thirty. I need to see Jason. Funny how having a kid around changes your game plans. Is five thirty okay?"

"I'll be there. Pat, try to calm down. I'm not sure you should be driving."

"So pick me up. You may be right."

Pat? The most hard-headed, independent woman he knew other than Danielle, reluctant to drive? They hung up, and Alan stood looking at the phone, swallowing the alarm that was triggering random alarms through his gut.

Pat was tearing around fixing a quick supper when Jason came in, his friend Sean right behind. Both boys looked as if they might shoot away like overfilled balloons let loose. "Pat," Jason called before he made it all the way into the kitchen, "Sean got this new game and the Andersons say I can come over and spend the night so we can try it out, if that's okay with you—"

"Pat? I'm Selina Anderson." A quiet, pleasant looking woman followed Jason and Sean into the kitchen. "The boys are both excited, and I'd rather have them at home than itching to make a break for it, so is it all right? Jason's more than welcome."

She was one step from totally freaking...

Pat reined in her churning emotions and fought to be logical. Just because it meant that her house was free for the night, and was so much more sensible and less staged than the Madison Inn, didn't mean letting Jason spend the night with Sean was the right thing to do.

Are you kidding?

Selina was here in her kitchen, for heaven's sake. Sean and his mother both looked and sounded like normal people. Why wouldn't she agree? "Are you spiriting him away right now?"

"If you're okay with it."

"Jason, go get your gear." Jason split, with Sean on his heels. Belatedly she offered her hand to Selina Anderson. "Pat Fraser. It's good to see Jason so enthusiastic, so yes, that's fine. I'll need your address and phone number, and you'd better have mine, too." She pulled a scratch pad out of a drawer and

225

scribbled her information on it. Selina, it turned out, had calling cards, and handed her one. "Wow. Elegant."

"Pretentious," Selina said with a laugh. "But they do save time, and I figure they're less likely to get lost."

"Have a seat."

Pat joined Selina at the table. The women chatted about Northside Elementary and the delights of twelve-year-old boys until they heard the stampede coming from Jason's room. Then Selina rose and everyone got bundled off, leaving Pat in her kitchen with a partly prepared supper, a stomach full of writhing caterpillars, and Alan due on her doorstep in half an hour.

23

Pat opened the door to Alan, who looked grim.

The last time he stood there, you sent him away.

"Come in."

"You wanted to go to the Madison Inn?"

"Turns out Jason's been invited to a sleepover." She stepped back to allow him to pass her, then closed the door and leaned on it.

He bent to take off his shoes—why did men refuse to wear boots until the walks were impassable?—then stood up and looked at her. "I'm assuming we're not talking about Landmark here?"

"No."

"Then you'd better tell me what's going on. I had the distinct impression you'd kicked me out of your life."

"I had. That was before." She squared her shoulders. "I may have been wrong."

His brows drew together as he studied her. It was the look she'd seen so many times before, the look of a man who came out on top, expected to, and did what he had to do to assure the outcome. If she had any sense she'd be running for the hills.

Instead, she found herself wondering for the first time what lay behind that look, if there was a man in there who was as unsure as she was at this moment. She suspected that was the case. She'd been in the business of reading unspoken messages for a while now, and she believed the one she'd read that day in the Social Services conference room. This wasn't Alan using Pat. This was more, for both of them.

All that made it through her head in a fraction of a second. He turned away. She'd swear that time had recalibrated to slow motion as he took off his coat and hung it on the hook on the wall. Then he turned back.

"Wrong about what?"

"You. Us."

His study of her turned into a bewildered stare. She hoped to God she'd remembered to brush her hair, brush her teeth, brush whatever needed brushing. She was sure she'd changed clothes, so she was tidy at least. Jeans contrasting to his slacks, but of course he'd wear dress slacks and a white shirt; he always did. Her hands had clasped the hem of her knit top; she unclenched them and wiped them on her thighs.

"Come on." She led him into the living room, sat in one of her big chairs, then bounced up again and moved to the sofa.

Alan watched her. She wished he'd park his eyes somewhere else.

"Please sit down. This is hard enough without you hovering."

He sat, on the sofa but not close. "Hard how?"

The laptop was set up on the coffee table; she leaned forward and clicked, and his voice came through the speakers.

When it was done, he frowned. "I know it wasn't my finest moment, but Pat, I'd just been blown up, I'd just seen you..."

"Not the language. The words. That Landmark is your life. All that matters."

She saw the light bulb come on behind his eyes. "That's what this is about."

"Yes. Or was. Or—I'm not sure."

Get a grip, woman.

"You wonder if I meant it."

"Maybe. Do you want a drink?"

He took a shaky breath. "Please."

She went to the kitchen, grateful that he couldn't see how wobbly her smile was, and came back with two short glasses,

228

each bearing somewhat more than a standard jigger of amber liquor.

"Scotch?"

"Bourbon. Don't ask me why I even have it. At the moment, I'm glad I do." She took a sip, coughed.

They didn't rush, and didn't speak until both glasses were empty.

He put his on the coffee table and faced her, twisting around on the sofa. "Tell me why I'm here, Pat."

Ah, liquid courage. "In raw terms? You're here because I need you to kiss me. And maybe make love to me."

The air changed, developed eddies, became thicker until it was harder to breathe. She watched him. Watched the pause, the resolve.

"I don't think so."

No?

Her heart contracted, sending all her blood flooding to her face. She looked away.

You can do this.

"Why not?" Not her strongest voice, and spoken to the carpet, but at least she'd gotten words out.

"Because that's never been all you want. What I don't understand is why you'd even say something like that."

Pat put her head in her hands and stayed that way.

"You want the truth?"

She nodded into her hands.

"You've thrown me. Every time I start to understand what's going on, something else happens and I'm stumbling again. When I realized...." He leaned back on the sofa. She heard his voice change direction, registered the slight give in the cushions. "When I realized how I felt about you, my heart stopped. I was called a vulture recently, and it's true. I'd started to believe I'm not the sort of person you should want in your life, whatever my feelings. And then you say that."

"I know your life hasn't been golden. Foster care." She spoke into her hands. "I know you were married and now you're not."

229

"Let's leave it that I learned early not to trust. Anyone. And to be prepared to claw my way to the top, because that meant security. I'm not sure I can change that."

She couldn't look at him to save her life. She spoke through her hands. "Why? Who betrayed you? Your wife, you told me that. What else happened?"

"Pat..." He swallowed and gave her a crumb. "Foster care's no picnic. I ran away. Twice, and for good reason."

"The report says you were abandoned."

"Don't do this."

"I want to find out what's underneath." She might never have the nerve to take her hands away from her face, convinced as she was that she'd completely misplayed this, that he'd bolt and never come to her again, but she could still talk.

He stood. "Look at me."

When she didn't move he put his hands on her arms and pulled her up, then released her and stepped back. Her eyes developed an urgent fascination with the carpet. She was suddenly, overwhelmingly convinced that she'd played the wrong hand, that she was in the middle of a monumental screw-up.

"Why, Pat? Why am I here?"

She shuddered, and he moved close enough to her to put his hands on her shoulders. He gave her a little shake. "Tell me. Talk to me."

Her eyes locked in the vicinity of his knees; she couldn't force them any higher. Her voice, when she finally found it, quavered. "Because I realized—sort of realized—that maybe you didn't mean it the way it came out."

One hand left her shoulder and held her chin, forcing her head up. "That recording—are you kidding me? Of course I didn't. I'd just staggered out of the hospital with every inch of me in agony, ten minutes after I'd fallen in love for the first time with a woman who was lying in there unconscious. I'd been hit by a sledge hammer. Those microphones weren't looking for personal revelations, and as far as business goes, it was true. Up until now, my work's been all I've had. I wasn't kidding when I told you I need help. I don't know how to handle this—this new thing."

Alan pulled her against him, held her head against his shoulder. She noticed—oh yes, every nerve ending in her body noticed—when one of his hands shifted to her lower back and pulled her closer still. Until they touched, head to knees.

"Are you sure?" he said into her hair. "Absolutely?"

"Sort of."

Say it. Say the words.

"Sort of isn't good enough." He tipped her head up and kissed her. Not a thorough kiss, more like a preliminary exploration to see what might lie beneath the surface before committing the heavy machinery.

"Sure?" he asked.

"Getting there." *Getting there?* On a cellular level she was well past 'there'. The chemistry between them triggered serious agitation followed by melting, and the process had started, threatening to explode.

"Then put your arms around me." This time the kiss wasn't preliminaries. This time it was tongues doing a Latin dance, lips tasting, mouths sucking, heads adjusting to deepen the contact. Time continued, if you measured in infinities, before they broke apart—but then time didn't have meaning anymore.

Now it wasn't only his mouth that was done with preliminaries. His hands dove under the pullover top she'd chosen for that purpose; hers became talons, trying to dig into his back, then fighting the shirt out of his waistband. Both of them desperate but cautious, aware of lingering wounds.

No going back. If Mandy's wrong, this is going to hurt like hell.

She sort of wished he'd smiled, at least once, before the kissing started.

He pulled away again and studied her. His voice was uneven. "I'm not a robot. If this goes any further, I'm not promising I can stop."

She twisted away. The short break in their contact restored the courage she'd misplaced. After a labored breath or two, she faced him again. "It's going further, Alan. Count on it."

Then she had her hands on him, frantic to get the shirt free, frantic for his hands to find more of her, for his mouth to follow where the hands had gone. She pressed against him, felt him hard against her, shimmied and was rewarded with a groan. His mouth moved to her breast, over her bra but heaven knows what had happened to her pullover top. She gasped, "Horizontal might be better?"

"Safer," he managed, his voice in a low pitch she hadn't heard before. "Speaking of which..."

"Seen to. I'm a thoroughly modern woman."

"Thank God."

For the last time she broke away from him. "Come on," she said, and wobbly-kneed she led him to her bedroom.

Alan awoke in the pre-dawn and lay on his back, acutely aware of the sleeping woman beside him.

He'd never experienced a night like the one just ending. He wondered if he'd ever recover from the sheer bliss—not to mention the erotic system overload—of sex with Pat.

The first time had got it out of their systems, he'd innocently believed. Until she'd met his eye with what, in retrospect, he had to call an evil grin.

"You're always in control, aren't you?" she said. "Always the boss. Let's do something different this time."

This time?

And then she'd straddled him. He could have dominated her, but... *are you kidding?* She'd even pinned his hands while she tormented him, both of them getting so overwhelmed in the lava flow of sensation they created that they couldn't have communicated in any way other than with their bodies.

He'd loved it. He'd given up control to her, and he'd loved it.

She'd slept, after. Until sometime in the middle of the night she'd shifted and poked him in the ribs, waking him. "Come on."

"Come on" turned out to be the kitchen table, where she'd served them both bowls of chocolate pudding. "Jason made this," she said. "I'll have to make it up to him. I was hungry."

Somewhere along the line she'd put on his shirt, an erotic vision, even eating pudding.

Intensely erotic. She noticed his reaction. "Like what you see?"

In answer he'd reached under the table and run his hand up her bare thigh.

They did manage to finish the pudding. Just. Afterwards, he'd sunk into one of the most contented sleeps he could remember.

Now, lying there in the dawning day, he was very sure he wanted to experience more nights like this, a whole string of them. With this woman.

Who knew that one of the side effects of being in love was mind-bending, soul-satisfying sex?

He turned so he was facing Pat, asleep with her hair spread over the pillow. *I did that,* he thought. *The tousled, sweaty hair, the flushed face, the half smile...*

The open eyes. Those eyes surveyed him. Then she sat up and kicked the covers back. "I want to admire."

Her frank gaze over his body had its effect. He grinned at her — and in the back of his mind wondered when he'd last found anything to grin about. "You do realize I'm forty-seven years old," he said. "I'm not sure I can take much more."

"Oh, you can."

They missed the dawn.

Jason was due home at ten, and neither of them was ready to add him into the mix yet, so Alan left after a quick breakfast.

Pat slumped in one of the big loungers in her living room and wondered what she'd done. Her libido had never gone so completely ballistic.

Worth having, she concluded. *Get him out of his eternal dress shirts and the man had the broad shoulders and tight tush a woman dreamed of. Not to mention that getting-craggy face, and those hands…*

Well, yes. His hands…

Whoa! Overnight I have a man and a boy. Holy Moly.

Pat had a cup of coffee and a few minutes to kill before Jason got home. The plan was a trip to the mall for spring-oriented clothes. Boys don't mind shopping, she'd discovered, if it was for them. And Jason's wardrobe had been hand-me-downs and others' discards for too long.

Where Alan was concerned, she'd deal with what to tell him some other time. When she was sure it had stuck. Because she wouldn't put it past Alan to bolt, and she couldn't let Jason be subject to another disappointment.

Involuntarily she closed her eyes. And didn't open them until Jason hovered over her, shaking her shoulder to wake her up.

24

"We found her," Linda said, right after they'd both arrived at the office Monday morning. "She's not coming back."

"Her? Who? Can we get coffee? I'm brain dead." Pat figured she had valid reason to be foggy, but she wasn't admitting to it yet, so blaming it on the need for a caffeine fix was a reasonable strategy.

"I can't get away, I start client meetings in an hour. Go get your fix and get back here."

Pat went to their break room, returning with a doughnut left over from Friday and her office mug full of coffee strong enough to keep her awake for a week. *Not a bad choice when Alan's around,* she mused, then kicked the thought to where it belonged, on a far back burner.

"Who's not coming back?" she echoed, dropping into Linda's guest chair.

"Here's the report. Illinois Social Services caught up with her." Linda dropped a familiar file on the corner of her desk. Pat set down the doughnut and picked it up.

Jason's file.

"His mom's legally abandoning him," Pat whispered after she'd read the new report. And realized she would have understood Linda from the first if she weren't so besotted from Saturday night.

Jason. Abandoned. No mother. Her boy. The thoughts piled up, tumbled over each other.

Linda nodded. "She and her daughter are in a town south of Chicago. Seems Mom thinks she can make a go of life in a big city. Or more likely she figures she can get more social

235

assistance there, I don't know. Whatever, she said she's willing to sign any papers we send to dump Jason in our laps until he's eighteen." Linda sighed and leaned back.

"So I can have him," Pat said softly.

Linda's eyes shot warning signals. "He's already damaged, and this will make it worse. Be careful what you take on here."

Pat shook her head. "Too late for that."

"He'll have scars so deep even you won't be able to root them out. You're looking at years of heartbreak."

Pat took a bite of the doughnut, cringed, and dumped the remainder into Linda's trash basket. She gulped the coffee, then said, "Maybe not. I'm looking at Jason, not the next six years. Or thirty years, or whatever."

"Social Services will want to place him in a home with a male influence, you know. For the long term."

"They won't find one. You know that as well as I do."

"They'll try, now that we know what his status is."

"Will his mother communicate with him? Try to get him to see it from her perspective?"

"No. I'm not sure it would be in Jason's best interests, anyway."

"I want to adopt, Linda."

Linda was on the move, arranging the files she needed for a day in the field. "I'm not hearing you. Talk to me again in a month. In the meantime, I need to tell Jason."

"I can do that."

A fast shake of her head as Linda moved around her cubicle. "No, you can't. I'm his social worker. You know the rules."

"When, then?"

"I'll come to your place after school, if that's okay. Three thirty? I'll want you to make yourself scarce for half an hour."

My kid. "Is there any way to soften it?"

"Sure." Linda put on her coat. Pat stood and stepped into the corridor. "She can't support two kids, he'd have to leave his friends, the usual. It won't work, but I'll give it a shot."

"Let's get it over with."

Pat went back to her own cubicle, torn between her own elation and her boy's heartbreak.

By noon, on overload from the news about Jason, Pat gave up any pretense of work. She canceled an appointment and went home.

A new construction trailer sat on the vacant lot. From her driveway she looked along the gap between houses across the street and saw Alan talking to the crew installing it. She walked over.

He saw her coming, said something to one of the men, and started along the path to meet her.

Her face gave her away. "What's wrong?"

"It's Jason."

He showed none of his usual impatience to focus on the job, and listened while she poured out the story.

"Your place," he said, and turned her around. When they got in her front door he stood there, his hands at his sides. She shed her coat, letting it drop to the floor, and stepped close to him. His arms came up—*robotically,* she thought—to wrap around her.

"I'm overwhelmed. Between you and this new thing with Jason... for heaven's sake, take off your coat. I need you to hold me."

He tensed. "Pat, I don't have time..."

"Not for that. Just to be close."

He unbuttoned the coat and his arms tightened around her, but something was missing. She wasn't feeling him, wasn't sensing him there with her. She shook her head against his chest. "I need you. I'm scared, Alan."

They stood there a minute in her little entry, locked together. "You were scared Saturday," he commented.

"So were you."

Alan stepped back from her. The businessman was dominant, the lover gone. She kept her hands on him, grazing his sides, seeking the connection.

237

He said, "The point is, you can handle it. You're one of the strongest women I know."

She shook her head. "I told you before, I'm not so tough. For myself I can be, I guess, but Jason—where he's concerned, I'm a marshmallow. I'm so afraid of doing the wrong thing. To be abandoned like that—he'll need so much help."

"Or he might bury it so deep inside you never even know. At least he has a home."

Pat sighed, a long, shuddering sigh, and let her hands drop from his sides. "And I'm the adult around here, aren't I? I may not have a lot of free time in the next little while. I mean, assuming…" She broke off, confused.

"I understand. We're hitting the final push on Landmark, so I won't have much time either."

"Oh. Right." She should have known. Alan's newly discovered human dimension was nowhere to be found.

"I have to get back, Pat."

Wordlessly she stepped aside, kicking her own coat out of the way, and watched him open her door.

"We'll be in touch, right?" he said.

"All right."

He left, and didn't look back. Not even once. Pat stood in the open door and watched him until he'd crossed Maple and started up the path between her neighbors' houses, then stepped inside and closed the door, very gently, behind her.

When she'd needed him, he'd left, without so much as a promise to return.

She had a bad feeling, almost a premonition. Things had changed, yet again. She supposed she shouldn't be surprised, but where she'd find the reserves to cope with his remoteness, she simply didn't know.

Walking back to the construction site, dealing with the contractors, then later at his desk at Brandon Caine Realty, Alan couldn't get his brief time with Pat out of his mind.

He cursed himself for a fool. Not to mention a despicable coward.

Because he knew exactly what Jason needed right now, and he suspected that he knew what Pat needed, too. And instead of supporting them he'd frozen and fled.

Love.

This was why he didn't get involved. Why he'd avoided any relationship that might lead to complications. Because he couldn't do it.

He could fight, and win, any corporate battle that came his way. He could wrangle blueprints, acquire funds, create technical specs, manage construction crews blindfolded. But he couldn't help a twelve-year-old boy whose life story was so similar to his own.

He hadn't even been able to tell Pat that she was exactly what the kid needed. The warmth, the stability. The love Pat felt for the boy. All the things Jason`s biological mother not only couldn't provide, but cruelly had put out of his reach forever.

But none of it was his concern. No reason for him to be involved.

The thing with Pat? He wouldn't let her expect anything from him that wasn't there for him to give her. She might as well know it now.

Later that day Alan answered a vaguely familiar number on his phone. "Mister Carmichael? This is Tom at Happy Trails."

He had to think a moment to place Happy Trails. Of course. Pete. Once again he'd forgotten.

"We've had a bit of a disaster here. There was an electrical fire, and we lost our main building. The dogs are all fine, but we'll be closed for a few months while we rebuild. I'm so sorry, but we can't keep Pete any longer."

Alan closed his eyes. How the hell was he supposed to manage a dog with everything else going on in his life? But what choice did he have? He wouldn't dare try to sweet talk Astrid into taking him again.

Tom continued to talk. "Could you come pick him up? The sooner the better. We're struggling to take adequate care of the animals without sufficient housing, so any of them we can send elsewhere—"

"Fine. Great." He wondered if his total lack of enthusiasm carried over the phone to the man at the other end. "I'll come by first thing in the morning." If he had another appointment, he'd cancel it. He was constantly rescuing the mutt from one threat or another. This time he'd see to the dog himself, if he could figure out how.

"Wonderful. I can't tell you how pleased I am. Not all owners are so responsive. We had one over the holidays..." Once again the man—Tom?—settled in for a chat. It took Alan a couple of minutes to get him off the line.

So, what did a dog need? He found the address of a pet store not far from his house. They'd be able to help him stock up for his unexpected guest.

25

Alan was growing to hate his house in Columbus. Even Pete didn't seem to like it. He spent most of his time under a dining room chair, emerging for food or to whine at the door.

The elegance of the place, the pricy furnishings, didn't mean a damn thing to him anymore. The shabby furniture and cramped space of a house in Calter Creek effectively obliterated his appreciation for his refuge.

And who was he kidding? It had nothing to do with the building. It was the woman. And the kid.

Alan paced the kitchen, sipping at the glass of scotch in his hand — a drink that held less appeal as the evening inched toward a time he could reasonably go to bed — and wondered if he'd be able to find the courage to do what he longed to do. Because like a bolt from the blue, sometime in the middle of the previous night, he'd seen where she was going with her talk about compassion and relationships. And how little any of it had applied to his life. It was no surprise she hadn't believed he could live up to her expectations.

The potential for pain nearly paralyzed him. The risk of failure was a living menace that haunted him. He'd refused to contemplate failure for most of his life, always driving forward, claiming what he wanted.

But he'd never considered what he needed, assuming that his needs would be met as he fulfilled his wants. And now the truth was as clear as the scotch in the glass he held. Quite apart from wanting her, he needed Pat.

And that meant letting go of his carefully constructed persona and facing his demons.

His house was so silent it echoed. He set the glass on the polished concrete countertop, with enough force that the liquid sloshed up the sides. He planted his hands on the counter, hung his head and closed his eyes, and stood still for long minutes.

When he straightened, he'd accepted that he was out of options. He went to his home office and fired up the computer. Surprisingly, Pete followed him and sat by the corner of the desk, watching. He canceled a meeting for the next day, then scrolled through Internet listings for psychologists in Columbus. He wasn't so much of a fool that he'd try to handle this alone.

Whatever it took, he'd do. And he'd be on Pat's doorstep tomorrow morning, praying she'd be there.

She was there. Pat's eyes were red, the skin around them swollen. She'd pulled her hair into that awful ponytail and dressed in shapeless sweats. No one could say she looked desirable, but to him she'd never appeared more necessary.

She closed her eyes and clung to the door, leaving them in a freeze frame for a moment before opening her eyes and facing him. "I don't think I can take any more of this, Alan. Please... just go away."

"No." This little house encapsulated everything that gave life meaning, and he couldn't afford to leave. They had to sort this out between them. Today.

When she didn't reply, he said, "I made a mistake."

"Some admission." Her smile was, at best, wan. She wheeled and disappeared into the living room.

He closed the door and followed. She hadn't opened the drapes, making the room more like a murky cave than the bright, cheerful place he remembered. He accepted the gloom as a further clue into her state of mind.

"I didn't expect to see you again." Her gaze fastened on the closed-off window. "You shut me out. The way you walked away Monday... as if you were walking out of my life. Ending it."

"Monday... I didn't know what I was doing. I panicked. This won't be easy, Pat. I wish I could say otherwise, but that's the reality." He swallowed and wished he had a printed script, a rehearsed speech, to fall back on. But even though he'd spoken to her dozens of times in his mind over the last two nights, none of those words fit now. "Until I figure this out, I'm going to panic, and I'm going to run."

"A hell of a way to live." Pat sank into a corner of the sofa. A tear trickled down her cheek. He didn't have the courage to wipe it away. Not yet. She looked at him, her face weary. "You didn't need to run. There's nowhere to run to, anyway."

"Yeah, I worked that out." He shed his coat and joined her on the sofa, keeping his distance.

Pat immediately stood and left him sitting there. When she returned after a few minutes, her face looked scrubbed and she'd brushed her hair, leaving it loose. She held out a mug. "Ballast," she said.

Alan doubted coffee would help, but he accepted her offering. "Isn't the idea to get through without ballast? To just intrinsically know what to do? How to handle things?"

"Let's try an analogy. Did you build a shopping center your first solo job?"

He almost grinned. "Actually, I did. A little strip mall, ten units, from stock plans. I doubt there are any canned blueprints for this."

"You learned from it, though. Some people are instinctively giving and compassionate. For others..." She shrugged. "You make mistakes, you learn. You don't give up."

"I need your help." How many years had it been since he'd last admitted need, beyond the technical skills he contracted out? He was aware of the tension in his body, but was almost too weary to care. "It worries me that I may be too old to learn. I'm exhausted, Pat."

"You're here. It's a starting place." She settled into her corner of the sofa, her hands wrapped around her mug, but made no move to taste the coffee. "But I can't keep watching you leave. I mean it."

"I get that. It's damn scary." Because it was easier, Alan focused on his mug instead of her. After he'd drunk half the coffee, he faced her again, not that she was looking at him. "I understand now, or I'm getting closer to it. Everything you've tried to tell me about how to live. I want that."

Now she did focus on him. Her expression was obscured by the gloom of the living room, but he sensed her eyes, assessing. "You mean it?"

"With you." He swallowed another mouthful, then set the mug on the coffee table. "I can't do it alone." His face heated at the admission, but he let it stand.

"That's one thing you never got, that nothing about this, whatever it is between us, is in a vacuum. Or a solo effort."

"I like the sound of that. But I know I'm going to hurt you. I wish it weren't true, but it is."

"That cuts both ways. I'm no saint. Inevitably I'll say and do things that'll hurt you." Her gaze seemed focused in the far distance, past her dining table.

"If only we could run away, go somewhere. Just the two of us, to get our feet on solid ground. I'm not sure I can make sense of it, with Landmark—"

"And with Jason. Barbados sounds more and more tempting, but it's impossible."

"Mornings with you? Afternoons?"

"We both work."

"Not today?"

She shook her head. "Called in sick. I'm sort of a mess."

"I don't want you to be."

"Good." At last she met his eyes. "Because you're the only one who can fix it."

The permission he'd waited for. He moved across the sofa and pulled her against him, feeling her trembling body, resting his head against hers. Speaking was beyond him, so he let his arms carry the message.

"I'm ruining another shirt."

"Please do. If you have to cry, this is where I want it to happen."

She spoke into his chest. "Honest?"

He put his hands on either side of her face and kissed her mouth, kissed her nose, kissed her eyes and the tear track on her cheek. "Yes. When I can keep the panic at bay, you're what I need. Holding you feels right."

"Oh, it does." She settled against him again. They sat together in the quiet obscurity of her living room, clinging to each other, until after an indeterminate time he said, "Give me a minute? I have to get something from the SUV."

She pulled away and shot him a puzzled look.

"I think you'll like him." He kissed her and darted outside, not bothering with his coat. Why would he, when all the warmth he longed for waited for him inside?

Pat and Pete bonded instantly. Alan watched the woman on the floor laughing, the dog ecstatically licking her face and running in circles. Pat opened the curtains before she returned to the sofa, flooding the room with winter light. Pete disappeared to sniff around the house, then settled on the living room carpet, as if he'd finally come home.

As we both have, he thought. *As we both have.*

They stayed together all morning, talking, touching, holding each other, until hunger chased them into the kitchen for lunch.

Pat finished what she had to do and put Jason's computer back on his desk. She hadn't wanted to put the extra restrictions in place, but he hadn't given her any choice.

Just like he hadn't given her any choice about grounding him, watching him like a hawk, sitting with him while he did — or mostly didn't do — his homework.

While she listened to his language. Listened to him trashing her, Linda, his mother, and everyone else in his world.

Her efforts to talk to Jason were like talking to a stuffed brontosaurus. He'd sit there unmoving, unresponsive. As far as she knew — and she knew plenty, because she was in regular touch with the school — the only emotion he'd shown in the face of his mother's defection was hostility.

She'd been upfront with her private clients, explaining that because of her personal situation, she couldn't be what their kids needed, and referring them to other psychologists in town. That gave her lots of free time to brood, lucky her. The Social Services work paid the bills, so she stuck with it. The smile and balanced, calm demeanor she showed the kids in her circle were a total lie.

These days, she thought grimly, it's a matter of surviving. Linda's warning about Jason had been more accurate than she could bear to remember.

She spent a minute staring out her picture window. It had been a week since Alan had walked out and miraculously come back. Across the street, the surveyors were at work, both the government ones to confirm the municipal boundary and the ones marking the final footprint for Landmark. The trailer was in constant use. Soon they'd shunt it over to one side or park it on Sycamore, out of the way while they built their mall.

It was so close now that they'd scheduled a groundbreaking ceremony in a couple of weeks, although it would be a while yet before they could bring in the heavy equipment. The groundbreaking was an opportunity for the county administration to strut and shine, for Alan and Brandon to present their vision and gather the accolades.

She'd turned away from the window and put on the kettle when the doorbell rang. Pat bolted for the door, flung it open, and threw herself into the arms of the man waiting there, a three-legged dog at his feet.

Nothing pleased Alan more these days than to find Pat in his arms, pressed up against him as if she'd never let him go. Pat affected him, her opinions, her sass, her willingness to call him on his bullshit. Her body. He'd learned he was better off not thinking of her pale, lightly freckled body when he had work to do, or for that matter when he was likely to be in public. Remembering his times with her, working on the plans and walking the site, tucking her in on that damn sofa the day she came home from the hospital, watching her smoothly control the round table meetings with no one but him any the wiser.... Every thought about Pat fed his contentment now.

The feeling of rightness surprised him again every time he saw her. He'd thought it would be a form of hell, but the more he talked to her, the more he wanted to talk, because she never mocked or scorned or made him feel like the failure that still lurked in the deepest parts of his consciousness. He might never give her the full picture of his early days on the streets, but the rest of it... she'd become his repository, his comfort.

And his complete, total satisfaction, like now. Because after she grabbed him at the door and dragged him in, they didn't waste any time with talk. Making love in the daytime, watching the sun play over her, the dog snoozing in the sunlight on the floor, more than payed for the painful times when the old fears still overtook him.

The workday was long over. He was alone in the construction trailer. He'd taken Pete out for a walk—a new experience and one they were both adjusting to—and now his dog slept under a chair in the corner, twitching periodically. To his surprise, Pete had proved to be a good companion, always falling in with his plans, rarely kicking up a fuss, and slavishly glad to see him again whenever he had to go away for a few hours. Pete provided reliable companionship for minimal outlay of effort. He'd grown attached to the animal, and didn't know how it had happened.

It was probably around ten o'clock; he wasn't paying attention. He had no wish to go home, and couldn't go to Pat's. He and Pete frequently turned up for supper, a fact Jason greeted with suspicion rather than welcome, but beyond that he and Pat kept their relationship private.

So tonight he was battling one of his recurring panics about the changes in his life, alone. He knew some of it had to be dealt with on his own, he couldn't use Pat as a crutch, but it left him off balance and irritable. He'd poured a scotch and killed the lights, sitting in the dark with his equally dark thoughts.

He heard a noise outside and put down the glass.

Alan could move like a cat when he had to, a skill he'd picked up when he was not much older than Jason. He silently

247

stepped out of the trailer and made his way around to the other side.

It was a kid with a can of spray paint. He cursed to himself. About to launch a major construction job and he was dealing with punk kids? But he'd handled worse, and this was a pretty small punk.

The kid was bundled up for winter with a heavy hat on his head and didn't hear him until it was much too late to escape. He pounced, pinning the kid with both arms. "You fight and I'll take you down," he growled, then he frog-marched him around to the door and into the trailer. He closed and locked the door, flipped on the lights, then yanked the hat off the kid's head before releasing his grip.

Jason. He should have known. Alan sighed. "Now, why did I suspect it was you?" he asked. "Sit." At the boy's hesitation he added, "Now." His voice was pure intimidation.

With Jason in a chair, looking terrified and defiant at the same time, Alan took the spray can out of his hand, put it on a shelf, and said conversationally, "I take it you're not happy at Pat's?"

"What's it to you?" the kid muttered.

"Because you're sure as hell trying to get thrown out of there and sent to that group home place. Doesn't seem like the best plan to me, but what do I know?"

Jason was silent.

"Okay, let's try another tack. Why are you attacking me?"

"Ain't."

"You are. This is my trailer. And this is the kind of thing that led up to the explosion, which if you remember caused Pat and me both a lot of hurt. Are you planning on blowing something up next? Because I'd be happy to throw you over to the police if I think that's where your thoughts are going."

The kid looked at him with disdain, as if he should know better. Which, Alan supposed, was the truth. He knew, right down to his fingernails, why Jason was outdoors at night with a can of spray paint.

Jason held on to the sullenness. "I don't do stuff like that."

"Could have fooled me." Alan sat across from the boy. He gulped the remaining scotch, then took out his phone and tapped speed dial.

"Who you phoning?"

"Figure it out." He waited, and when she answered he said, "I've got him."

"Got him? Alan, what are you talking about?"

"Go check his room."

"He wouldn't have—I *told* him..." Pat was on the move. He heard two taps, then she must have opened Jason's bedroom door because he could hear the fury in her voice. "Where are you?"

"At the trailer. Don't come over. I'll get him home in one piece. But he and I have a few things to clear up first."

"He's my responsibility."

"It's my trailer and the door's locked. Wait for us." He hung up and faced Jason again.

"Let me guess. Your grades have plummeted. You're in trouble at school. You're making Pat's life hell. Am I right so far?" When Jason didn't answer, Alan stood and leaned across the table, getting right in the kid's face. "Let's get this straight right now. I've got all the power. And I'll stay here all night if I have to. But if I have to, you will be very, very sorry. So, am I right?" He sat, but never took his eyes from Jason's face.

"Yeah. I guess."

"Because some dipstick of a woman decides she'd rather not have you around. Tell me something. Tell me exactly why you'd want to be with her?"

He'd finally pushed hard enough. Jason exploded. "She's supposed to want me. She's my damn mother." He started to get up but Alan reached over and yanked him back into his chair.

"Biology isn't everything. Now, you're going to sit there while I tell you a story. If we both get lucky you'll learn from it. You want water?"

"Nah."

"Okay, here goes. A thirteen-year-old kid, very much like you. Mother hadn't been in the picture for years. Father mostly ignored him, occasionally knocked him around. Until one day father didn't come home, and guess who was at the door next? Social Services. But that was after a couple of weeks of the kid trying to scrounge food on his own. Not like your situation, with a warm house and lots to eat. Food was a day-to-day business at the best of times, and times suddenly got worse in a hurry. Before the social workers turned up, the power and water were turned off—dear old dad must have decided not to pay for them anymore."

Jason's eyes were narrow; he was studying Alan, taking in every word. Alan intentionally let the silence stretch out, knowing the kid would break first.

"So, what did he do?"

"Went with the social workers. What choice did he have? He was dumped in a foster home with five or six other kids, in a different school district. It was a dead end, in every possible way. No possessions, no privacy, no free time, no friends, no adults he trusted. So after six months he ran away."

Jason was into the story now. "Yeah? Did they catch him?"

"The first time. His foster dad beat hell out of him. The second time, by then he was fifteen and he knew more. He stole money and got out of town. He made it to Toledo and lived on the streets. He did whatever he had to do to survive. You don't want to know some of the things he had to do."

"How do you know all this? You know this kid?"

"Yeah. I know him."

They eyeballed each other for an eternity. Alan felt stripped to the bone, waiting for the boy to figure it out. "You're making this up."

"No. I wish I were."

More silence. Then, "What happened to him?"

"He woke up. He was nineteen and a bum. One lousy spring night his sleeping bag and his clothes got soaked in a storm, he was freezing, and he woke up. He was a smart kid—like you—and he figured he could do better. So he got cleaned up, he found help through one of the local soup kitchens. He got his GED—"

"What's that?"

"What you get if you don't finish high school the usual way. Then, he went to college. He studied and worked non-stop, graduated. Made a career."

Jason shrugged. "Doesn't sound so bad to me."

"It's bad, Jason. Because the kid learned never to trust anyone. Ever. He's a grown man now, and he'd like to be a part of a family, have a wife and kids. For years he didn't believe it was possible for someone like him, and he's still struggling, every day. Because of what he learned on the streets."

Their eyes met. Jason's voice was quiet. "What did he have to do to survive?"

Alan told him. Watched the boy go pale.

After another silence, Alan said, "Now. Are you like that kid? Or is there a chance you'll wake up and realize you've got everything he didn't have? A home, food, warmth, clothes, someone who cares about you, even your own electronic toys. And you're acting up because of some ignorant woman who doesn't deserve the name mother? Kid, grow up."

"That other kid — where is he now?"

"Where do you think?"

The silences were killing him. Alan thought he might crawl out of his skin, crawl right up the exhaust pipe in the ceiling and down into the dirt like a bug. He clenched his hands into fists and waited.

Finally the kid got it. "It's you."

"You're the first person I've told any of this to, Jason. No one knows all of it, especially not Pat. I suggest you think about it. You don't want to grow up to be like me. Or go through what I went through."

Jason squirmed; he was embarrassed. "I want out of here."

"I'll be taking you home. Get that? Home? Did you hear a word I said?"

The attitude was back. Alan waited. "Yeah. You had a rotten childhood. Big fat hairy deal."

"It is, when you're in the middle of it. And you're in the middle of it, because you're choosing rotten over pretty damn

251

marvelous. If you have a brain in your head you'll reconsider your choices."

Jason slumped deeper into his coat. He'd held onto it like a safety net around him. Alan recognized the coat. It was the one they'd bought while Pat was in the hospital.

"Okay, kid," he said. "Let's go."

"You're nuthin' to me," Jason said, struggling to sneer. "You think you're so damned important, but you're nuthin'. Just 'cause you got money and power, you think you're so hot. I bet you don't even know what my name is. You always call me kid. I have a name, you know."

"Jason." Alan stood.

"Half right. I told you once and you've forgotten again, haven't you? You're chicken-shit, man. You're not worth a damn thing."

"Pete. Come." Alan snapped his fingers, and the dog flew to his side from the corner where he'd been lying under a chair, watching the man and boy. He took a leash from a hook beside the door and attached it to Pete's collar. Then he turned, opened the door and went down the steps.

Alan looked at the angry boy hovering above him. Pete bounded past them, handling the steps as if he had four legs. The boy followed and squatted by the dog. Pete nuzzled Jason's hand, then did an ecstatic, full-body shake and head-butted his leg.

Boy and dog. Another dream he'd never lived.

"You know what? You're right. I don't know your legal last name. I guess I always thought of you as Jason Fraser. Pat's kid."

"Pat's kid?" Jason looked up from the dog.

"Yes. Aren't you?"

Alan held out his hand. Surprising him, the kid took it. With his free hand, Alan passed the leash to Jason, turned out the light, and locked up. He led boy and dog along the path to Maple Street.

Pat was at the door, no surprise there. Neither of them gave her a chance to speak. Alan hauled Jason around and said, "Room. Now." He took the leash and unclipped Pete.

The kid got out of his outerwear and fled, the dog on his heels.

Alone with her in the foyer, Alan spoke quickly. "I love you, you know that. And it's time I moved in, at least for a while, because Jason needs a man around. He won't accept discipline from a woman, however much he might love her. It was a woman who betrayed him."

Pat stared at him, open-mouthed. Then she swallowed. "You'd better tell me what happened, Alan."

"I'll sleep on the sofa if you don't want to share your bed, but I'm inclined to think Jason's smarter than that, and our sleeping together will make more sense to him than not sleeping together. Your call." He turned and went toward the kitchen. "I need a drink," he said without looking back at her. "Do you have anything?"

She followed him into the kitchen. "White wine, maybe sherry."

"Wine will do. Pour two, then sit down."

"You're bossy tonight."

"Yes." Alan sank into a chair. "I've had a heart-to-heart talk with your young man, and it was the hardest thing I've ever done."

She filled two wine glasses and put them on the table, then sat opposite him.

"I told him about my past."

"Which you haven't shared with me."

"You know some of it." How could he tell her that it was too ugly, that he couldn't bear to defile her with his story? "Trust me, there are parallels. Maybe it got through, I don't know. What did seem to sink in—I admitted I don't remember his legal last name. That I'd always thought of him as your kid. Jason Fraser. The look on his face when I said that—that's when I brought him home."

Alan told her about the spray paint. He was still off balance after the cathartic episode with Jason, and he was sure his voice sounded cold, but he couldn't help it. Maybe his words would go where his tone couldn't. "I'm exhausted."

He pinched his eyes closed, ran a hand over his face, then leaned an elbow on the table and shielded his eyes with the hand, blocking himself off from her. It was the only way he could get the words out. "Stay close, Pat. Let me stay here. It's not only for Jason."

"I guessed."

"I want to believe there's someone in the world who'll stay, even if I don't deserve it."

He glanced up, watched the emotions flicker across her face, then shielded his own again.

"I want you to stay," she said. "But right now I have to see about Jason. He may not let me in, but trying counts."

Pat left the kitchen. Alan sat there with his wine and waited.

When she came back a few minutes later, she circled his chair, draped her arms around him from behind, and rocked gently, her head resting on his crown. To be held by Pat, simply because it was what he needed... he leaned back against her, letting it happen.

In her bed later, her arm across his chest, snuggling herself against him in the dark, she said, "It was that bad? Your childhood?"

"Don't, Pat."

"One day, though. I want to understand."

"Don't push. I'm raw."

He started to turn away, but she resisted him. "I'm right here, so get used to it." She rose up on an elbow. He could feel her eyes on him, even though he was sure she couldn't see him.

He spoke into the darkness. "You probably know this, but I'll say it anyway. When you're a kid, and the people who are supposed to love you abandon you instead, you never get over it. You don't trust, even if someone else steps up. You never really believe you'll ever be loved."

"I know it academically, but I haven't lived it."

"I need time. I mean it." He shifted his arm to lie parallel to hers across his chest, let his hand tangle with her fingers.

254

"Remember this. You may be here for Jason, and you don't know how grateful I am. But I'm here, too. If you need me."

"I'll remember." He knew he sounded distant and dismissive, but it was the best he could do. The emotional toll the evening had taken still singed his nerve endings.

She settled back down beside him and kissed his shoulder; he felt that lovely silken hair on his skin. Her fingers wrapped around his, then she was still.

26

Waking up in Pat's little bedroom, in her little house, every morning for the last two weeks, was unlike anything Alan had experienced. He'd lived in his share of small places, once upon a time, but none of them had had Pat in them. Or the kid.

Even eating breakfast, instead of skipping the meal or grabbing takeaway, was new. Most days it was nothing fancy, but Jason had made pancakes once, and Pat had produced an omelet the previous Sunday.

Taking Pete for walks—at his house in Columbus he'd just let Pete out into his fenced back yard. That wasn't an option here. Jason and Pete had bonded, so morning and night one or the other of them explored the neighborhood with their dog. Sometimes they'd both go. Those were the times Alan liked best.

There was never enough space in the house. He'd tucked the things he'd brought from Columbus into corners of several closets. Pat had offered to make some of her own stuff disappear so he'd have room in her tiny ensuite bath, but he and Jason between them had agreed to share the larger main bath.

To his dismay, he'd found out a few days later that he shared responsibility for cleaning it.

That first night she'd taken him at his word, and they'd held each other until they both fell asleep. Although she'd been still, he was sure she was still awake, like a mother bear, as he drifted off. When he woke up she was curled next to him, her hand resting on his chest.

The next night they made up for lost time, but quietly. Pat had chuckled when she realized that he'd hauled her bed a few more inches away from the wall, just in case. Having the kid in the house certainly changed the dynamic.

Now, standing on the front porch, his dog at his feet, watching the activity across the street, he felt like shaking himself. He'd become part of a family, and a tight one at that. The kid had settled down, although the attitude hadn't completely died out. He was no fool, Jason, and sometimes boys needed to have the facts laid out for them, then be given time to digest them their own way. He'd worried that Jason would resent his presence, but instead he'd find the boy at his heels when he prowled the site, and Jason turned to him instead of Pat for help with math.

No engineer, this one, he thought. *I wonder where he's going.*

One thing Alan knew for certain, he intended to be around to find out.

And Pat? He wasn't going anywhere, even though he worried that it wasn't fair to her. Watching her with Jason, he recognized that his own need was as great as the kid's, to be reassured, for once in his life, that he had someone's love.

He'd been for his first appointment with the psychologist in Columbus. He'd try it, for Pat and for Jason. And for himself, because he had a vision now of what he wanted to be, a normal man with a normal family. Pat had hugged him when he told her, and asked no questions.

She drove up and maneuvered into the little one-car garage, then she joined him on the porch. "You could put one of yours in there instead. They're by far the more valuable."

"Ever hear of one step at a time?" he asked linking an arm around her shoulders. Her hand went up to take his. The day was mild but not warm, typical early April, so she wore a light jacket over her work clothes. "I'm just watching," he said, nodding at the field across the street.

He felt her sigh. "It won't be long now. I wonder how it'll be, where I'll run, what the view will be —yes, I know what it'll look like," she said, giving him a full-body nudge. "It's never the same when it's real."

"Would you ever consider moving?"

"Not soon. Too much change in my life already. I'm hanging on by a thread."

"I've got you."

"I know, I've got you, too, but I still don't quite believe it. Is Jason home yet?"

"Getting his homework out of the way before cooking class tonight. Pat?"

"Hmm?" She was close. So close.

"Thank you."

"Thank you." She turned her smile on him, then slipped out of his grasp. "My turn to make supper. I'd better get cracking if Jason's going to get there on time."

"I'll take him, if you like."

"He'd love it. He's still not over those cars of yours. I expect trouble when he gets his license."

Pete went inside when she opened the door, probably looking for Jason. The old-fashioned storm door closed behind her, and Alan stood alone on the porch.

Yes, he'd be around when Jason got his license. When he got his first car. His first girl. When he figured out where he was going with his life.

He'd be around.

The month since Alan had caught Jason at the trailer had been so full of heaven and hell that Pat wasn't processing very well.

Well, what do you expect, with Jason's drama and Alan moving in.

And a dog? She'd never pined for a dog. What did it say about Alan that out of nowhere he'd produced this sweet, three-legged pet? Alan would sit on the living room floor in the evening, stroking Pete or scratching between his ears — whenever Pete wasn't holed up with Jason. She'd heard the story and suspected the universe of playing a massive joke on Alan, leaving him with no choice but to take Pete in. Kind of like with the two of them, when she thought about it. He obviously didn't know what he was doing where Pete was concerned, but he and the dog had forged a bond.

As had Pete and Jason. When Alan wasn't home, boy and dog were inseparable.

While Alan's days were full of the groundbreaking ceremony and the last touches on the plans, trying to figure it all out kept her mind occupied and her body tingling whenever she wasn't busy with her foster kids. Evenings, the three of them sharing a meal, she watched the cautious regard growing between the two males filling up the house. Her life had done an abrupt turn, down a road she'd seen in the distance but never taken before.

Get it together, Pat.

She'd talked to Alan the night before. These days Alan had a better handle than she did on where Jason's head was. "Is it time? Do you think it's too soon?"

"No, it's not too soon," Alan had told her. "I think it'll help. Give him the assurance you're a permanent fixture in his life."

Now, Pat tapped on Jason's half open door and put her head in. "Need to talk to you."

"'Kay." Jason sprawled on his bed, computer under his nose and Pete curled up next to him, dozing. While she made her way across the littered floor to his desk chair he hauled himself upright, his eyes wary. "Am I in trouble?"

At least he asks, instead of clamming up.

"Not as far as I know. In fact, after the chicken paprika last night, I'd say you're stuck with me forever."

He grinned, and Pat felt something enormous and hard release from her insides. She loved his grin, she realized, and it was still a rare visitor. "Yeah," he said. "I thought so, too."

"In fact, that's sort of what I want to talk to you about." She hesitated. However much she might be sure of what she needed to tell him, the words had deserted her.

Jason fidgeted.

"So here's the thing," she said. "I want you to have the facts, up front. I've talked to Linda." She'd dropped all effort to call Linda 'Ms. Gonzales'; it was too much work. "Jason, this is

259

your decision, and you need to know that there won't be any negative repercussions. It's got to be what you want, no pressure."

"Jeez, Pat, could you get to the point? You're making me nervous here."

She grinned; he was sounding more like a teenager and less like an obnoxious twelve-year-old every day. "Okay, in one short sentence. I love you, and I want to adopt you."

That caught him. "Adopt?" he echoed faintly.

"It would mean that legally you'd be my son. You could change your last name if you wanted to. You'd be out of the system for good."

What he said next surprised her. "If I said no, would you adopt some other kid?"

She almost joked about it, then caught herself. "No," she said with a shake of her head. "I don't want anyone else. You're it, I'm afraid."

"Wow."

"Yeah, wow. I've been thinking about it for a while now, so I guess it's your turn. I've got the papers ready to be filed, if you agree. You can talk to Alan if you want to."

"Should I?"

"I think so." Jason and Alan periodically withdrew and talked, but neither of them ever shared with her. After spending time with Alan, Jason seemed calmer, more in balance. So yes, she'd gamble on his talking to Alan.

"You can talk to Linda, too. In fact, you'll have to, for this to happen. But Jason." She paused. "If you're better with the status quo, then that's okay, too. You're a part of this family, and you'll always have a home here, whether you're fostered or adopted. You understand that?"

Jason had a strange look on his face, one she couldn't interpret. Perhaps it was being caught on the horns of uncertainty, fear and joy at once? Plus, being a boy his age, not wanting to let any of that show.

"You want me to go away now? There's no rush."

"Yeah. I feel funny."

"So do I. Plus I have to start supper." She stood and risked mussing his hair as she worked through his room. "Incidentally," she added from the door, "either way, the mess on the floor gets cleaned up, right?"

He turned a sheepish grin on her. "Oh, yeah. I kinda forgot."

"See you in bit."

She didn't go straight to the kitchen. She went to her bedroom — *their* bedroom — and closed the door, then sat on the edge of the bed and closed her eyes. Sought the strength to give this boy, and this man, what they both needed so badly.

It was the grand finale, short of actually putting the buildings up. After a symbolic groundbreaking on the site, they were at a banquet at the Madison Inn, where Alan and Brandon would make speeches and celebrate with the county officials, the mayor and council of Calter Creek, and anybody who was anybody for miles around. The round table members were there, and the Chamber of Commerce.

Pat sat at their table, Jason trying not to fidget beside her. She dutifully stood with the rest of the committee when a beaming county commissioner acknowledged the round table's hard work, their dedication, and every other positive attribute he could dig up. Then she settled back to hear what Alan and Brandon had to say.

She hadn't seen the plans in a while. She hadn't wanted to. As if an invisible line had been crossed, she and Alan both shied away from Landmark when they were together. That worked for her. They had enough to contend with, with the shifts and changes the three of them were living through. Pat had reached the point where she just wanted the thing built and done with.

Alan's role would change now. While Brandon ceased to be an active partner and returned to putting up housing developments, Alan would be the man on the ground, holding it together until Landmark was a reality. She could sense his anticipation, getting his hands dirty again, at home on construction sites. He might have made his fortune in

261

boardrooms, courting investors, but there was an eagerness now to put himself between a hardhat and work boots.

Interesting. If she weren't living with him, she might never have noticed this change, subtle as it was. But it told her something about the real man, something he himself might not have fully realized. His enthusiasm colored their lives these days.

After the pedantic county commissioner, Brandon cut quite a swath as he took the podium. They might be building for the second coming, the way he extoled the virtues of the mall. Pat did her best not to snicker while Brandon wooed the crowd. Oh yes, the man could speak and charm, no doubt about it. To hear him talk, you'd think he'd been the driving force rather than a mostly silent partner. Vision, inspiration...well, this was Brandon's bread and butter, so let him have his day. Pat was getting lots of practice in tolerance.

The speech ended. Pat jolted awake from her daydream and applauded politely. Jason had gone quiet. She glanced at him and saw that he was thumbing his phone. She looked more closely; he was reading.

Alan took the podium next, and Pat felt a tickle under her breastbone. *Déjà vu,* she thought. Been here, done this. He looked good up there. She was used to his being around by now, but she hadn't seen him at a distance, in his official role, since the whole thing started.

He scanned the gathering, caught her eye, and winked.

So much for déjà vu. Her heart did a funny little tap dance. This was nothing — *nothing* — like last time. She stifled the explosion of laughter that fought its way up.

Then he started talking, and this time she let herself become wrapped up, embraced, by his velvet voice.

Alan said the usual things; she knew the theme he'd be pursuing. The vision, the desire to build something as unique and beautiful as it was functional. Mostly platitude — except that she now knew he meant it.

Then he looked straight at her and said, "This project has been the driving force in my life, the work I've been learning for, growing for, for twenty-five years. Everything in my professional life culminates in Landmark Center." He paused before going on. "I won't say it's the most important thing in my life, because it's not; I'd put my family in that spot. But professionally, this is it. And so we—Brandon and I, the county administration, the volunteers who've worked so tirelessly—we've done our best to make Landmark something you can be proud of, and use. That will become a part of Calter Creek, not merely a shopping destination but integral to the life of the community..."

Pat never heard the rest of his speech. She'd caught the message he'd sent out. In public, straight to her and Jason.

He's come out of the closet. He means it.

Her heart filled up to bursting.

She nudged Jason, whispered, "Back in a minute," and fled. She needed a few minutes in the ladies' room to get through this sudden need to cry, to convince herself it was real.

Oh, it's real, all right.

After the dinner and speeches, Jason found a chair along the wall and returned to the book on his phone. Alan slipped up next to her, handing over a cup of generic punch. Their eyes met, and the understanding darting back and forth between them might have carried her through the next century if Millicent hadn't come bustling over.

Well, power to Millicent, who'd taken on the role no one else was willing to step up to, and managed it with grace, even if, in Pat's opinion, the round table had been mainly window dressing. She and Alan welcomed her and chatted; Millicent had no idea that there was a tight little circle, right in the room, and only two of them could fit in it.

Or maybe they were more transparent than they thought. Before Millicent wandered off she pulled Pat aside and whispered, "You know, we're all so happy to see you with dear Mr. Carmichael. It took him long enough, but we knew he'd realize eventually what a jewel you are."

Pat turned pink. Stammered out a thank you, although for what she wasn't sure. She relied on residual manners to squeeze Millicent's arm in a polite goodbye gesture before darting back to Alan.

He stayed by her side for the rest of the reception. They congratulated round table members and schmoozed county commissioners, tossed around possibilities with the Chamber of Commerce and risked an occasional private smile. Part of the game, for him. She'd attended her share of these punch-and-cookie things, and she'd endured rather than enjoyed most of them, but she'd never, ever, been so eager for one to end. But since it wouldn't be over for a while, she smiled a bit mistily and kept her hand on his arm.

Later, when they were alone at home, he touched her nose and whispered, "I've always loved your freckles. I'm not sure I've tasted them all yet."

After that, the rest of the evening was a no-brainer.

"So it's kind of funny, don't you think? You thought it'd be intimidating and it's been a fairy tale." Pat stretched her legs out in Amanda's kitchen. Alan and Jason were having a men's night, possibly talking about the adoption bomb, and she wasn't welcome, so she'd sought refuge in the McKinnons' big, cozy house for supper and the kind of talk she and Amanda hadn't had in much too long.

"You're going a step too far there," Amanda said dryly.

"Trouble in paradise?"

"No, just the expected merging pains. Plus not feeling one hundred percent."

"Throwing up every morning isn't much fun, I suppose."

"You could tell me I look radiant, even if you'd be lying. Jacob's not saying so, but he's secretly dying to get to the glow stage and out of the hold-her-while-she-pukes stage."

If all went well, Amanda would be a new mother in November. The thought awed them. Although they both had kids now, neither of them had ever been pregnant before.

"And I thought my life had taken a radical turn."

Amanda laughed. "More than mine has. At least we'd planned this. Once I get through the mornings I'm fine. And ravenous." Amanda sipped her tea. "You might want to follow in my footsteps," she said. "I've got to tell you, with all those pregnancy hormones, the sex is cataclysmic."

Pat sputtered, put down her wine glass, and laughed until tears coursed down her face. "Mandy, you'll have to tell me how you manage it with Norah in the house. We sort of tiptoe around so Jason doesn't get an earful."

"Spare room downstairs. And she still goes to her grandparents in Columbus for the weekend every few weeks."

"Don't look so smug. I'll keep that in mind, though. Alan wants a larger house, and it's probably a good idea." Pat returned to her original train of thought. "I honestly believed that once I found the man, life would be fairy lights and magic, and here I am with the man and the kid, who was supposed to come later, and sometimes it's hard. It's all I ever wanted rolled up into one crazy package, but the pressure's insane."

"Why's it hard, Pat?"

She retrieved the wine glass and watched as she twirled it. "It's... they both need so much. I'm not sure I have enough in me, sometimes. Plus, they've got this bond, and I'm not a part of it. Sometimes they closet themselves in Jason's room and I'll hear them trying not to yell at each other, as if they don't want me to hear. I want to intrude, but I don't.'

"But you can live with it?"

"I can, yes. Whatever the two of them have going, it's good for them both. I'm not the only one supporting Alan in his quest to be fully human, you know. A lot of it's Jason. Maybe most of it."

"Because Jason needs him. You do too, but in a different way. You'd survive without him, but Jason might not."

"It's still a lot to carry."

"Between the two of them, they must have clued in by now that you need them, too."

"Alan's told Jason about his childhood. I've heard bits and pieces, enough to put a picture together. But it's weird, that my son knows something I don't."

"Sounds like your men are protecting you, Pat."

"I guess it contributes to this bonding thing. I'm grateful for it, but it's... weird." Pat sipped her wine. "Jason's going from being unwanted kid to wanted kid, which is humongous. Plus he's about to turn thirteen years old — and that confirms my basic insanity. Where Alan's concerned, whatever his history, for him to let himself need anyone, anyone at all, that's major. Daytimes, he's in a constant battle with himself, and when he loses he goes on this macho, I-don't-need-anything-from-you kick that drives me nuts. The idea that Jason needs him has him freaked, but mostly he's coping. I think he sees himself in Jason—I know he does."

"Nighttimes?"

"It's different. In the dark he can let go, at least some."

"Jason's not giving you any clue what he's thinking about the adoption?"

Pat shook her head. "He seems more comfortable though, like he's really at home, not a hanger-on who could be given the boot any minute. What I think is, telling him I want to adopt him made a difference. Maybe it's the most I dare to hope for." She shrugged. "I've got him. Most likely I'll have him for the duration, one way or another."

The women sipped their respective drinks, thoughtful.

"Work okay?"

Amanda brightened. "Yes. The energy's different in the new warehouse. Jacob has a couple of contracts right now—he's joking about being a house husband when the baby comes."

"If he can work from home, might be a good idea."

"Maybe. How are things at Social Services?"

"Same as always. One of the foster mothers told me the other day that life's more peaceful since her kids started coming to one of the circles, so that's good news. I thought I might get back to my private practice, but lately I've got enough caseload in my living room. I need to petition the county for more hours, though, if I give up my private practice."

"Ever thought of sitting back and being supported?"

"Don't be provocative." Pat grinned, then settled back, reflecting. "At times I figure he owes me. But when I think about what he's taken on, living in my little house instead of his mini-mansion, basically changing his whole lifestyle, I guess it evens out. Sometimes I send them to get groceries, just so I can sit back in an empty house and put my feet up on the kitchen table and indulge in some of this." She raised her wine glass.

"And you should have seen Alan's face the day he realized he'd have to clean a bathroom."

Amanda's laughing eyes reflected Pat's amusement. "Are you doing much with the mall these days? You haven't mentioned it."

Pat shook her head. "I've done all I can, and the round table's finished. I'd had enough. It won't be the disaster I was expecting, so I guess that has to do."

"I hope you're not at loose ends," Amanda said, frowning. "You're inclined to get into trouble. Taking me bowling and things like that."

Pat laughed. "I'm not taking anyone bowling who'll be shaped like a bowling ball in a few months." The laugh died. "I'm not bored. I'm tired, and not just physically." The smile returned. "Though come to think of it, I don't seem to get as much sleep these days."

"You'll adjust."

"It's Jason's fault. I have to restrain myself. No screaming, for instance. I can't meet Alan at the door in a negligee."

They exchanged grins. "You're right," Amanda said. "It does feel like a fairy tale. Not always, but enough of the time."

"Good. And I'm going home." Pat stood and put her empty wine glass on the counter. "You're a positive force in my life—thanks for holding me to just one of those." She nodded at the empty glass. "My guys have an idea that men's night means they don't have to clean up. I figure men's night is more important than dishes in the sink, so I'm going home to a kitchen with my name on it."

At the door she turned and wrapped Amanda in a hug. "You're the best friend in the world, you know that, right?"

"So are you. Sisters forever, I think we promised that once?"

"Even better than sisters. I'm out of here—this is getting mushy." Pat headed for her car, throwing a wave to her best friend, watching from the doorway.

267

That weekend Jason spent the night at his friend Sean's, so they had the house to themselves. Pat was thoroughly sated by the time Alan rose up on one elbow and looked down at her. "I want to show you something. It's a present. For you."

She yawned and stretched, giving him a glimpse of what he'd be missing if he really insisted they get up. "To show me, not give me? Can't we just go to sleep?"

"No, we can't. And I can't give it to you because, one, it isn't mine to give, and two, it doesn't exist yet. Come on, lazybones." Alan swung out of bed and strode across the room, returning the favor where the view was concerned. He tossed her bathrobe to her. "Move, woman. You'll like it. Then we can pour cognacs and come back here."

"I'm taking that as a promise," she mock grumbled, but tied herself into the robe and padded out of the bedroom with him.

On the dining room table he took sheets out of a tube and unfurled them, using knick-knacks to hold down the corners. "Here. The second floor elevation of the office block. Tell me what you think."

What she thought was that it didn't look a thing like the last time she'd seen it. Alan had incorporated Jason's idea of cantilevering the second floor. She traced it, then looked up. "You saved the creek?"

"I did. Look again."

It took her only a second to see what he was showing her. That the cantilever provided glass walls for a large room. With wheelchair access outside, as well as stairs and elevator. The blueprint was bare bones, but in her mind she could see easy chairs looking out over the creek, kids in a circle, shelves and shelves...

"The library," she said, almost a whisper.

"We signed the lease today. Until then I couldn't guarantee it. You got your library, Pat. And it's the making of Landmark Center. Look, there are meeting rooms over here—"

She looked from the plans to him. "Sweet Jesus, I love you," she whispered.

He pulled her up and hugged her. "I love you, too. But you're not getting much value from me for a while, so let's hit the kitchen."

She straightened. "Always the voice of reason. I think I'd rather have hot chocolate. This is a hot chocolate kind of moment."

"Does brandy go with hot chocolate?"

"In the absence of the resident cooking genius, I expect the only way to find out is to try it." She let him take her hand and lead the way to the kitchen.

Epilogue

Pat stood at the entrance to the library and looked across the big, open space to the windows. It had been over a year since he'd shown her the plans. Now, at the height of summer, the place was bustling. Reading in the kids' area, a craft activity in the large meeting room, adults with books and newspapers, short lines at the automated check-out booths.

And a man sitting in one of the easy chairs by the big windows, reading a magazine.

Alan didn't sense her eyes on him, which was unusual. These days, it was as if they had radar installed in their brains to tell when the other one was around. He had on khaki slacks and a red golf shirt, with sandals. The man who lived in either business attire or hard hats, with no middle ground, had gotten lost in the last few months.

Whatever he was reading absorbed him, until another man came over and spoke. Alan stood and they shook hands. After he'd put the magazine back on the shelf, the two of them headed for the small meeting room.

She recognized the second man, and knew what the meeting was for. The upcoming United Way campaign, and her husband—*her husband*—was one of the prime movers and shakers this year.

The husband thing was new, brand new, and sudden. There'd been technical challenges they hadn't expected with the site, so while the office block was open, the shopping mall still had a way to go. He'd come home dead tired from the construction site a month before, collapsed in a kitchen chair, and said, "Pat, I need you to marry me."

Not the epitome of romance, maybe, but was it even a question? Two weeks later it was a done deal.

They'd kept the whole wedding thing very low-key, although she regretted not being able to stick Mandy in a ghastly matron of honor dress. Her parents were there, and her brother Adam and his wife, who'd flown in from the west coast. Jason had stayed with Amanda so they could get away for a long weekend. Alan's face, when they'd exchanged vows, had made up for any romantic deficiencies in his proposal.

This afternoon Jason was off playing pickup basketball at the middle school. He'd been her kid, truly her own kid, for four months. The day the adoption was finalized they'd gone before a judge, then the three of them went out for dinner at a nice Italian place on the way to Columbus. Now Alan and Jason were discussing yet another adoption. Step by slow step they were formalizing what they already were, a family. She could thank whatever powers that be, on her knees, for that.

Alan had another six months, minimum, before Landmark was finished. After that? He refused to give up his Columbus office because of his office manager, a woman he both dreaded and relied on. But they were exploring the possibility of a bigger house, one large enough for a home office, so it looked like they were in Calter Creek to stay.

Someone tickled her in the ribs. She yelped and spun around. "You," she said. He caught her hands before she could counter-attack. "I saw you go into the small meeting room."

"Shh! Library," he said back to her. "I snuck back out. They said they'd wait. Very understanding bunch." Alan swept her up, that was the only word for it, literally swung her around before he put her back on her feet. "Like it?"

"Love it. Loved it more when this good-looking guy I know was part of the view." Alan might never get enough reassurance, but she was giving it her best shot.

"Prove it?"

"Shall I check you out a book?" She gave him an innocent smile.

"Not sure I'll have time or energy for reading."

"Jason's learning to make doughnuts or something tonight."

"Good. See you at home." He whispered something in her ear that turned her scarlet, then gave her a gentle swat on the fanny and loped off to his meeting.

To My Readers

Hello, and thanks for choosing *Pat*. I hope you'll be inspired to check out what else is happening in Calter Creek, where Amanda and Mel both have their own stories of romance and discovery.

If you enjoyed this book, well, I don't need to tell you how much reviews mean to writers.

To keep up with upcoming romances, visit my website, http://lizanncarson.com. There you'll find notices about book events and my musings about life as both a writer and an inhabitant of the real world.

Happy reading,

LizAnn

About LizAnn Carson

It's interesting, trying to condense who you are into a paragraph or two. For openers, there are the basics: husband, three kids, and three kids-in-law, with a shifting grandkid count. I live in Victoria, British Columbia, a smallish city that's large enough to have all modern conveniences, but not so large as to have hours-long traffic jams or heavy duty pollution. I can follow a trail to my local supermarket, or I can be downtown in twenty minutes.

Yes, I spend most of my time writing (and editing, formatting, critiquing for other writers, battling computer problems, and occasionally tearing my hair out). But beyond that, I enjoy a variety of crafts. I love the new craze of coloring books for adults—in fact, almost every woman I know loves to color. I walk a lot and enjoy weight training and yoga. Once, a long time ago, I owned a yarn shop, and for a while I taught English as a Second Language. My career, on the other hand, was in the world of computer systems development.

You can follow some of my explorations on my website/blog, http://lizanncarson.com.